The Lutist

One

Her slim, fluent fingers, flickered with an easy elegance across the strings. She played in Capriccio, in the Renaissance style, with eloquent Lute craft. It was a clever piece, arch and deviceful; it was her own inspired composition; conceived there and then. They were rare these pieces and they emerged when they were least expected, when her mind flowed away and the burning inside her head ceased completely. She did not know how they originated in her, but there was always a little darkness about them and an element of glee; wasted in her current environment, she decided. She ceased to play with a dismissive hard strum and her trademark double knock on the soundboard.

The Lutist ended her set. She glared, as though defying them not to applaud. Though there was no gathered appreciative audience for her skills. Just bodies on the move; lots of office and shop assistant types on lunches; shoppers, and yummy mummies and dross in equal numbers. She cast a contemptuous glance at the accumulated tribute cast into her open lute case. Four one-pound coins, a generous, discerning five-pound note and a couple of pounds in small coins. She stooped and put her Lute aside, laying it on the folded woollen overcoat that she had got for a song in a charity shop; she raked her takings out of the case and stuffed them into the front pocket of her black skinny jeans.

'If you glared less, you might earn more.'

She turned her beautiful diamond-form face towards the voice. Her large suspicious eyes were as green as a cat's, fierce and almost affronted. They appeared to flash as she blinked a challenge. She narrowed them and peered.

He studied her, derisively she thought, as he chewed down on his lower lip. He allowed it to slide from between his teeth and grinned at her, revealing the whiteness of his teeth. It was not a friendly grin she decided. And he owned uncharitable eyes; these were cold and very pale blue. He was hunkered down in hand made black leather shoes, with pointed toes, he balanced on the balls of his feet, over her Lute, just a few feet away. His lean black hands hanging over his knees. There were four large gold rings on his fingers, two on each hand, and a heavy gold curb chain on his left wrist. A gold Jaeger-LeCoultre watch and bracelet on his right. He caught her look as it lingered on them longer than she had meant. Usually she was sharper, not one to give herself away, but the high of playing was quickly diminishing and hunger was making her lightheaded. It was not real hunger, she would never lay claim to that, just the lack of a meal in the last thirty-six hours. Though that was her own doing.

'Nice, aren't they? But you'll never be able to afford anything like them.' He was unkind, he even had the bad grace to smirk.

She studied his angular face resentfully. He was almost good looking in an unforgiving way. He looked mid to late forties. He had obviously cultivated the sneer to a fine art. There was no charm in his eyes or expression at all to mitigate his unpleasantness. He filled his expensively tailored grey suit well, with wide shoulders and a lithe muscular physique. His jaw was stubbled out of choice, it scraped the collar of his white shirt as he moved his head. His skin was smooth, shiny, and black. She watched his eyes as they calculated her. Then her own eyes widened in horror as he reached for her Lute. He straightened and examined the instrument, turning it over in his hands, stroking the patina of the wooden body, gliding over the ribbing and the tautness of the strings with his long fingers.

'Please put that down. Be careful.' Her voice had an element of depth, though it was not too deep, it had a pleasing timbre.

His head was bent over the Lute, he did not raise it to look in her direction, rather turned it to smile mockingly at her.

'I prefer the Mandolin,' he told her. 'More diversity. More flexibility.' He looked her up and down: somehow, she knew that he was playing with the words inside his head as he regarded her. She thought for a moment that he was about to articulate his thoughts and she flushed. He expelled a short breath, contempt spreading across his mouth.

'Please, put down my Lute.'

He plucked several of the strings with his thumb nail, listening to the tone or making a pretence of doing so. Her heart had begun to thud in her chest; she was stressed, her breathing elevated, but not yet to the level of panic.

'This is an expensive instrument,' he remarked. 'How did you manage to afford it?'

'That's none of your business.'

'Maybe you stole it.'

'No, I did not.' She spoke resentfully.

'Maybe I should call the police and tell them about the girl with the stolen Lute.'

'I play here all the time. They know me. The people in the shops know me.' She was beginning to feel anger, and a very palpable sense of unease.

'Then tell me how someone like you came by it.'

'I shouldn't have to.'

'Answer my simple question and save yourself a world of hassle.'

She breathed hard through flared nostrils; her lambent eyes were baleful as they flashed a hint of defiance, but it was temporary; her energies were depleted, and her head had begun to throb, a precursor to familiar discomfort, and the defiance withered away to be replaced by brimming tears. Her face worked in frustration, fighting them back. She sniffed and wiped her nose with the back of her woollen fingerless gloves, the tip was red with the cold of the early December day. She nodded, looking miserable in almost genuine surrender. *Why was he doing this to her? Some twisted Entertainment at the expense of the needy girl?*

'Alright, if this is what you want, we'll do it your way.' Her voice became gruff; she cleared her throat. 'It was my mums.'

'See, that wasn't so hard, was it?' He compressed his mouth. He became thoughtful and his expression altered, hardening. 'You know, if we are going to get to know each other, you must learn to answer me truthfully without hesitation, get rid of your resistance.'

'I don't want to get to know you.'

The look in his eyes became chilling and she began to feel genuine fear. She realized that she was shaking and that could not have escaped him. Now she simply wanted to get away, put distance between them, but he was still in possession of her Lute.

'Yes, you do; you just don't know it yet.'

'I don't know what you mean.'

'You will Saskia.'

'I'm not called Saskia. I'm called Stevie.'

'Don't lie to me. I know that your name is Saskia Challoner. I did warn you about answering me truthfully. Do you want me to smash this Lute to pieces on the ground? Because I will, never doubt me!'

'Okay, yes, I am Saskia Challoner. Stevie is my middle name. Please don't damage my Lute.' Her eyes pleaded with his. A familiar burning sensation inside her head had ignited.

He shrugged and compressed his mouth; he twisted his lips hard in deliberation. He looked to be having an inner struggle; almost unwilling to relent. Then with a shrug, he rested the body of the Lute upright, on her overcoat. He allowed the instrument to fall over; the nose of the peg box smote the paved ground hard, causing the strings to vibrate.

Saskia leapt for the instrument, grabbed it up and clutched it to her black pullover. The man regarded her with contempt, he fixed her eyes with his while he searched inside his trouser pocket. He drew out a few coins in the palm of his hand; he selected one and tossed it into her Lute case. It was a fifty pence piece.

'I've nothing smaller,' he told her callously. 'I knew it was your mother's Lute. I just wanted you to say it.'

'No, you didn't! How could you?'

'I knew her, before you were born in fact.'

'I don't believe you.'

'Sam Challoner. Your mother's name was Samantha. You had just turned five the last time I saw you. You're still as sulky.'

'You could easily have found out our names.'

'Why would I want to?'

'Precisely.'

'I already knew who you are, and what you are.'

'What do you mean by that?' Saskia was by now very scared. The burning sensation inside her head had intensified, and her neck and shoulders ached with tension. She felt drained and shaky. She wanted to bolt, but she suspected that her legs would not support her right then, if she had.

'What am I?' She heard herself say, ashamed of her small childish voice.

'Your mother informed me the last time we saw each other, that you had recently acquired the coercion of static, at five years old. No mean feat.' He wagged his index finger at her, meaningfully. 'I was ten before I acquired it.'

'How...? Please I just want to be left alone. What can you possibly want from me?'

'Compliance.'

'Compliance? I have nothing you could want.'

'You have more than you know.'

'I've no powers. No intent. You really must believe me.' She was desperate for him to believe her.

'I do believe you.' He fell silent at that point and raised his index finger to his lips, requiring that Saskia too be silent. The pupils of his eyes expanded almost filling the centres, so that only a thin aura of pale blue encircled each. She thought that he appeared to be listening.

'I am meeting someone. In fact, they are not far away, and approaching us. It's best for you if they don't see you. Safer for you If I am honest. Meet me here tomorrow morning at eleven without the Lute, then I'll tell you about all the benefits that knowing me can bring to your, at present, squalid little life.'

'I don't think that I will.'

'You will Saskia. But if you fail to turn up, I will find you, and I promise that I will not be this friendly.' Abruptly he turned and walked away.

Shaking, Saskia examined the nose of her Lute, her mouth made a thin line in a worried face; she saw there were abrasions where the peg box had impacted on the ground. She rubbed them with her slim fingers.

'Dickhead,' she growled; her resentful eyes watched him as he merged with the pedestrians on the precinct. She saw Gilly, Daryl and Nob detach from the entrance to Tanner's yard Arcade and follow him. They were low level criminals undoubtedly attracted by his showcased opulence; she avoided them.

Occasionally they entertained themselves at her expense, sometimes they hit on her, but they were the wrong colour for her preference, and thick. She cased her Lute and pulled on her overcoat, she buttoned it up and turned the lapel over. She was cold, and she realised that the day was becoming colder. She had heard someone say it might snow. She extracted a black thermal beanie from her coat pocket and pulled it over her short dark brown hair down to the level of her brows, which were equally dark and un-plucked. She swung her Lute over her shoulder and took a deep breath. Her anxiety had peaked and was on its way down, but she still felt shaky and lightheaded; she had a small bar of chocolate in her pocket, she unwrapped it and snapped a section off between her even white teeth; she munched it as she walked. She crossed the thoroughfare diagonally, weaving between the afternoon pedestrians and circling the recently erected Christmas tree at the centre. She moved awkwardly to her annoyance; her usual crowd skills seemed to have deserted her. She accidentally barged into a few people and a couple of them felt suspiciously for their wallet or mobile phone after the collision. She felt almost drunk and that coupled with the cold, and the intensity of the burning achiness in her head, made her feel dazed. She forced herself to concentrate and hoped that the chocolate she had consumed might begin to help. She had lost sight of Gilly and co but that did not matter to her. She was content to be on the other side of the street to them and out of their line of vision. What mattered to her was finding the blue eyed black skinned stranger and gaining some information about him that might prove useful, if she could; anything. The things he had said to her had resonated powerfully with her. She entered the old part of the town centre, the old market square; it was long and enclosed, sloping from right to left; It had two access roads; one of them pedestrians only led from the modernized shopping precinct where she had just emerged and the other entering from the lower corner at the same end. This swung left and up; at the top it established the end of the pedestrians only street; it continued right, along the top of the square, it exited through the buildings and eventually joined an outer road which was never that busy; there were plenty of easier routes out of town. The centre of the square was occupied by a single storey structure built of faced stone; a clock tower steepled out of it, similar to an outsize grandfather clock she often liked to think. The structure had an antique ironwork arcade with a coloured glass canopy. The building had been many things over the years, it was currently a restaurant with pretensions, named Jacobs, its prices intimating at exclusivity. It boasted external seating partitioned in the pavilion, which admittedly was stunning. She had almost given up on finding her quarry; she almost felt relief; she needed food and warmth. Then she caught sight of Daryl; he appeared at a stroll from behind the pavilion. His attention was on his two companions who were waiting outside the King George public house. He smirked and nodded; then all three of them disappeared inside.

    The wooden pierced partitions looked like they had come out of a church; the adapted pew like seating confirmed it. It was warm in the pavilion, there was some cool air being pulled in from outside, but overhead heaters generated a warmth that she desperately wanted. She told the woman at the counter hot chocolate as she entered, to avoid speech at the table, and slipped quietly into the stall next to his. She had placed her Lute on the pew on the other side of her table, out of sight. There were a few customers; a few more inside. The sky, which had been uneven and overcast for most of the day, had just begun to blacken and bulge from the south.
    A woman had joined her tormentor; she was not easily discernible through the partition. Though she had seen that she was slim and blonde; dressed in a smart grey coat. When she had appeared from inside; Saskia had hung back whilst she settled next to him.
    'That's better. Too many office coffees. My face is burning, that's what it does to me if I have more than a couple of coffees.' She spoke in a clear educated voice. Her tone was crisp, even precise, but pleasant.
    'I ordered for us like you said,' he told her. 'Tea and toasted teacakes.'
    'Sounds marvellous, I haven't had a toasted teacake in months. No sign of her then? Shame.'

'No, I'm sorry to say. But I will search again tomorrow. It's a wasted journey for you though Claire.'

'Not really, just disappointing. I needed to visit our office here. It's been six months since I was over. It was a busy meeting, hence all the coffee. And I haven't finished. I'm going back.'

'I booked into my hotel for a couple of nights. I'll stay more if necessary. Why don't you join me for tonight? It's been over a week since I saw you naked.'

'I'm tempted. Room or a suite?'

'A luxury room, great bathroom.'

'Okay. I'll phone Graham and tell him I won't be home tonight.'

'You didn't take much convincing.'

'Are you complaining.'

'Not me.'

'I'm shaking up our sister office in Newcastle in a couple of weeks. Care for a trip to Newcastle?'

'I might.' They were quiet for a time. Then Claire spoke striking a sombre note.

'It's important we locate this young woman, Nathan.'

'I know. The information we are given must be accurate though.'

'Zimpara is a good finder. She doesn't often get it wrong.'

Nathan, eh! The name suited him. A waitress appeared with Saskia's hot chocolate right then. Saskia smiled her appreciation. The waitress continued to Claire and Nathan's table, setting down her tray.

'Thank you,' said Claire. 'Mm! hot buttered teacakes. When the woman had moved away, she said: 'I hope no one got to her before us, that would be a bugger.'

Saskia had removed her fingerless mittens; she cupped the hot chocolate in her hands, relishing the warmth. She smiled thinly at Claire's comment. She wondered what her reaction would be if she knew that this Nathan had lied through his teeth to her. But she felt genuine concern that other people might be looking for her too. And why would they be looking for her? Nathan had frightened her. What if the others were more intimidating than him? She pushed the side of her head up against the partition and listened even more intently.

'When we've had this, I'll go and search the Arcades again. I'll ask about her in the shops and I'll ask if anyone else has been making inquiries about Saskia Challoner.'

'Okay. It really is worth the effort. We don't want her slipping through our fingers. We cannot afford to let one of the Orders get their hands on her. As much for her safety as for what is potentially at stake.'

'I'll do my best. I will keep looking Claire.'

'Thanks Nathan. Any means necessary, yes?'

'Of course.'

'That teacake was lovely. I'm almost tempted to have another.
But I won't. I'll have this tea and I'll go.'

'Are you coming to the hotel?'

'Why don't you meet me at the office. Say five-thirty.'

'Okay. I might have news by then.'

A few minutes later they got up to leave. Claire waited while Nathan went to pay. She had got the impression that someone was occupying the stall next to theirs, but it was unoccupied now. Not even an empty cup and saucer on the table.

The square which had showed a level of business when she entered it, never buzzed like the main shopping zone, and was populated by just a couple of dozen people now; the brightly decorated pre-Christmas shops were beginning to look empty. Saskia felt exposed. She held onto the strap of her Lute case which she had again swung over her shoulder and stalked quickly across the square. She headed for the higher ground where the eye level was split by the raised one-way road which serviced the various outlets along the top of the square, including an assortment of banks, estate agents, country clothing, furniture, and an art shop. A stone block wall retained that section of the road. Saskia jogged up a flight of well-worn sandstone steps and crossed the narrow tarmac road. She cast about for temporary concealment, prepared to shoot into the cover of a shop if she had to, or into Penny Black Lane mid-way along. She felt horribly exposed.

'Stevie.' She recognised the voice. She glanced towards it, recognising it as Travis Bonner's. A tall casually well-dressed black man of about thirty had appeared from the Midland bank. She gave him a brief smile and impatiently gestured him over. He frowned and shook his head irritably; he was already approaching her.

'What are you up to?' He was over ten years older than her, and she credited him with a maturity that she regarded as not a given in most males. He called her Stevie because that was the name that he knew her by. Saskia had made a habit of using her middle name, Stevie, since she had moved to the town two years previously. Travis was useful to her; he was a go to when she needed sex; and in the past, occasionally money if she had been in desperate need of funds. It had never been a handout, he had always expected it to be repaid.

'It's going to snow.'

'I know, but apparently the weatherman said it wouldn't lay on low ground.' The conversations of passers-by always proved a good news source. 'Stand right there in front of me. Do not move.'

'What for? Oh okay, keep your hair on. It's getting icy cold and it's going to be a shitty evening. Come back to my flat; I'll get us a Chinese.'

Under other circumstances she might have been tempted, she was starving, and his apartment was warm and stylish, but she had commitments elsewhere. He dealt in substances, but was too clever to use, and the occasional sex was always okay with Travis, he was a powerful male and she liked to be placed. But she also knew he wanted more, which was a turn off, even more so because his would have been the dominant role in any relationship; and if she was brutally honest, he was not in her league. She preferred older men anyway; to be honest men like Nathan; who had progressed from, in her view, the nappy wearing phase of most men under forty, and many over. That of course was if the choice was limited to men only; not that she wanted a relationship, she could not think of anything worse that could happen in life. Temporary connection was her preference, then you could get back to being who you really were.

'No, I have something on. It's important. Just stay where you are.'

He was tall and his padded jacket made him bulky, and he kept her hidden from view.

'Are you in trouble?'

'Not yet. Stand still.'

She saw Nathan and Claire appear from the restaurant. They paused for a moment continuing their conversation. They looked on the point of parting company, otherwise why remain stationary.

'Listen to me, carefully because there is not a lot of time. Someone has taken an interest in me. I don't know why. I have not done anything. It's a mystery to me. I'm following this guy who has been looking for me, but he's met up with a woman now. I listened in on their conversation in Jacobs, and it was about me, though I didn't hear anything specific. Now I want to follow the woman, but I also need to watch the man. Look round you can't miss them. Black guy, blonde woman.'

Travis peered over his shoulder, knowing not to stare directly at where he was really looking. He glanced at the clock tower, in a pretence of checking the time, knowing that it was four minutes slower than the accurate Tag Hauer on his wrist.

'Will you watch the man? While I follow the woman. He knows me you see, she doesn't. Will you do this for me Travis please?'

'Okay. I'll do it. But you will owe me.' He had nothing better to do and he had grown curious.

'Then I'll owe you. They've separated. Give them a few moments. And be careful, I think Gilly and his two mates are interested in the guy; he was flashing more gold than Jimmy Savile. They were following him; they're in the George. Shit they're coming out now.'

'Those bastards? Look Stevie if anything kicks off, I'm not getting involved; I'm not a match for any one of them.'

'I don't want you to. Stay out of it. Stay out of their way. Meet me back here at four. Okay? Thank you, thanks Travis.' Her expression had become disarmingly coy.

Nathan and Claire went their separate ways. Nathan back towards the shopping precinct, whilst Claire walked across the square and along the road that fed into the square from below. She passed Nathan's stalkers on the way. Saskia followed, taking the shortcut down the alley at the side of the George; she had given the three hard looking young men a wide berth and Claire was now some way ahead of her. She examined them stealthily; they were mean young men, confident of applying the intimidation or violence required, but their game plan was based on opportunity, Nathan had to present them with that. The acquisition of the high value items on show and anything else that might be on him, would be well worth the risk they would be taking. It was a game, and they had to be philosophical about its outcome. They would probably waylay him where he had parked his car, she thought, or if he strayed somewhere deserted without CCTV. None of her business. Beer fug filled her nostrils from the back of the George, she avoided slipping on the greasy cobbles, and strode over the guava beneath the span of the building where the pigeons roosted, to appear on the other side. Claire was twenty metres ahead of her at the crossing. Saskia hung back, cautiously following.

Across the road, they had built a Morrisons, beyond that lay the bus station and the railway station. Serviced by a large carpark sprinkled with shrubbery. Elsewhere, a swish modern building block housed offices and a large country pursuits outlet. Saskia kept the distance between herself and Claire, there were a few people about but not enough for her to lose her amongst them. She studied her enviously, admiring her style, posture, and her easy elegant walk in expensive high heels. Her grey coat was smart and slim cut, falling to her knees. She had good legs and ash blonde hair in a short jaw length bob. She entered the largest of the offices contained in the block. Jackman, Bosola, and Wuddery, whom, their window signs read, specialized in Wills, Probate, conveyancing, and family law. Other offices in York, Leeds, and Newcastle.

Saskia needed to sit, she needed more to drink. She bought a litre bottle of sparkling spring water at Morrisons and sat on the bench outside sipping it. A massive black sky loomed above, lights began to stand out and car headlights flashed on, hurting her eyes. The burning inside her head had intensified, becoming hot ugly pain, but it had been that for years. It was another thirty minutes before she was due to meet Travis. She capped her water bottle when she had drunk half of it and set it next to her on the bench. She breathed deeply and evenly and allowed her eyelids to slowly close. It was never dark behind one's eyelids, but imagination could make darkness, and imagination was one of the few talents that remained to her; that had not been stolen from her. She visualized a black cold sphere at the very centre of her head. She saw it turning slowly as she whispered the repeated words of the mantra *nam-myoho-renge-kyo*. She visualized the sphere spinning faster as she increased the tempo of the mantra. She fell silent removing her voice from the repetition; the mantra continued, the sphere continued to revolve, she saw it expand, as it filled her; she imagined it to be as cold and soothing as meltwater. She woke with a gasp, the hand of a spectre on her arm.

'Are you alright?'

Three years previously a schoolgirl Donna Treadman had been murdered a few hundred yards from there, along the railway line close to the river and the ruins of the old priory. She had been stabbed an alarming number of times. Her body had not been found until the next day; her killer had never been caught. Saskia had seen her ghost several times, usually when she had been on a bus or waiting for one; she often saw ghosts and occasionally wished that she could not; it was an ability she had possessed since she was about twelve. On two occasions and she did not know why, she had followed the ghost of Donna, but on both occasions, it had dissolved before it came to the place of her physical body's last moments.

'Yes, I'm alright,' said Saskia. 'I fell asleep.'

The schoolgirl was sitting next to her, slim and dark haired. Quite solid. Feeding on her energy. Saskia felt cold, but that was not necessarily caused by Donna. The schoolgirl's ghost stood. She was in uniform, blouse and skirt, dressed for the weather of another season.

'I must go, or I'll be late. I don't want to keep her waiting.'

'Her?'

'Sometimes I think I should go home you know.'

'Maybe you should,' said Saskia. But Donna Steadman's ghost had been swept away in the headlights of a taxi as it pulled into the nearby pick-up point. Saskia stood, it was dark, and she was probably late. She felt unsteady but the burning sensation inside her head had mostly relented. It began to snow, filling headlight beams with slanting flurries; she turned her pale face up towards the overarching dark to briefly watch the flakes come tumbling out of it. She put her Lute over her shoulder, picked up her water, and hurried off to meet Travis. She did not bother with the light at the crossing; she paused for a council gritter wagon to go by, then darted across. She was late, but he had waited for her. He looked unsettled. Nervous, there was even a hint of fright working its way into his eyes too. At the periphery of her vision, she saw a police car glide onto the pedestrian precinct and turn along cooper street, its siren was silent, but the blue lights were flashing.

'You're lucky. I was about to go. You really do take the piss sometimes.'

'I'm sorry. What's happened?' she asked.

'Who is he?'

'What do you mean?'

'The guy in the suit.'

'Why?'

Travis took hold of her arm and propelled her with him as he moved further along the pavement towards the far end of the square. When he halted, she yanked her arm irritably from his grip and peered at him questioningly.

'He beat the crap out of Gilly and Daryl. I've never seen anything like it. I've never seen anyone move so fast.'

'Describe to me what happened.'

'You know he set off along the precinct?'

'He was supposed to be going to make more inquiries about me. But he was lying because he'd already found me.'

'Yeah, well he didn't go back along the precinct, he turned into Cooper gate.'

'What's up there? restaurants, the night club and casino, a couple of flash hotels,' Saskia puzzled. 'Was he going back to his hotel?'

'Let me finish.'

'I'm sorry.'

'He led Gilly and his mates behind Blunts. Yes, I did say led. I thought he was a fucking idiot, playing into their hands; there's just bins, walls, and graffiti round there. I was hanging well back, but I saw how excited they got. I hesitated about following them. I got a bad vibe from the whole thing. But I didn't want to let you down'.

'Bollocks,' she said quietly, and without sarcasm. 'You were curious.'

'Maybe I was. The bins behind the Maharajah stink but that's as far as I was prepared to go. He knew they were following him.'

'Maybe he knew before he met his lady friend. Fuck! He was so relaxed in Jacobs.'

'Yeah, well I can understand why. Cause they didn't worry him. He was waiting for them behind the casino. Just standing there, smirking.'

'He likes to smirk.'

'I couldn't hear what was said, but Gilly pointed at the guy's hands. All the gold, flash bastard, no wonder they got interested in him. He just grinned. They closed in round him. They enjoy what they do, you could see in their body language they were intending to have fun, see how much blood they could get out of his face and make plenty of dosh at the same time, joy. But it didn't happen for them. I didn't see it properly, it was a blur, just like my eyes were smarting, and I got pressure in my ears. I think I was stressed, I'm not violent unless I need to be. I know they moved in; I know he must have hit them, but I didn't see it. Three seconds, tops, it was over. I saw Gilly pitching over, blood flying out of his mouth. Daryl just dropped, he was on his front, I think he was having convulsions. Nob was okay, he screamed, squealed, and ran back towards me. I got out of there fast. That happened about forty-five minutes ago.'

'I'm sorry that you had to wait so long.'

'I didn't. I went back. I almost reached the precinct before he came out; I was watching for him; he looked about as disturbed as if he'd been for a piss. He turned right; the Cowell's along there and the Malden hotel.'

'Why did you go back?'

'My conscience wouldn't let me just walk away.'

He frowned as he noted Saskia's expression. There was no understanding in it and a complete lack of empathy. He peered into her green eyes; a large flake of snow caught on her eyelash, and she brushed it away. He was reminded of his mother's black cat, Moomi, when he visited; the eyes simply watched him, green and soulless.

'They were still there. I didn't touch them. I could see Gilly's teeth all over the ground. He was covered in blood and his jaw looked like it was shattered. He just lay there gasping. He'd pissed and shitted himself. I could smell it. Daryl was just laid there; he was so still. I could see a big delve in the side of his head, there was a lot of blood and I'm sure there was a bit of his skull jutting through his hair. He'd pissed himself too. I couldn't get out of there fast enough again; I slipped and nearly went over. I went to a payphone and called for an ambulance, anonymously.'

'So that's why the police are sliding about. I'd have left them to it. They're low lives.'

'I'm not like that, I had to get them some help. You worry me sometimes. The ambulance hasn't come back out yet. Would you genuinely not have got them any help?'

'I don't believe I would. I have no compassion for people like them. I can't help it, that's me.'

He frowned, suspecting that her lack of sympathy for his actions might also hint at contempt for what had prompted them. He looked down at her tired white face, she was tallish, five foot six, even so he was six inches taller than she at least. She was shaking with the cold and through tiredness; she looked drained. Though he was not that sympathetic, his thoughts were on sex; he was turned on by the vulnerability, that, and her habitual moodiness. She always had a resentful look, occasionally mean, even cruel; it was part of her attraction. He enjoyed the hint of deviance in her nature; she was permeated by a sulky sexiness, it was dark and nuanced, reflected in all her actions no matter how slight; in her expression, in her eyes and in her voice, though it was never deliberate. She had few boundaries in bed, and he enjoyed watching the sight of orgasm flood those moody eyes. There was no relationship per se just a casual hook up now and again. There was an age gap, she was nineteen, eleven years younger than him, but he always got the impression that it might be the other way round. From the very start after he had first seen her playing her Lute, that thought had occurred to him. Even then, he had wanted more than just occasional sex. He was good looking, he had plenty of money; had his share of pretty women, but Saskia held a powerful attraction for him, way beyond any of them. Money spent, an investment, tidied up, she would be superb, a genuine trophy. Travis Bonner was smitten, but it was not emotional, or so he told himself, it was not love, its roots were clawed deep down in a splicing of kudos and lust, and he was glad of that because lust was much easier to manage. He had the knowledge though, and it made him bitter, and it was always there whenever they met; he was simply not in her league.

They watched an ambulance appear from the end of the precinct, blue light flashing. Its tyres crushed into the thin wet snow, leaving black tracks as it passed Travis and Saskia. Its siren chirped out, squeezing at their ears, then began in earnest as it increased its speed and exited the square onto the main road.

'You're cold, come on back to mine.'

'I've something I need to do.'

'I'll come with you.'

'No. Give me half an hour. I'll see you at your flat.'

'Okay.' He knew better than to remonstrate with her. And he knew that she was lying to him. He smiled sardonically. She had no intention of coming to the flat. He shrugged, turned, and walked away.

'See you Stevie,' he called over his shoulder.

'Travis!' she called after him. But he did not turn round he continued to walk away; his footprints darkened the mushy veil of snow. She shook her head and exhaled hard through her nostrils. *Fuck! People were hard work.*

Saskia exited the bus one stop early to pick up a takeaway she paid for a vegetable korma and a chicken Dansak, then went next door to the off license and bought vodka. The snow had almost stopped falling and there was only a thin layer. She went back for the takeaway and ten minutes later she kicked bits of snow off her boots and shot the door bolt to Beehive cottage.

'Roger I'm back!' she called out. She heard his gravelly cough and equally gravelly voice respond from the living room.

'Curries as promised, I'll dish them up. Do you want tea?' He always wanted tea, but she always asked. One day he might shock her she supposed. Roger Lavery more than her landlord, he was a true friend, and in her life, friends were in short supply; he was perhaps her only genuine one. She was thirteen when she met him, she used to visit a car boot in the summer at York racecourse, when he was still well enough to travel the hours journey from his home, to have an antiques stall. He was in part responsible for her enthusiasm for antiques, which was genuine, though her interest pre-dated the friendship. She had lived in his cottage for almost two years, since she had left care and come to his hometown to find him. In exchange for lodging, she kept house; kept the garden neat and made sure the household bills were paid; ensured that he was okay. She gave him his meals and kept him supplied with cigarettes. It was an arrangement she liked; it kept her under the radar, she did not want a job and she did not claim benefit. She knew that it was an arrangement that could not last indefinitely, but it gave her time to breathe and plan; she did have plans, they were simply badly defined. At present it suited her. She went to the kitchen and prepared their meal.

Saskia removed her boots, she opened the door of her room and stood them and her Lute inside the doorway without entering; she made a play of rocking on the creaky floorboard outside her room and then closed the door loudly, jarring it in its frame. She waited, composed herself, then padded in her socks to the little back bedroom where Roger Lavery kept his old stock from the days when he traded in antiques. That was before he developed his 'lung problems,' which though they had not curtailed his smoking, had ended his career. Saskia knew where to place her

feet to avoid the creaky floorboards along the corridor; she knew to open the door just wide enough to slide her body through the gap to avoid the squeaky hinges, and step across the first two boards inside the room; then she had a safe island of six boards, because after that the room was a nightmare of creakiness. She did not turn on the light because it made the rest of the lights in the house dim. Her only light was from the naked bulb in the corridor spilling into the room past the part open door, leaving most of the room in thick shadow. An old iron framed bed stood next to the wall; it was piled with a variety of polished wooden boxes and small suitcases. Several more suitcases were jammed under the bed, but she had never disturbed these, extracting them would make more noise than she was comfortable with. Quickly and carefully, she removed one of the suitcases from the top of a stack on the bed and set it down in the weak light of the doorway. She shivered slightly and felt like someone had applied an ice cube to her spine, sliding it from base to neck. She glanced around and saw the dim form of a woman in a house coat in the corner. She was watching her, she never did anything but watch; Saskia could not make out her features properly, but she knew that they would be expressionless as always. It was Roger's wife, Jenny; Saskia recognised her from photographs around the house. She had died eight years previously, though she
had divorced Roger before that. Roger saw her occasionally too, though not as often as Saskia; he couldn't work out why she had turned up as she hated the place. Saskia rolled her eyes and raised her finger to her lips in a playful gesture of silence. She released the catches on the suitcase and raised the lid. It contained boxes, well packed but not tightly, some were cardboard boxes and there were three old wooden cigar boxes stacked at one end. She went quickly through the top layer, removing the tops of half a dozen of them. She extracted a silver half hunter pocket watch and chain, a silver vesta match case, and a Waterman fountain pen; then she closed the boxes, shut the suitcase, re-engaged the catches and returned it to its stack. She gave Jenny a little friendly wave and exited the room clutching her little haul. It was cynically done, and she was not exactly proud of herself; however, she mostly lacked a conscience and she told herself that

Roger would never miss it and hardly needed it. He was too comfortably off. She secured the items in her room, inside her knicker drawer which also housed her little collection of pleasure toys, and which she kept locked. Her bedroom was quite a barren little room, the wallpaper was to the taste of an earlier generation, and it was shabby. The room had an old wardrobe, a chest of drawers, a threadbare rug in the middle of the boarded floor, and an iron framed bed like the one in the back room, and a little bedside table with a lamp. With a nod to vanity, and she was vain, she had begged an antique cheval mirror off Roger which she had discovered in his shed. He had never dealt in furniture, but he had acquired as a matter of course; and anything ropey had ended up in his shed. Saskia had restored the cheval, stripping off layers of old paint to reveal its walnut frame. It had silvered glass which had deteriorated, but Saskia quite enjoyed looking at herself through its distressed surface. She stripped for a shower in front of it and gazed with critical dissatisfaction at her supple nudity; short unruly hair, small firm breasts, and narrow hips; she was slender, even fractionally undernourished at a hundred and eighteen pounds, but that was an oddly deliberate choice; like skipping food the previous day. She revolved her body to view her firm arse from over her shoulder, the lean flare of her hips from her slender waist, and the symmetry of her straight shoulders, and the dark elegant shape that was the cause of her suffering; this had been tattooed between her shoulder blades. It resembled in outline a finely turned ebony lace bobbin and was of comparative length; a fine red tattooed thread without breaks undulated end to end along it, crossing at seven points. It was called a fetter, and it denied magical power to the person in whose skin it was embedded. It had proved useful today, it had prevented her from being sensed by Nathan or Claire in the cubicle, and when she had followed them.

    She cursed softly under her breath and tears brimmed in her eyes. Anguish clawed its way into her face, contorting her features. Her mouth compressed, working as she fought against a surge of despair. Her fists clenched and she lifted one to the level of her face; she held it there as if she wanted to strike down on something; her fingers went white with effort as it held every pain and misery in her pathetic existence. She gradually overcame the despair, fighting it back down into herself by a relentless act of will. In control again, Saskia stalked out of the room, heading for the shower, she took a razor with her to shave her legs and edge her pubis, she was unsure why.

Later, propped on pillows her knees drawn up in front of her, she relaxed naked on the bed drinking the vodka she had bought, neat from the bottle. She laid her thoughts bare recognising that this had been no ordinary day in her life. That the black guy Nathan was a magician was unequivocal, she had decided. He wielded energised intent, in this case by a form of what was called desiring, in the imagined shape of a club or a hammer probably; this was called Grim intent. The way Travis had described events it could only be that, combined she suspected, with the declining of time, accounting for Nathan's incredible speed. The man had known her mother, or so he said; surely, he had no reason to lie. He had mentioned the acquiring of static coercion with easy familiarity. He was certainly dangerous, and he had an intensely scary vibe. But because of what he represented, his sudden appearance on the scene had begun to excite her, now that she had thought it through with a cool head and on a full stomach. God knows what he wanted from her; she had nothing to give; her magic had been withheld from her. But he had promised to tell her the benefits that knowing him could bring to her 'squalid little life.' If he had something to give that would offer her a connection to magic, she would take it; not that she trusted him.

Then there was the woman, Claire, what was her role in this? She was probably the mysterious other whose approach Nathan had sensed? If so, she must have magic too, or an intimate connection; their conversation had indicated that they were sexually involved. If not Claire, then who? Saskia recalled what Nathan had said: *I am meeting someone. In fact, they are not far away, and approaching us. It's best for you if they do not see you. Safer for you If I am honest.* It had to be Claire and for his own reasons Nathan was obviously intent on keeping them apart. Why was it safer if Claire did not see her? Smoke and mirrors? What had Claire said during her conversation with Nathan in the restaurant?

'Yes, what did Claire say during their conversation in the restaurant?' said Saskia, addressing the spectre of Jenny Lavery, who had appeared by the closed door. The room was centrally heated and warm, but she felt it grow cooler and she drew a blanket up over the lower half of her nakedness. She recalled Claire's words 'We *can't afford to let one of the Orders get their hands on her. As much for her safety as for what's potentially at stake.*' They had not exactly sounded like the words of someone who meant her harm; it had been Nathan who had threatened the destruction of her Lute. Bastard! She was halfway into the bottle of vodka; she could feel its fire inside her blood. It offset the burning inside her head, which admittedly was only just to say present right then. She raised the flat bottle to her parted lips, tipped it and heard the contents glug as the warm spirit entered her mouth. She would pay in the morning.

What was at stake? Why did they need her? She could always ask Nathan, but she decided that she would prefer to ask Claire. Saskia put down her bottle and picked up her music page pad, and a pencil from her bedside table. She suddenly felt the effects of the vodka. She shrugged in the direction of the spectre of Jenny Lavery and gave a little chuckle of laughter.

'You really don't approve of me, do you? Well, I don't really care.'

She drew a deep breath and played back the composition she had created impromptu that morning, inside her head. Had she left it until the following morning it would have been gone. But tonight, she could summon it up and hear it with total recall and clarity. Fifteen minutes later Saskia set her pad aside, exhausted; Jenny had disappeared, returned to the ether. She lay back, closed her lambent green eyes, and fell asleep, her bed side lamp still lit.

Saskia almost missed her bus. She had woken up with a brute of a headache which seemed to want to punch the backs of her eyes through their sockets. She almost cried out as she lifted aside a window curtain to examine the partial snowiness of the day, and the light from outside flooded her brain, with a sustained close range camera flash that continued until she dropped the curtain. She was late, she realised. She threw water on her face and sprayed her body with body spray. She dressed in black, socks, knickers, skinny jeans, boots, and fine knit v-neck pullover, all black. Coffee: black; she preferred tea; right then it was essential, along with a palmful of pain killers. Any thought of having breakfast made her feel sick, but she prepared scrambled egg on toast for Roger, who was in situ, in his customary armchair beside the fire in the living room; had he been to bed? she wondered. She would watch that. She brought in a heaped scuttle of coal from the coal bunker at the back of the house. The fire was already alight, if it had even been allowed to go out! She re-ascended the stairs and returned to the bathroom; washed her hands, listerined her mouth and brushed her teeth; she glanced at her paper-white face and hollow eyes in the bathroom mirror with six minutes left to catch her bus. She threw on her black leather jacket and stuffed her little parcel of plunder into one of its side pockets. She clattered down the stairs and was about to go out the door when Roger's gravelly voice called out to her.

'Saskia.'

She threw back her head and closed her aching eyes in disbelief. The bus stop was right at the end of the road; she had four minutes; tops.

'Yes Roger?' she replied, allowing no impatience to enter her voice.

'Stick out for a decent price my love. But remember they must make a decent profit too.'

On the bus she did not know whether to laugh or cry, so she chose neither.

Saskia hung around outside the offices of Jackman, Bosola and Wuddery for half an hour after they opened, waiting for Claire to arrive; she watched the staff as they came into work, but there was no sign of Claire, and she began to have doubts that she was coming in. Saskia was beginning to feel very cold, and she wished that she had put on more clothing; she also wished that she had not consumed most of the contents of a bottle of vodka the night before; the morning would have been less challenging. She drew a deep breath through her mouth, compressed her lips and exhaled it through her nostrils; she decided on an alternative strategy. She unzipped her leather jacket and hands in pockets pushed open the glass swing door into the offices with her shoulder. She appeared much more confident than she felt. A lithe girl with a river of auburn hair occupied the reception desk, she was sliding printed documents into A4 envelopes and laying them out for collection or posting. Saskia sauntered up to reception and allowed a flash of appreciation into her eyes and across her features, as she engaged with her; Hannah, her name badge informed. Saskia smiled a small understated uneven sided smile, with closed mouth conveying the message, hopefully, that she just wanted to say wow. Her green eyes flickered to the name badge and back to Hannah's face with obvious interest; not too much, best not to overdo it. Mostly it worked, sometimes it ended badly. In the case of Hannah, it did not need to be forced.

Hannah's ears crimsoned at the tops of their shells, and she smiled shyly; surprisingly there had been a hint of recognition in her expression. Saskia did not remember meeting her before.

'Good morning,' said Hannah. 'Can I help you?'

'I certainly hope so,' Saskia had an educated voice, though by no means high class; she allowed warmth into its timbre as she spoke to Hannah.

'I spoke to a lady from this firm yesterday, I can't even remember how we got talking, and I told her that I'm going to need some legal advice in the future. She gave me her card and told me to make an appointment to see her, and like an idiot I've lost it.'

'We all lose things. I do regularly. Parent's dog. Little sister.' Hannah said disarmingly.

Saskia gave a smoky chuckle of appreciation.

'Thank you for being kind.'

'Do you remember her name? What was she like?'

'Blonde hair, nice looking. Late forties. Her first name Claire.'

'We don't have a Claire working here.'

'She said that she was only here yesterday and for this morning.'

'Oh! You mean Mrs Bosola. She's one of our big three. She was going to be in this morning but there was a change of plan and she had to go back to head office. That's in Leeds; so, she hasn't come back in. She's brilliant.'

'She was ever so nice.'

'There are some excellent people here who can help you, I'm sure.'

'I'm in Leeds regularly, now that I know she works from there I can make an appointment to see her.'

'Would you like me to make you one now, over the phone?'

'That's kind. I'm not really prepared yet. I need to build up to it.' She drew a deep breath and firmed her mouth, revealing a soupçon of vulnerability.

Hannah opened a drawer under the counter in front of her and extracted a business card. 'We carry all our main executive's business cards out of every office. All our offices do. Here is Mrs Bosola's, to replace the one you lost.'

Saskia could be many things; charming, attentive, seductive, whatever the situation needed when she wanted, right then she was appreciative and impressed.

'You're ace.' She accepted the card and slipped it into her pocket.

'You're the girl who plays the Lute aren't you?'

'Yes I am.'

'You play beautifully. I love that type of instrument.'

'Thank you, it's nice for my music to be appreciated. Sometimes I don't think that it is.'

'I always put something in your case, I wish I could afford more. Do you go to the music college? You said you were often in Leeds.'

'Yes.' Saskia lied, suspecting that Hannah might be the secret donator of five-pound notes.

'Say hello next time, we can have a drink together.'

'I think I would like that very much.'

Stella, a pleasant full-bodied woman with ringlets and fingers weighted down with gold rings, always gave Saskia the best price. Her antique shop was the last one at the top of Penny Black Lane, which on better days was a thriving little Antique quarter; they made up eight out of the ten shops on the little thoroughfare. Beyond that lay Steeple Road and on the other side of that the old cemetery, which Saskia tended to avoid. Stella opened her shop at ten-thirty; by then Saskia was almost frozen, and fretting. Stella greeted Saskia with her customary 'hello luvvie.' Then: 'Ooh you look frozen.' Saskia was sharp but she was never sure if Stella was genuine. Not that it mattered. 'Have you heard about the two young men who were attacked behind the nightclub? One of them died I heard!' Saskia said that she had not heard, how awful. There remained plenty of time to do her deal and make her meet with Nathan, but she felt that it was cutting it fine. She exited Stella's with ten minutes to make her meet and with seventy-five pounds folded in her skinny jeans front pocket next to Claire Bosola's business card. Nathan seized her by the scruff of the neck as she appeared. He propelled her with uncompromising strength across Steeple Road, which was habitually deserted even in warm weather. She did not cry out which puzzled him, not that it mattered to him if she had. Instead, she kicked out, and struck at him with her fists surprising him with her strength. He skewed her around and hit her in the face with the heel of his hand; pain exploded, and she experienced the firework flash of the impact. With contempt he pitched her backwards over the low cemetery wall, into the still gathered mushy snow on the other side; the snow and long grass cushioned her fall, but it knocked most of the wind out of her. He eased over the wall and crouched on his heels beside her; he smiled down at her unpleasantly. He placed his hand firmly on her chest and held her down. He had watched her from a window in Jacob's restaurant, where he had enjoyed a very pleasant breakfast after buying a pair of green Le Chameau wellingtons in a country clothing shop. She had paced, with her shoulders hunched in the cold for a half an hour keeping her eye on Penny Black Lane; when she disappeared into the lane, he had followed her.

'I told you that I'd find you. I told you that I wouldn't be friendly.'

'Fuck you!' she snarled. Blood was trickling out of both nostrils where he had struck her and there was blood in her teeth where they had cut into the inside of her lip.

He could feel her body giving little jerks of fear. She was scared but her lambent eyes were defiant. He grinned enjoying that in her.

'I'll enjoy making you compliant,' he told her; she frowned and shook her head. He began to unzip her leather jacket. Saskia felt panic; she struck at him with her fists, but he seized her wrists and held them down easily, one handed above her head in the snow. She writhed and twisted, kicking out; he punched her in the ribs, a short jab that made her whimper in pain; when she continued to kick, he punched her again, harder. She moaned, sobbed, and became still. He finished unzipping her jacket and released her wrists; he turned her on her front and pushed her face hard into the snow with one hand pressed down on the back of her head then yanked up her jacket and pullover, exposing her back up to her fetter. Saskia gasped as her midriff came into the contact with the cold snow and its wetness seeped into her pullover.

'Just making sure.'

He gave her head a last hard shove down into the snow and released her. He stood and shrugged his coat into place on his shoulders and flexed his elbows; he straightened the cuffs of his shirt and jacket. Then he regarded Saskia's still form.

'Get up,' he ordered her. He pushed her rear with the soul of his boot, leaving a half print of snow and mud across her right buttock.

Slowly Saskia raised her face out of the snow, she studied the bright blood in the whiteness in the collapsing imprint left by her face. She was breathing hard, fighting back emotion, she was determined that she was not going to cry for him; he had already humiliated her. She got to her knees and adjusted her pullover and jacket, re-zipping it. Her eyes anxiously roamed the lines of headstones. She focused on a couple of dim manifestations. Moochers was how she referred to them; they hung around most of the graveyards she had come across. They never bothered her, and she never bothered them.

'I haven't got all day.'
'I don't want to be here. I don't come this way.'
'What are you looking at?'
'I see ghosts fuck face. And other things.'

He scowled at her, he looked almost tempted to hit her again, but he let the insolence pass and he followed her gaze. He did not expect to see anything, but he knew people who could, and he had no reason to doubt that Saskia could see forms; she would take after her mother in that.

She braced herself against the little cemetery wall and eased herself to her feet, gasping at the pain it caused in her side where he had punched her. She turned a white face to him; there were still bits of melting blood-stained snow adhering to her skin and trickling down it. Her green eyes were resentful, and her mouth was compressed into contempt. She was breathing hard and rapidly through her nostrils, the coldness of the snow seemed to have stopped her bleed.

'We need to go.'

She was aware of an entity that came out of the old plague pits, and she did not want to encounter it. It had once followed her as far as her bus. After her energy, she presumed. She had stopped coming any closer to the cemetery than Stella's after that. She threw her leg over the wall. 'There was no need for this. I was coming to meet you. I still had time.' The timbre in her voice had deepened in resentment.

'Maybe. It was more entertaining this way. Go on,' he jerked his head for her to precede him as he clambered over the wall.

Saskia was taking long strides, she kept looking back. Nathan threw her a curious look. She had begun to interest him.

She was shaking from cold by the time they reached the Cowell hotel. Her jeans and pullover were damp from contact with the snow and the icy air had cut through her clothing. She felt frozen, and her face and ribs hurt. She dived for the radiator in Nathan's high-end room; and dropped to her knees on the floor next to it, relishing its warmth. Nathan took off his overcoat and dropped it on the settee; he sat in one of the matching padded chairs and studied her dispassionately; he rested his elbows on the leather arms of his chair, and steepled his fingers in front of him. After a few minutes, her shivering stopped, and she became more relaxed, and she levelled a look in his direction that he felt was best described as acrimonious.

'I need to pee,' she told him.

'The bathroom isn't hidden. I'm going to order coffee.'

'I'd prefer hot chocolate. You find that amusing?'

Nathan's compressed lips curved derisively, and he shook his head, looking away to the side. 'You make me smile, not in a pleasant way. It's something about you. I'll order you hot chocolate.'

He watched her get off her knees; she leaned on the radiator to push herself up. She slipped out of her jacket and tossed it onto the couch.

'Wash your face while you're in there, it's a mess.'

She returned ten minutes later with a face washed clean of blood; she had on a white bathrobe and her socks.

'I used the fresh robe they left for you. It was folded on that heated shelf on top of the towel rail. It's nice and warm; if you don't like it, tough. I've hung my clothes on the rail to dry.' Her face was still drained of colour and bruising was starting to show across the bridge of her nose.

'You are a bastard,' she told him coldly.

He had leant back in his chair. He locked his fingers behind his head and met her moody eyes dispassionately, staring her down until her gaze fell away in defeat.

A buzz from the direction of the door indicated the arrival of room service. Nathan paused momentarily, as he considered sending Saskia, then issued smoothly from his chair. He brought back a tray and set it down on the coffee table, then dropped back into his chair. On the tray stood a pot of coffee and a pot of hot chocolate and cups and saucers.

'Oh God a pot,' said Saskia appreciatively.

'I like my coffee black. One sugar,' said Nathan.

She scowled at him; for a moment he suspected that she was going to tell him to get it himself. But she slid from her chair onto her knees, wincing a little as the pain of movement gripped her ribs; she poured him steaming coffee into a cup. Very deliberately she scooped a single spoon of brown sugar from the bowl and tipped it into the coffee. She placed the cup and saucer on the table and pushed it towards him.

'My name is Nathan Xavier,' he told her as he watched her carefully pour hot chocolate into a cup.

'I believe you understand what I am capable of.'

She added a little milk to her hot chocolate, not too much, and stirred. She lifted it to her mouth and sipped, wincing as the hot drink made first contact with the damage on the inside of her lip; she swallowed, sipped some more; she held it in her mouth for a brief appreciative moment, then swallowed again. She lowered the cup a few inches, licked and deliberately sucked in her provocative lower lip.

'About time you told me,' Saskia responded, poker faced. 'No. I have no idea what your accomplishments are, You've only implied. You might be bullshitting me.'

'Why would I do that?'

She shrugged. 'So, Mr Xavier, why do you want me?'

'First things first. Tell me what you know about magic? How much did your mother pass on to you?'

'As little as possible, meaning virtually nothing. She told me to avoid any contact with it because it's dangerous.'

'It is dangerous. It's not for the spineless.'

'I prefer faint hearted, to spineless.'

'I see.'

'It should never belong to the overzealous or the malign either.'

'You can say that about any form of power, I'm sure the malign and zealous have other opinions. So, you know nothing about magic.'

'I didn't say that. I said my mother refused to tell me anything about it. How did you know her?'

'I was under the impression that I was questioning you.'

'A little give and take,' she said reasonably.

He shrugged, deciding to indulge her. 'We were members of the same Order; before it was disbanded. That happened over twenty years ago. We were sexually involved. And we practised sex magic together. We tried to break the sixth seal. I failed, she succeeded. She became strange after that. Does that shock you?'

'Why should it?' Saskia felt an odd sense of surprise at this revelation from her mother's past. It was a lot to take on board her mother being the person she was. She wondered at the significance of the breaking of the sixth seal.

'I'm surprised though,' she admitted, 'that she was a member of an Order.'

'Things were different with her then. She enjoyed her talents.'

'What happened to change her?'

'I am as much in the dark about that as you. If she did not, who taught you about magic?'

'Auntie Ben. She knew so much; she had elemental and energised intent. She knew both Alchemies. There wasn't much about magic she didn't know. We lived with her for a few years. They were in a relationship. My mum was in a lot of pain; she home schooled me, and it tired her; while she was sleeping, and she did a lot of that. Ben, filled in 'the gaps in my education' that's how she described it. I know what's out there. I was twelve when they split up and we left; I didn't want to leave. They were both supposed to have rejected magic, but I don't think auntie Ben was as committed as my mum. In retrospect, I believe she only committed herself to it because she loved my mum.'

Nathan's malevolence appeared to have become diluted for the present.

'Your mother stayed in touch with me after the break-up of our Order. We met every few weeks at first, then every few months; I think I was more committed to it than she was. She never said she was with anyone, she didn't speak much about her life at all, apart from referring to it as normal. She talked about you. On a few occasions she brought you along. You were with her when she told me you had static coercion and on a couple of times previously. Don't you recall me at all?' Saskia shook her head.

'That was the last time I saw you. I met Sam occasionally for a few years, after that she told me she planned to fetter you when the time came.'

'You could have asked to see it you know,' Saskia told him.

He ignored her and continued. 'Then we stopped meeting, her decision. I didn't know she had died until a few weeks ago. Where were you living all that time?'

'Just outside Knaresborough. They ended their relationship because of me. My mum became odd. Angry. She used to rage at me when I talked about magic. I remember having energised intent for a time. I didn't have vis ultima and my intent was erratic.

But I certainly owned it; I wanted it. My mother refused to tutor me and screamed at Ben not to. She took me to see a man she called a Bran, I'll never forget his name, Tadgh Byrne. We stayed overnight; she hadn't told Ben obviously. I was twelve. I had no idea what was happening. She said he was an old friend; we ate with him; mine was obviously drugged. When I woke up, I was in pain, and I was fettered. I was distraught. Then I was furious. I never forgave her. I still haven't forgiven her, even though she's dead.'

'You are very bitter.'

'I am. It was my choice, and she took it from me. I didn't want to be fettered. I wanted magic.'

'Where did you go to visit this Bran, do you recall?'

'Yes. It was in Wilmslow, in Cheshire. Apparently after I was born, she had the Bran fetter her. But that was her choice. My mum and Ben had a terrible argument about me after she had me fettered. They wouldn't speak to each other. Mum took me away with her after that and we went to live near York; to the best of my knowledge, they never saw each other again. Mum home schooled me until she died. And she taught me to play my instruments. It's the one thing I'm grateful to her for.'

'What killed her?' Saskia searched for a hint of regret in his tone. But his face and voice were equally hard.

'A brain disorder. She slept for longer and longer periods. Eventually she didn't wake up. I believe it was the fetter that killed her. It's what makes my head burn inside; that began as soon as I was fettered. How did you know that I was fettered?'

'I told you, your mother said that she intended that for you. But these things leak out, from other connections of your mother say, or this Ben. Everybody looking for you may know that you're fettered.'

'Everyone? Why?'

'Where did you go when Samantha died?'

'I'm not telling you that.'

He shrugged; he did not really care.

'What if I told you the fetter could be removed? You could have use of magic again.'

Saskia's eyes widened.

'Mum said that was impossible. The fetter is permanent.'
'She lied to you.'
'You are saying that I can be unfettered!'
'I am but expect a quid pro quo.'

'I'd do anything to restore intent. I did look for Ben, I wanted her to teach me the subtle practises, all the lesser stuff, talismans, glyphs. I know that for those I don't necessarily require energised intent. Though I did need a proper magician, not someone fantasizing that they were one; Ben was the only one I knew. I went back to her house. Other people were living there. Our only neighbour Mr Coolidge said that Bernadette O'Hare had left years ago and good riddance; she had become pregnant and sold up.'

'Bernadette O'Hare?'
'He refused to call her Ben; he insisted on Bernadette.'
'Bernadette O'Hare?' He repeated.
'Yes, do you know her then?'

Nathan surged from his chair; his face had become malevolent again and expressed a wolfish hostility. Saskia felt genuine fear. She eyed him cautiously, her breathing quickened, and her heart hammered.

'Are you still in contact with Bernadette O'Hare?'
'No. I haven't seen her for over seven years, I told you.'
'Don't lie to me.'
'I'm not lying.'
'Have you spoken with her? Do you exchange letters? Emails?'
'No. No. No.'
'Why should I believe you? stand up!'

Suspicious and scared; shaking her head, Saskia stood.

'Take off the robe.'
'Why?'
'Do as I say. Show me!'
'Show you what?'
'Your body. Show it to me.'

She shook her head in confusion astonished at his sudden ferocity. Angrily Nathen seized the robe by its lapels and jerked it from her shoulders and down her arms, baring her.

'Fuck you.' She said sotto voce. She fought tears but they spilled down her face which had become fused with resentment.

'Show me your arms. Extend them.' He examined each slender arm in turn from shoulder to hand. He was thorough. He inspected the slim curve of her shoulders and upper arms he ran his strong fingers across the hairs of her forearms, viewing her skin with an intense scrutiny. He peered at the backs of her hands, her palms and between her fingers.

'Raise your arms above your head.'

'You could say please.' She said showing some fight.

He stared her down with a look made of stone. Reluctantly she raised her arms above her head. He examined her arm pits; then her sides; he was oblivious to the red bruising on her ribs where he had punched her into submission. He calmed as he worked. He became preoccupied with his task; he was thorough, and not gentle.

'What are you looking for?' Saskia demanded; she was quickly regaining control.

Nathan did not reply. He continued examining the outside of her legs and her rear. She gave a little gasp as he pushed apart her buttocks.

'You're looking for glyphs, aren't you? I don't know how to make them.'

'Bernadette O'Hare is a powerful adept of elemental magic, particularly the art of Designing, of glyphs. What did she pass on to you?'

'I knew that she was yes, but she kept those skills away from me, she said I was too young, that it was dangerous. She told me about talismans, and sigils and glyphs. And designing intent. But she never taught me them. I've read stuff about them in books but it's mostly crap. Lesser stuff. I don't know how to use any of them properly. What are you looking for on my skin? It must be ridiculously small.'

'Not necessarily small. I'm looking for device. Drawn in black, white, or translucent pigment, even white marker, and charged.'

'But I'm fettered,' Saskia protested. 'I have no power; I couldn't charge a glyph.'

'There are other ways; energised intent is not essential. Just vibration, ingredient, and command.'

'I've none of that. Why would I?'

'Why wouldn't you. Why should I believe you?'

'Do you think I would be playing the Lute for change and freezing my arse off if I had any magic?'

'You might have a moral aversion to using it for gain, many have.'

'Well, I wouldn't!' Saskia shouted.

'Take off your socks.'

'You take them off.'

He surprised her by pushing her down into the chair his hand forcing down on her shoulder. He had uncompromising strength, and she did not resist. He hunkered down and yanked off her socks. Then he examined her feet, peering at her soles and intently between her slim toes.

'Open your legs.'

Saskia weighed up the choice between a demeaned look and a distraught look; she settled for demeaned. She separated her legs bending her knees and raising her feet to the chair seat. He scrutinized her inner thighs, then between the dark down of her pubic hair. He separated the lips of her vulva with his fingers with cold indifference. She turned her head away, tears spilling; quietly pleased that she was not overplaying it. He searched the inside of her legs. He stood back, straightening.

'Now open your mouth; it shouldn't be difficult it's rarely shut.' Saskia set her jaw and stared at him with a grim defiance; but she recognised his determination, and she knew that he was cruel; her resolve melted away and she opened her mouth. He turned her face to the light holding her jaw hard in his clamped fingers. He peered inside her mouth; searching tongue, cheeks, and roof; she gagged as he thrust a finger inside her mouth and prised her tongue down and to each side; eventually, he appeared satisfied. Saskia started laughing through her tears, suddenly seeing humour in his intensity. Her face became as mocking as she had seen his. The deviant in her had come out to play.

'And did you really think that I might have had a murder glyph written up my arse or in my vulva?' She laughed contemptuously.

'It has been known,' he replied grimly. He jerked her head back with unnecessary roughness and released his grip on her jaw. He resumed his seat and regarded her sullenly, again staring her down.

Saskia fixed her gaze on her hands. She remained like that for several minutes as though holding emotion. She was trembling, and she waited for it to stop. She was intensely aware of her nakedness under his scrutiny, and intensely aware of the energy of connection that she was building between them. More conscious of it than him, though she sensed that she was unsettling him. She withdrew her fixed gaze from her hands, tilting its emphasis to Nathan. Looking at his body, lingering on his hands on the arms of the chair. Powerful fingers, she imagined them on her body with sexual intent, not his recent indifference. She allowed her eyes the briefest examination of his face; him a glimpse of their sultriness; they were emotional, still even a little resentful. She looked away again. Her head had cleared of the pain of hangover, but the burning inside it had returned, it was subdued however, slow to increase in strength now that she could combat it for a time with purpose.

She got out of the chair, she went to him and crouched beside his chair. She lay her slim folded arms along the cushioned leather arm. She tilted her head resting her cheek upon her forearm. She stroked the leather with her fingertips, studying their stroking movements. She extended her hand to rest her fingertips on his abdomen; she prised open a button of his shirt and slid her fingers inside; she drew her sharp little nails across his skin over the contours of his superb abdominal muscles. He watched her; he made not attempt to prevent her.

'I'm impressed,' she commented.

He frowned. His eyes continued to express the routine contempt he had for her.

'Do you want me in the bed? You aren't indifferent to me. I can see the effect this is having.'

'You don't like me.' He remarked.

'I don't like you at all, there's nothing to like; what has liking you got to do with it? How do you want me, submissive? I'll be submissive.'

He raised his brows, mocking her; he exhaled contemptuously.

'Do you find me amusing?' Saskia asked husky voiced. 'I don't care; humiliate me. Do you want my compliance? I'll comply to everything you want if you can remove my fetter and give me back my magic. It is all I want.'

Saskia gambled. She rose to her feet and walked to the bed; aware that his eyes would be following her naked form. She did not like Nathan Xavier one little bit, but the idea of him, the fact that he scared her, gave her a sexual buzz. She turned back the covers of the bed, catching the scent of Claire Bosola still lingering on them. She climbed into it. She propped herself against the pillows, legs drawn up, knees parted, her wrists resting on her knees. She regarded him coolly, deliberately.

His studied her for more than five minutes in silence, his cold eyes played over her, always derisive, but there was interest there too. He stood and approached the bed, almost surprising her; the hairs on her neck rose, her heartbeat increased. He took his time, carefully hanging his clothing on the stand provided by the hotel. Physically he was impressive, like a middleweight boxer at the height of his prowess, all steely strength. He could see her eyes running over his body, they stopped at his long, circumcised penis. When he climbed into the bed, he was predatory, a thing of menace; she knew that this was not a place of equals. He kissed her once, his mouth possessively covering hers, one hand locked in her hair, the other passed under her arm, and high behind her back, his fingers pressing hard into her spine over the fetter. He ended the kiss after some time, he forced back her head, his fingers twisted in her hair. He grinned at her; he had the eyes of a timber wolf she thought.

Saskia had never experienced anyone as sexually accomplished as Nathan Xavier. She realised quickly that her body was nothing more than an instrument to him. He was contemptuous of her; he lacked any tenderness and that suited her. Compared to Nathan, Travis Bonner was an effete novice. Nathan induced an element of pain, his strong fingers compressing her and probing her existing injuries; he induced intense pleasure too and in the flood of endorphins and dopamine she found that pain felt as good as the pleasure. She came half a dozen times, intensely; laughing and crying out as she experienced the velvet clawing of orgasm. He had climaxed twice; both times inside her. His body surged as he held her with uncompromising strength, her arms twisted up behind her back, her wrists in hands like vices. The second time he climaxed ended the encounter; he had her folded beneath him, his eyes fixed on her face. He had watched Saskia's climax flood her eyes, consuming her. He grinned mockingly as her fingers clawed at his skin. As his own pleasure engulfed, his expression became malign. She felt him ejaculate. He ended it immediately; he swung her legs from his shoulders and pushed her away from him across the bed. She flashed him resentment and he gave her a baleful look in response. He was panting; glistening with sweat; they both were. He swung his legs from the bed and stalked to the bathroom, a minute later she heard the shower. Her hair clung round her brow and neck in little damp points, her skin felt hot and damp. Saskia pushed herself up on one arm, she waited, listening for the shower to finish; she controlled her breathing. Her body felt drained, worked. Her brain felt awash with pleasure chemicals, and the burning had been extinguished. He had not kissed her again after the first time; she had suspected that he would not want to hold her, and that was good; she didn't like to be held, not by men. She did not really like men. She waited and sat up; some of his semen running out of her onto the bed. She hated semen; it was loathsome stuff. Opportunistically, she decided to search his pockets, any information was useful. She found half a dozen black plastic cable ties in his coat pocket which she felt was a little disturbing. In his inside jacket pocket, she found a leather wallet holding his credit cards and two hundred pounds in notes. In the side pocket of his jacket, she made what she considered to be an intriguing find. A small antique snuff box, made from horn. She had not had him down as a snuff taker, but it rattled slightly when she moved it. She pushed open the tight-fitting lid and peered inside. She frowned then and tipped the contents into her palm. Seven slim tapering spikes of hardened black wood lay across her head and fate lines, they were dusted in a fine residue of the old snuff which remained in the box. Each spike was about threequarters of an inch in length. Her mouth compressed into a thin line; her eyes recognised; they were seven blackthorns, cut from a branch; she had seen similar in Roger's Garden; they might have been fire hardened but there was no charring. She felt a tingling sensation from them, and she felt that they were shifting in her hand though she saw none of them move. She huffed. Magic of some sort. She dropped them back into the snuff box, closed it and replaced it in Nathan's jacket pocket. She heard the shower go off then. She brushed her hands together dusting off the residue of snuff; she made sure there were no visible signs of snuff on the cloth of his jacket and climbed back onto the bed. Nathan appeared from the bathroom, towelling himself dry, a few moments later.

'Shower. Get dressed. Then we can talk,' he was dispassionate; business-like. He might have been addressing a hooker. She nodded impassively and left the bed, as she walked to the bathroom her legs felt shaky. She had not eaten again all day and the sex had been hard on for almost two hours. She enjoyed the power of the luxury shower as it washed Nathan from her. She had peed in the shower to help wash away his semen. Her vulva felt sore as she bathed it; it ached; her body ached. Nathan had not gone easy on her. She was aware of the burning gradually intensifying in her head again.

She towelled her body dry, then towelled her hair; leaving it damp; it was shortish, it would quickly dry. Her clothes had almost dried on the heated rail. She dressed, she really needed to be clothed now. She felt released after the sex, somehow more confident. If only the burning would stop. She could about ignore it for the present. She had no liking for Nathan, he intimidated her, scared her in fact, but she wanted the sex, she decided; she would want to repeat it. She returned to the main room and found her socks and boots. She threw Nathan a look, a tight half smile. He had finished dressing.

'Is there bottled water in your mini bar?' She needed to drink.

'Help yourself.'

She chose sparkling water and resumed her chair; she crossed one knee over the other, the toe of her boot pointed towards him; she was still on a nervous high and it moved quickly up and down. He watched her from his chair as she swallowed the bubbling water; his left leg barred across his right knee in the traditional figure four, his fingers were steepled under his chin. She felt like she was being appraised. The water refreshed her.

'How tall are you?' He asked.

'I'm five feet six.'

'What do you weigh?'

Saskia lifted her brows and shook her head.

'You need to put on a few kilos and build some muscle.'

'You mean I'm a skinny, unfit little bitch.'

'Something like that.'

'Why am I important?'

'You assume that you are?'

'Don't fuck around; you came looking for me remember. It certainly was not about any finer feeling you may have felt for my mother. That's not in you. How old was my mum when you fucked her?'

'How old are you?'

'I'm nineteen.' She would be twenty in three weeks.

'Samantha was twenty. You take after her; she had no barriers either. Though you might be more partial to pain.'

'I'm going to be covered in bruises. You simply enjoyed hurting me. And I let you.'

'You have tiny cuts on your shins and in your armpits. You shaved last night. That is vanity.'

'I am vain.'

'Boyfriend?'

'No, I don't want one.'

'Yet you enjoy sex.'

Saskia shrugged. She wanted to say *I prefer girls*, but she held her tongue.

'You shaved because you expected to go to bed with me, didn't you?'

Again, Saskia shrugged. 'If that's what you want to think. Okay. So, tell me what have I got that you want? That you are willing to get rid of my fetter in exchange for; what's the quid pro quo; I'm sure it isn't sex. Time to tell Mister Nathan Xavier.'

Slowly he stroked his stubbled jaw and inclined his head. His mouth curled into its default sneer. He shrugged.

'Okay, you're right, yes, it is, and I need you onside. You've inherited something, something old, that was originally intended for your mother. But when she died you were made the recipient.'

'Who died?' Saskia demanded suspiciously.

'A man called Trevor Challoner, a cousin of yours, of a kind.'

'I've never heard of him. Are you lying to me?'

'What would be the point? Really?'

'I don't know. Did you know him personally, Nathan?' She used his name deliberately; he had not yet addressed her by hers.

'Slightly.'

'Did you kill him?'

'I did not.' He seemed amused by the question. 'He was old; I believe he died in the bath. Don't worry I need you alive. I won't be your best friend, but your survival is imperative.'

Saskia continued to shrug. 'Maybe you drowned him,' she quipped. 'What is the legacy? An antique? You said it was old.'

'An Artefact. A powerful one. It can't be sold; it can only be bequeathed.'

'But what is it specifically?' She was fascinated, but she remained cautious even though her mind was racing.

'You'll see it soon enough.'

'And you want me to give it to you?'

'It can't be given. I want use of it for a period. And that is within your gift. It would remain yours and in your possession. That is an immutable fact. An arrangement between us would benefit you, as much as me.'

'Yes, but what can it do for you?'

Nathan sighed. 'The Artefact can enable me to do things that at present I am unable to do. And enable me to acquire things that at present I am unable to acquire.'

Saskia smiled sardonically, accepting his caution. 'Okay I'll change tack. I presume from the way you spoke yesterday, that there are others looking for me?'

'A handful, and that's enough. You have become an accomplished ghost. There is no record of you since you left care almost two years ago. You dropped off the radar. But everyone leaves a trail.'

'I wasn't trying to hide. I was just getting by on my own terms. Why should I trust you more than them?'

'Because we all want the same thing, we'll all make you the same offer. And I got to you first. I intend to advance my own interests; I have no intention of doing evil.'

'I don't care. How does this work, what sort of guarantees have I? When would my fetter be removed?' Saskia's mouth had become dry, she moistened her lips. This was important to her; more important than anything else. She felt emotional and it was a struggle not to reveal it.

'You would come with me. We would enter a temporary pact agreed between us and satisfactory to both parties as soon as your fetter is removed. I would help you regain your intent, but I would expect your compliance in return.'

'And when would the fetter be removed?' Nothing else really mattered more than that.

'You will be rid of your fetter in a matter of days. Then we claim the artefact; it's location for the time being stays my secret, until we have an arrangement.'

Saskia felt her heart beating hard, and her anxiety levels soared; the burning inside her head intensified, becoming like a small molten core at the centre of her brain. She breathed deeply; she hoped she appeared calm and in control. She wanted the fetter gone more than anything; but the thought of consequence disturbed her, everything resulted in consequence; it attracted her too; she was aware that she had a dark little soul. This was not a good man, and she would be placing herself into his hands.

'What sort of compliance? You said that you would expect my compliance.'

'By the time I am finished you will excel in the skills I can teach you. Energised and Grim intent, the declining of time; there must be compliance on your part; for that period, you would be my apprentice with benefits.'

'And if I don't want to be compliant?'

'Then you will have to find someone else to guide you. And that is not easy to do, particularly not one so powerful or as resourceful as myself.'

Saskia placed her fingertips to her brow. She felt weary; unwell. 'When would we begin?'

Nathan was silent for a moment as though caught unawares by her question. 'Tonight. Now if you like. There's time.'

She wondered what he meant. Time for what. 'I can't. It can't be before tomorrow.'

'We should begin as soon as we can, others may come. Why not npw?'

'I'm a Carer. Not officially. For someone who is unwell; an old friend; I've lived in their home since I left care. They depend on me, and I must make some arrangements for them if I'm going to be away. And I've done something wrong, and I must answer for it to them too. This is not negotiable.'

Something in her determined expression made him realise that she meant what she said. He had her now; if he pushed her, he might lose her and then he would have to take more extreme measures, which he preferred to avoid if possible. He nodded, agreeing.

Saskia stooped to pick up her leather jacket; she drew it on and considered the darkness beginning to form outside the window. She went to the door and stood with it open while she looked back at him. She shook her head conveying an element of regret.

'I must go.'

'I'll drive you,' he offered, he made to stand. 'Then I'll know where to come to pick you up tomorrow.'

'No. I have errands.' Her face was tense and uncompromising. 'I'll be back here by ten tomorrow morning.' She paused in the doorway. 'I need this Nathan, I genuinely do. I liked the sex,' she added truthfully. She left the room and closed the door silently behind her. Nathan relaxed back into his chair; broodingly he regarded the closed door. He debated if he should have simplified the process by the simple expedient of tie wrapping her ankles and wrists and throwing her into the boot of his car. It would have saved him the annoyance of waiting around on her terms. The girl was odd, strange; even refreshing; unexpectedly fascinating. Eventually he frowned and shook his head; he was dwelling. He needed a drink and he decided to go to the bar; there might be a pretty woman with whom he could entertain himself for the evening; for the night as well maybe.

Saskia thrust her hands into her jacket pockets, her mouth curved downwards in distaste as the freezing air greeted her. The darkness had formed outside, dispelled a little by the hotel lights, but they were soon behind her, and a rich cold dark consumed the world around her. She avoided Cooper Street and Steeple Road; she had no desire to meet Daryl's or Gilly's ghost, whichever one of the Nathan had killed. The Cemetery held too many restless occupants. She wanted to make her bus and she took the shortcut at the top of Cowell Street, down Shape passage. It was a narrow way mostly squeezed between the stone wall of the Rectory Garden on one side and the walls of buildings on the opposite side, including a Masonic lodge and a building which had been originally a Workhouse. Shape passage descended in six flights of worn sandstone steps with the slight decline of a cobbled expanse between each flight. It was poorly lit by old lamps with metal hoods, relics of the nineteen-fifties. Saskia could see the gleam of ice beginning to tighten over the cobbles. She almost changed her mind but taking that route would halve her journey to the bus stop. She was joined by a dark little tabby cat that tripped along the top of the wall, keeping pace with her, jumping between the growths of ivy that spilled over the coping. Her breath was white vapour, and her boots slid on the icy cobbles; she avoided surviving patches of thin freezing snow. She took her hands from her pockets, in case. There was a metal rail, but this too was coated with ice. She did not want to rip the skin from her fingers by gripping it, she knew it happened; was it freezing enough for that? She decided not to take the chance. Her feet slid away beneath her when she was about halfway down, and she fell heavily; she twisted her body as she fell and threw up an arm to protect her head and face. She went down with bruising force on her arm and hip. 'Fuck! Fuck! Fuck!' she hissed in distress and pain. She lay propped for a moment collecting herself and hoping she had not fallen in any dog shit. She climbed shakily to her feet and flexed her leg and arm and rubbed her hip; nothing broken she decided. There was no sign of the cat.

'Are you alright?'

The voice came from the direction of a narrow passage lost in total blackness between the lodge and the workhouse. A woman's voice, its tone husky; deeper than her own.

'Yes, I'm fine...thank you,' Saskia replied.

'You must have hurt yourself; you are only slender.'

'A bit. I'll be fine.' Saskia was still massaging her right hip and rear; she peered into the darkness. She thought that she could make out a darker shape even in the pitch black. The darkness appeared to shift a little and she caught just the glimpse of a white pretty face peering at her; then it was gone. And she wondered if it had been her mind playing tricks on her. She decided not.

'Come and join me,' said the voice, invitingly. 'It gets lonely.'

'It's too cold,' Saskia replied. But there was a strange dark part of her that wanted to go, the same drew her to Nathan, and had it not been so bitterly cold she might have been tempted. She began to walk away, still glancing at the passage.

'I don't feel it,' the voice told her.

After a few steps, the cat re-joined her, bounding along the top of the wall, and keeping her company to the bottom, where it sat down neatly, showing that it had come far enough. She gave it a little goodbye wave and continued to her bus stop; she was limping a little and cautious of the patches of ice. She was only just in time to catch her bus; she sat at the back, grateful for the warmth.

Saskia weighed one hundred and eighteen pounds. She knew that because she had weighed herself in the local department of Boot's only the week before; having removed jacket, shoes, and pullover; she had been tempted to take off her jeans as well, but that had not gone well on an earlier occasion. She had put on a quarter of a pound in fact since she had weighed herself the previous month. She had not felt inclined to reveal her weight to Nathan when he asked her, though she was not sure why she had withheld the information. She considered herself to be too thin, though she did realise that she was not some elfin waif. She must have looked like one when she had first turned up on Roger's doorstep, when she weighed not much more than a hundred pounds. At that time in her life, she had found herself displeasing, imperfect. She hated her appearance then and was dissatisfied with it still; she envied other women their appearance, unaware that many of them envied her appearance. She had preserved a mental image of the look she wanted, mostly from glossy magazines. She had a name for it; stylish Parisian chick; she supposed chic was more correct, but she personally preferred chick, and it really was at her discretion she told herself. But that still did not make it any less than a million miles beyond her reach.

She was worried about Roger because his health was in serious decline now. And when Roger was gone what would happen to her? That was why she was putting money aside, squirreling it away. She knew that it was selfish to think like that, but the reality had to be faced, and now he knew that she was stealing from him. This was the part of her day that she had been dreading. She took a long breath of icy air; she held it as she turned the key in the yale lock and let herself into Roger's cottage.

Saskia loved precious things. Beautiful things. Antique things. Those that could be contained in the hand and their inherent charm considered and appreciated; or standalone things to put on a shelf and blow you away. She was a fan of Bargain Hunt though most of the choices annoyed her, and the more recent program Flog It. When her mother moved them to York, she quickly discovered the Knavesmire car boot and Roger Lavery. He became the nearest thing to a proper friend she had. His illness had begun to manifest even then, and each year there was less of him. His condition was a gradual deterioration, and recently it had worsened considerably.

Saskia had been taken into the care of the local authority when she was fifteen and a half. She had been placed in foster care. she attended school for a few months; then sixth form when she was sixteen. Intellect and her mother's home schooling had made her easily the equal of anyone there. It had been a nightmare for her; a place populated by children! And they assumed that they were adults. She worked; she got a couple of A levels. She had not mixed. The boys did not like her because she laughed at them, most of the girls avoided her because she used to hit on them, often just for the hell of it; other than that, she had kept her head down until she became eighteen. Then she had simply just walked away because no one could prevent her. She went to find Roger Lavery. She had his address, his town. His phone number. She did not phone him though; she wanted to surprise him; but she also wanted to see him unprepared. She had not seen him in a year, and she knew how unwell he had been the previous year. Half the man she remembered opened the door to her. He had medication yes. But he did not want anything more, his mind was made up. Saskia respected his decision. They had never revisited it.

She had made beef stew in the slow cooker two days earlier. Quite a lot remained in the fridge. She put it in a Pyrex dish in the oven; Roger did not like the microwave unless it was a ready meal. She had not announced her return, though Roger would know she was back, he always sensed it. She waited for a time, standing in the kitchen, steeling herself.

She sat down on the sofa and leaned forward her elbows on her knees, the fingers of her hands clutched tightly into each other in the space between. She twisted at them suddenly feeling stressed and very pathetic. She gazed miserably at Roger. He regarded her with slightly amused blue eyes. The rims were pink. His skin had a slightly greyish tinge, it looked thin. His grey hair was collar length where Saskia maintained it. He was in corduroy trousers and moccasin slippers. He wore a triple layer of woollen garments over his shirt; he mostly felt cold, despite the flickering fire in the hearth. The coal scuttle was almost empty Saskia noted, he found putting coal on the fire a hardship, but he managed; Saskia felt guilty about the days she was not there, though there was a health visitor.

'I'm sorry Roger,' she told him. 'What you must think of me. Do you want me to leave?'

'That's a silly question. I don't expect silly questions from you.'

'How long have you known?'

'Since you began in the Summer.'

'How did you know. I was so careful.'

'Jenny told me, she's becoming more present; while I was dozing.' Roger knew that Saskia saw ghosts, she had confessed when he had told her about his wife's visitations and that she whispered to him.

'Yes of course she did, she watches me. I haven't spent any of the money. I'll give all of it back.'

'Jenny said you hid it all away. Under a board in your room. That's not very imaginative, is it? It's a bit of a cliché. I don't want it back. How much have you hoarded by the way?'

'Including todays; nine hundred and sixty pounds. It felt very strange today, knowing that you knew.'

'You went through with it. I thought you might wimp out.' He chuckled. He coughed, racked by it. Grabbing tissues from a box he coughed into them and threw them in to the fire. Challoner thought she saw blood.

'I had your permission. It will never happen again.'

'What's it for, the money? I think that I know.'

'I don't want to say.'

'That sort of confirms what I already suspected.'

Saskia shook her head and shrugged at the same time, both tiny gestures. She tilted her head a little, regarded him despondently; her mouth compressed into a tight line.

Roger turned in his chair wincing in pain; he winced so much more these days, Saskia thought. He reached up to the mantel piece and took down two creased white envelopes; they had not been there in the morning. He breathed hard, just that effort had taken a lot out of him; he was better in the mornings. He held the envelopes out to her; she took them, gazing at them suspiciously. Roger's cough rattled out again and he reached for his cigarettes and lighter where he kept them down the side of his chair cushion, his hands trembled.

'Go on, top one first,' he told her still coughing as he lit a cigarette.

Puzzled, she opened the envelope and slid out the contents. There was a document and a covering letter from a Valerie Leeman, Solicitor, addressed to Mr Roger Lavery. She was pleased to enclose a copy of the will she had recently drawn up on his behalf. The date on the letter was June 12th, 2003. Roger was able to get about in a limited way back then; his illness had hollowed him out in the months since.

'Look at it.' Roger rasped.

Saskia unfolded the copy of the will and read the contents.

'Oh Roger. Everything!'

'Everything. Keep that, you can wave it under a certain person's nose when I'm gone.' Roger's only relative was a second cousin, an accountant; he never visited but had expectations. 'Now open the second one.'

'I thought you were leaving everything to cats?' Saskia's voice had tightened with emotion as she read the second letter, also from Valerie Leeman.

'I nearly did. I'm sure you'll do right by them once you're sorted.
Is that stew I can smell?'

'In the oven. It'll be ready in about ten minutes.'

'You're going to have some tonight, aren't you? I worry about you when you don't eat.'

'I did last night. But yes, tonight I'm eating as well. Wait and see. Roger this letter says that you had a new deed drawn up for Beehive cottage at the same time as the will. And that we are joint owners.' Saskia's voice twisted away, and her eyes blurred with tears.

'No ambiguity there then, eh? Copy of the deed is in the table drawer, that's where I had these. The original deed and will are at Leeman's. Saskia.'

'Yes Roger.'

'You know that you've kept me going, don't you?'

'And you'll be going for a lot longer yet.'

'I don't think so my friend. I've been waiting for the right time for the big reveal. Better now than too late. Have you been fighting?'

'I'll get the trays ready. Do you want tea?'

Two

Saskia felt odd getting a taxi to the railway station the next morning instead of the bus. She challenged her boundaries even further by buying a first-class ticket on the train to Leeds. She had dressed as smartly as she could; she did not know why, but it felt appropriate, and pleasing. She had chosen to wear a slim fit, long black jacket over a close-fitting charcoal mohair jumper with a V-neck, also her newest black skinny fit jeans and black ankle boots with three-inch heels. These were her smartest items of clothing and as she sat on the train watching the passing landscape through the window; she glimpsed her own partial reflection and for a time watched it; she appeared calm. and it came to her at that moment that it was Claire Bosola who she wanted to make an impression on for some reason, as much of one as she could anyway. Nathan had treated Claire Bosola with respect, deference even. And she had sounded nice. Saskia wondered if she owned magic. She wanted her to. How powerful was she? Was she too in the position to have her fetter removed? She had to be surely. Saskia as always was prepared to gamble on her instinct, and her instinct told her that Claire Bosola could give her everything that Nathan had promised and presumably had a direct route to the Artefact bequeathed to her; she might even have it in her keeping.

There had been a clear inner conflict though and she had spent an almost sleepless night engaged in it; she felt attracted to Nathan, or to the nature of the beast he represented to her. That she actively disliked him did not matter. In fact, it added a certain spice. He came with benefits that appealed to her darker sexual side. She found the idea of exploring that compelling. Her darker deviant self was urging her down that route and she found it was hard to resist.

It was of course Roger Lavery who had proved the deciding factor; she simply was not prepared to leave him to it. He needed her; and he was giving her so much. She still had her doubts even as she climbed on the train. If Nathan had somehow sensed her intentions and come to the station for her, she knew that she might have gone with him. She almost expected to see him; her eyes even searched the platform for him. As the train pulled out of the station a feeling of relief washed over her.

After her second taxi ride of the morning Saskia entered the offices of Jackman Bosola and Wuddery. The burning in her head was at six on a scale of one to ten, she felt stressed, and she had undermined her confidence with so much unrelenting uncertainty about her decision to seek out Claire Bosola, that it was in freefall. The incredibly fit looking girl at the desk was name-badged Ayesha. She had dark lustrous hair, undulating to her shoulders and dark beautiful eyes; her skin appeared to glow and was ultra-smooth and her makeup was beautifully executed. She had a wide pretty mouth and an ultra-sexy overbite, showing white perfect teeth with fine gapping. She was wearing a skinny suit with pants rather than skirt, cheekily with no top under the jacket.

'Can I help you?'

'God, I hope so.'

Ayesha's brows furrowed into a little puzzled smile in response.

'Are you here to see someone?'

'Yes, I need to see Mrs Bosola...she's...'

'It's okay miss Shah I'll see to the young lady now,' announced a woman appearing from a doorway to the side of the reception desk. She was carrying a flask. She looked to be in her late thirties, a striking brunette. She was of similar height to Saskia; her build was lithe and athletic but with perhaps a toned ten pounds more distributed over her limber frame. She did not look a stranger to the gym; physically she was how Saskia saw her ideal self.

'Thanks for that. I can't drink this office coffee, and I need decent coffee in the morning. I'm just pleased it was in the car and I hadn't left it at home.'

'You're welcome, Siobhan. I'll leave you in capable hands.' She smiled at Saskia and gave her a little farewell wave. Saskia saw, as she walked jauntily away that she was wearing black patent high heels on naked skin. Without high heels Saskia guessed that she would be around five feet three.

'I heard you say that you were here to see Mrs Bosola, miss...?'

'Saskia Challoner.'

Siobhan checked her computer screen. 'I can't find your appointment here. Have you got the right day?'

'I haven't got an appointment.'

'You need an appointment.'

'Mrs Bosola has been trying to find me. I think she'll see me.'

'Mrs Bosola isn't in today. You'll have to come back.'

Saskia saw her plan suddenly falling into ruins. This was not going well.

'Yes, she is,' Ayesha Shah had suddenly reappeared. She retrieved a dictation recorder from the top of the reception desk where she had obviously put it down then forgotten to take it with her.

'I saw her about fifteen minutes ago going into her office with a client. What made you think she wasn't in?'

'I heard someone say yesterday that she wasn't.'

Ayesha gave a little shrug. She looked slightly surprised as she walked away. The client would have come through reception and been greeted by Claire Bosola there. Siobhan Redland would have been at the desk at that time. Perhaps she genuinely did need that strong coffee fix in the morning to help her function.

Siobhan looked slightly annoyed Saskia thought, but she was not paying that much attention, she was too relieved by the news that Claire Bosola was in the office.

'If you take a seat. I'll tell Mrs Bosola you're here.'

She sat in one of the comfortable reception couches feeling very on edge. They were low backed and had tubular chrome frames. It took her a couple of attempts and a shuffle to finally get comfortable. She felt disappointed that Claire Bosola had not disgorged from her office the instant she knew that she was there; she watched the clock and kept glancing at the doorways for the first twenty minutes; then she picked up a harper's Bazaar and leafed through it; then a couple more glossies on the look for Paris chic. Meanwhile clients kept turning up at the reception desk and staff from various parts of the office met up for chats; mostly they came for documents from the open plan office pool to the right of reception; it was behind glass, then someone decided to open the doors and it became intrusively noisy, Saskia thought. People kept sitting in the sofas close to her before they were scooped up for their appointments and Saskia started to feel hemmed in by the whole unfamiliar environment. Only Siobhan's head and neck were visible above the reception counter, and she spoke several times on the phone. Saskia tried to tune in to what she was saying but there were too many intrusive voices for her to follow her conversations. Eventually Siobhan unexpectedly popped her head above the counter and spoke to Saskia.

'Mrs Bosola is still busy. She could be a while yet; are you happy to wait?'

'Does she know I'm here?'

'She will see you eventually. Would you like a drink? Tea or coffee?'

'No thank you. I'll wait though.' Saskia decided to remove her jacket.

Another fifteen minutes and Saskia's shoulders and neck had begun to ache with tension. She felt uneasy, something was not right; she could sense it. Siobhan received a call on a Nokia phone she retrieved from her bag, she bent down to get it. Saskia watched her curiously.

'Okay,' she said. It was all she said. She put the phone back in her bag. She looked relieved Saskia thought.

'Are you still waiting?' Saskia recognised Ayesha's voice. She was carrying a package, marked 'courier' clutched to her chest. She had appeared from the corridor down which the clients were led, Saskia noted. She appeared surprised and a little concerned. She continued to the desk where she had headed with the file and laid it down. She turned again to Saskia.

'Miss Shah,' Siobhan stood hurriedly, looking unsettled. 'Can I have a word.'

'Just a moment Siobhan,' said Ayesha. 'Has Claire seen you?' she asked Saskia.

'Not yet. But I'll wait. She knows I'm here.'

'Claire's just left by the back. She can't know that you're here, she wouldn't have just left without coming to see you. She's not like that.'

'What? Are you sure?'

'I've just spoken to her. No more than two minutes ago, she was heading for her car.'

'Miss Shah!' Siobhan spoke quite sharply.

'What is the matter with you Siobhan?'

'Where's her car?' demanded Saskia rising quickly to her feet; desperation had entered her voice. 'I must see her! I must!'

'It's in the office carpark at the back. There's a little road on the right as you go out, if she hasn't already left then you'll stand a better chance of cutting her off that way, but...'

Saskia was already arrowing through the doorway.

'...I'll get her on her mobile phone.' Ayesha tilted her head to one side and her brow furrowed into her second little puzzled frown of the morning. She crossed back to the reception desk looking pensive. She reached for a phone, but Siobhan Redland looking desperate clamped her hand down over it before she could pick it up. 'Nathan Xavier said we had to keep her here in the office until he arrived, and away from Mrs Bosola,' she told her weakly.

'Since when did Nathan Xavier tell us what to do? Give! On second thoughts.' She turned and rushed out of the office.

Three months into sixth form Saskia had discovered that she could run. She spent PE at her school on the grass track doing her own thing; mostly avoided by teachers and students alike. She had the idea that she would build up some stamina and start running after she left sixth form; to still her mind and cool the burning in her head which it did seem to achieve, a little. But she had never followed through with it. It was part of the imagined new order that she fantasised about bringing to her existence, but was too uneasy about or scared, to try. High heeled ankle boots she realised quickly were not designed to run in. She heaved open the glass swing door and hurtled from the offices of Jackman Bosola and Wuddery onto the solid concrete sections of the pavement outside. She winced at the successive impacts of three-inch heels into the soles of her feet as they hit the hard slab work, the impacts transmitting to the tender bruising on her ribs and to her hip where she had fallen in Shape alley. She cried out in pain and frustration as she tried to flow. Every pedestrian out on the bloody pavement, and there was not that many, thoughtlessly seemed intent on getting in her way. She did not even know the colour of the car

Claire Bosola would be driving, it might already have gone past her for all she knew. Saskia came to a halt; the pavement had ended at the little side street Ayesha had described, out of which Claire Bosola would appear in her car if she had not already; it disappeared between the buildings; there was: 'Private No Entry' printed in large white letters on the ground across the entrance onto the street.

She saw Nathan Xavier then; on the other side of the street; he climbed out of a dark blue Daimler; he had parked it half on the pavement. His eyes fell on her at the same moment, his mouth framing words, unkind ones; he paused as he looked for a gap in the traffic to allow him to cross over. He was standing in the road beside the Daimler and cars were having to go around him to avoid hitting him. Leeds's traffic was not inclined to pause or slow for a crazy man standing in the road. So, Nathan stopped it, including the shout of a car horn, turning it into a long mournful bellow and the cars into compressed chunks of blurred colour. Saskia thought at first that he had jerked his hand into a fist in frustration, but as Nathan passed through the traffic like a figure in fast forward mode, at an incredibly fast waddle, she realised that he had used intent to decline time. Her ears were ringing, they felt stretched inside. The car horn stopped bellowing and the traffic resumed its progress as the false god time jealously reclaimed its tenure. Saskia tensed staring uncertainly at Nathan who now stood in front of her, no more than a couple of metres separating them; his mouth was set like a poacher's trap and his wolf's eyes were furious, but they were not on her, they were glaring at someone behind her.

'Naughty Nathan,' said the voice of Ayesha. 'Declining in front of all these people. You are getting some very strange looks.'

'Fuck you and fuck them! She is coming with me.'

'Care to try to take her?'

Saskia watched a red Mercedes Benz cabriolet slide from between the buildings and come to a stop, its long bonnet extending over the No Entry warning on the road. A slim blonde woman in a smart grey shadow check suit climbed out. It was Claire Bosola, and she did not look pleased. She stalked up to their little group and inquired coldly.

'What just happened. Who used intent just now, in public?'

'Nathan just declined time,' Ayesha told her. 'Now he wants to fight a duel.'

'Stand down both of you. Who is this?' Claire stared towards Saskia.

'You've been looking for me,' said Saskia quietly, suddenly feeling very wobbly. 'Nathan found me, but he lied to you and said that he hadn't.'

'Oh my God!' Claire exclaimed softly; realization dawned in her striking grey eyes; they fixed on Saskia, fascinated, surprised, and relieved all at once. She turned a hard, resentful look in the direction of Nathan Xavier. There was a brief flash of hurt before cold contempt took up residence.

Saskia shifted her stance and swayed, she felt an arm slip around her waist and support her; she moistened lips that had gone very dry.

'Oh my,' said Ayesha, holding on tightly and peering sideways at her. 'You're the elusive Saskia Challoner.'

'That's me,' she smiled into the beautiful face, enjoying the fascination of notoriety.

'Take her back inside Ayesha. My office.'

'Come with me Saskia,' said Nathan, it was the first time he had used her name when addressing her. He extended his hand towards her, his eyes willing her to take it.

'You know what I promised you. It still stands; you don't have to stay with them.'

Saskia hesitated. She felt faint, pathetic. She was annoyed with herself and with her pain. Despite that the temptation to go with Nathan was strong, she could almost feel it owning her like an evil spirit.

'What has he promised you?' Claire asked.

'Don't engage with her Saskia, she's not your friend,' Nathan urged her.

'Nathan said he could have my fetter removed. Give my intent back to me.'

'You're fettered? But Nathan can't have it removed just like that. It doesn't work like that!'

'She's lying to you!' Nathan claimed bitterly.

'I will never lie to you. I'll never make you promises I can't keep either. Only you can find a way to remove your fetter, but I'll help you in every way I can.' The gambler in Saskia wanted to take a chance with her. The darker sexual side of her personality wanted only to drive away with Nathan.

'Saskia.' Nathan's hand was still extended. She could almost feel his will physically reaching out to her, coercing.

'I don't believe you.' She made the gamble and broke the connection; she felt herself walk free.

Saskia turned and walked away, back towards Claire Bosola's office. She drew away from Ayesha's supporting arm. 'I can manage.'

'Okay,' Ayesha shrugged indifferently, but she walked with her, keeping step.

'You've got your answer Nathan,' Claire said to him.

'Looks like you've got your puppet.'

'I'm not like you. God knows what you had in mind. Why did I trust you?'

'Because you are a cock-struck bitch like all the rest,' he said maliciously. 'Your husbands going to find out about us. I won't hold back.'

Claire shrugged. 'It's a marriage in name only anyway. Time to put it out of its misery. I don't want to see your face again. Leave Saskia Challoner alone, or there will be consequences.'

Claire Bosola's office, though high end, was not overstated, it was deliberately restrained. With a curved desk in one corner, and luxury seating for suspension of formality in the centre, around a large merino wool rug. It had a view of the city through a scenic window and modern art on the polished wooden walls. And its own beautifully appointed bathroom, which Saskia was grateful to make use of; she needed to pee and to wash her face and have a few minutes time on her own. She emerged and looked at Claire Bosola quite shyly. Ayesha Shah came back in at that moment and Saskia threw her a grateful look.

'I've re-scheduled my appointments for this afternoon; Jamie's taking half of them he's quite capable,' she said. She was Claire Bosola's paralegal and dealt with most of Claire's general workload, though she was well able to manage anything put in front of her.

'How long did Siobhan keep you waiting for me?'

Saskia shrugged. 'I don't know, over an hour I suppose.'

'It was two hours,' said Ayesha. 'I see Jan's brought tea and biscuits. Come on sit down.'

'Have you eaten anything this morning?'

'No. I was too stressed.'

'Are you still stressed.?'

'No, I feel released. I am my own worst enemy. I must warn you about that. I'll get something to eat when I leave.' Ayesha looked at Claire Bosola.

'I could eat. I should be about starting my lunch now. Sipping a crisp cold Chardonnay.'

'Okay,' said Ayesha. 'My Tofu will keep.'

She pressed the intercom. 'Can you get me Henry's.' Ayesha studied Saskia while she waited for the call. She voiced her thoughts to Claire Bosola.

'She's beautiful, you just know her teeth are clenched together behind that mouth. I thought she'd be a waif, or a bit fay. I'm impressed.'

'Looks like her mum. Taller; stronger. A Challoner though,' replied Claire.

'I'm actually in the room,' Saskia pointed out.

Ayesha smiled archly and answered the phone as it buzzed. 'Hi it's Ayesha. Can we have three sandwiches; with hand cut chips. Lots of trimmings. Brown or white?' she asked Saskia.

'White please.'

'Chicken? Ham? Beef? Cheese?'

'Ham.'

'Two brown mediums one white large, all with ham. Thankyou Rosie. There, ten minutes she says. The chips are gorgeous.'

'Thank you,' Saskia replied, trying for a demure smile.

'Saskia,' said Claire Bosola, she tilted her head to one side and smiled. 'Would you mind if we looked at your fetter? so fascinating.'

'Not at all.' Saskia surprised them both as she pulled her jumper all the way over her head and bared her upper body. She laid the jumper on the couch next to her and turned her torso around so that they could view the fetter between her sculpted white shoulder blades.

'I've never seen one before,' said Ayesha. 'Am I to understand that it wasn't your choice? As you are so desperate to get rid of it.'

'No, it was my mum's decision. I was twelve.'

'That is seriously not fair.'

'I've seen a couple of fetters,' Claire said. 'Both voluntary. But seeing this one, it makes me feel angry. What was going through her head when she had this done to you.'

'And what about these? What happened?' Ayesha dropped down onto one knee beside Saskia and carefully brushed her fingertips over the bruising on her ribs which had now turned very dark. Saskia turned and regarded her, enjoying her attention and her concern.

'And this?' Ayesha looked at the bruising across the bridge of Saskia's nose. 'What happened?'

'Nathan made them.'

'No shit! But he is a bastard. And your arm! Claire look!'

'My arm was my fault I slipped on some ice.' Saskia reclaimed her jumper, suddenly self-conscious, and slid her arms into it; she slipped it back on and as she pulled the neck down over her head, she saw that Ayesha's eyes were peering at the definition of her neat breasts through the mohair; she was aware that she had watched them as she had covered. Saskia made a point of staring down at Ayesha's breast which was visible under her suit jacket where it had rucked forward. She was braless too; it was a cool appraisal of pertness and coned nipple; she caught a glimpse of tattoo, in the form of a slender curl of what she thought might be a vine, it wound from midriff to breast and disappeared beneath her arm. Ayesha followed her stare; she smiled unselfconsciously.

'What are we going to do with her Claire?'

'Well, you are obviously interested in her well-being so I'm going to hand her over to you for the present?'

Saskia laughed, surprising herself. 'I can look after myself.'

'Let Jamie take over your case load. Ayesha is my paralegal' Claire explained; 'I can supervise. Are you all right with that?'

Briefly Ayesha appeared uncertain. She considered the request looking from Claire to Saskia. Eventually she shrugged, perhaps lacking in total commitment.

'Okay. But it depends on Saskia; how do you feel about me riding shotgun with you? I am capable.'

'Well, I'm going home as soon as I'm through here. Even if I must come back.'

'Then I'll be driving you. And I think that you'll be coming back.'   'I can't ask you in.'

'I won't ask you to. But wouldn't you be better off staying here in Leeds.' She took a deep significant breath before continuing. 'You can stay at my apartment. You'd be safer there.'

God I would like that, Saskia thought. But she knew it was not workable. With a sense of regret, she replied. 'I can't leave Roger on his own overnight, he's too unwell.'

'Who is Roger?'

'My landlord. But he's my friend too.'

'I think we are getting ahead of ourselves,' Claire said. She turned her head in response to a polite knock on her door.

'That will be our lunch. I think we eat and share.'

Saskia nodded in agreement; she could not have looked at food until a few minutes ago, now she felt seriously hungry.

Saskia ate and told them everything that she wanted them to know. A brief, edited history about her life, about her mother and about Bernadette O'Hare; that Clare metaphorically pricked up her ears, and her brows furrowed into a little pensive frown when she had mentioned that name, was not lost on her. She described her encounters with Nathan over the earlier couple of days, though she decided to keep the fact that they had had sex to herself. She described how she had listened to Nathan and Claire's conversation in the restaurant.

'You were in the next stall. I recall someone being there. You heard everything then? It was empty when we stood up to leave; I'm glad you were canny enough to follow him.' Claire Bosola's face gave nothing away. 'I'm surprised he didn't sense you; he possesses that skill; he can scent magic on the air like a wolf!'

'I have a theory my fetter prevented that. Yes, I heard everything. I followed you then. But I only decided to talk to you after I got home and had time to think about what had happened. I tried to see you the next morning, but you'd left.'

Ayesha listened to her attentively and Saskia was aware that she had been appraised with a casual intensity while she ate and conversed. She was unable to tell if it was personal interest or simply curiosity, she preferred the former. She took a covert interest in Ayesha, her look cool, appraising. She had not bolted her food, in fact she considered herself to have been quite demure in her consumption of the sandwich, so at least she had shown Ayesha that she was civilized.

'You are being kind to me, but is that because you want the same as Nathan wanted from me? and you are simply employing another tactic; playing the friendly card?'

'Saskia, we have nothing to gain...'

'Let me answer that, Ayesha. Saskia, we don't want anything from you. And if you want to walk away from this you can. I don't want you to obviously, there's a lot at stake, and you are in danger. But I will protect you, no matter what decision you come to.' Claire wiped her fingers with her paper napkin, balled it and placed it on her plate. 'We are not your enemy, and we would prefer to be your friends.'

Which amounted to a pretty speech, Saskia thought. She had decided that she wanted to trust them; she really did.

'Mrs Bosola, you remarked earlier that I was like my mum, only stronger. That implies that you knew her.'

'Call me Claire. Yes, I did know her. She was unpredictable, I considered her mercurial. You can conclude from that, that I was not a fan.'

'Were you in the same order?'

'Yes.'

'Are you still part of an order?'

'No, I am not. That was a regrettable period of my life. My experiences have convinced me that you can only trust a small number of them. They are insular. Monastic. Some are ethical, some are not. They are dedicated to a purpose, they have agendas.'

'Yet you're working with others. Nathan, Ayesha. There's obviously more between you than top lawyer and paralegal.'

'Ayesha and I are friends. But we have nothing to hide; we are both Archers of Lugh.'

'So, you are in an order.'

'No!'

'Not an order!'

'Never that!'

'We are a free association!'

'Okay, I believe you.' Saskia was taken aback by their animated response to her words.

'We are not an order. We are independent practitioners of magic,' Ayesha told her solemnly. 'Some of us choose to work together. But all Archers of Lugh are dedicated to a common purpose. To live well in magic; protect where we can, and to not do evil. For my part, I am not active, it's a name only sort of thing.'

'Until now,' Saskia said chidingly. 'Very laudable. So, what happened to Nathan?'

'Nathan is not an Archer of Lugh by virtue of his sex. I had no idea that he was so dedicated to an extreme purpose,' Claire said. 'He's concealed it well. He was always uncompromising, and we are all in a sense dark, it goes with the territory, but what he was intending was extreme action with potentially frightening consequences.'

'With the artefact that now belongs to me.'

'It belongs to you. But it's not an artefact Saskia. Nathan lied about that.'

'Nathan has pretty much lied about everything,' Ayesha assured her.

'So, what have I inherited?' Saskia felt apprehensive; she felt the urge to laugh but it was not funny. She suppressed it.

'How comprehensive was the knowledge that Bernadette O'Hare imparted to you about magic?' Claire leaned forward on her knees and peered earnestly at Saskia.

'There are gaps. Sizeable ones, I think. Some things she said I was not ready for, and that we would blow the dust from them, her words, another time. I was only young.'

'Fingers crossed then. Here goes, did she ever mention something called a Place to you?'

'Yes, she did. A young girl can find something like that very appealing. I still do.'

'What did she tell you.'

'Let me get this right!' Saskia furrowed her brows in thought. 'A powerful magician can create a hidden Place out of activated imagination. Between dimensions. Or between the atoms of a dimension. That was how Bernadette described it. But she was either not certain herself, which I doubt, or she was allowing for the fact that I was only eleven when she told me about them.'

'I am immensely grateful to her that I don't have to begin explaining it to you. You have inherited a Place. A very unusual one. I'm not even going to try to describe it to you. I'm going to show it to you. We are going to show it to you. Ayesha and I.'

Saskia experienced apprehension. It felt as if event was closing around her and eating her up. But if it meant eventually getting rid of her fetter and regaining her magic, bring it on she thought, bring it all on.

'Will you come tomorrow to see the Place that you have inherited?' Claire asked.

'Yes of course I'll come.'

'When you've seen it and when you come to understand more about it, then you'll understand Nathan's motivation perhaps. We all might.' She added a little enigmatically.

Saskia frowned, her mouth compressed into a thin straight line as she glanced between Claire and Ayesha. Eventually she sighed and gave a tiny shake of her head.

'He promised to teach me the use of my power, my intent, when my fetter was removed. In return I had to be compliant. I took that to mean among other things that I was to be sexually available.'

'To make you compliant is much more than that. It means that he would as good as own you Saskia,' Ayesha told her.

Saskia had already assumed as much; a little dark corner of her continued to find it attractive. She recalled the seven sharp blackthorns contained in the horn snuff box in Nathan's inner pocket; they had felt so active when she held them in her palm. She was pretty convinced by now that they were intended for her in some way. She decided for the moment to keep that discovery to herself. The moment would come. The moment for everything came eventually.

'Nathan lied to you throughout,' said Claire gently. 'He could not have your fetter removed. I know I couldn't. I don't know enough about it to know if it's possible. If there's a way, I'll find out I promise.'

'Thank you for being honest with me. I simply had genuine hope for a brief time.'

'Don't abandon it,' Ayesha told her. 'Never give up hope; I'm sure there'll be a way.'

'I suppose!' Saskia said without enthusiasm, her voice tightened, and she held back tears.

'There's some ordinary but important business to take care of,' Claire said gently.

'Ordinary business?'

'The rest of your inheritance. We can leave it for now if you want to. If you've had enough for the day.'

Saskia shook her head. She was curious.

'I'm here now. I'm tired but I've been tired before.'

'Okay, if, you're sure. I'll get your file. I'll only be a moment. Your documents are in my safe of course.'

Claire stood and made for the antique safe against the wall next to her desk. Ayesha cleared away the remains of their tea things, and sandwiches, utensils, and the metal hot-dishes that had held the chips. They had been nice chips Saskia thought, and expensive, but she had known better. Ayesha finished moving everything to one side of the table, piling them on the tea tray.

'Would you like some more tea?' she asked. Saskia had become lost in the moment. Absorbed by Ayesha's elegant, edited beauty. She was exquisite, she smelled exquisite. Saskia swallowed, responded, she looked into the beautiful inquiring eyes, and felt herself grow hot.

'Do you have a sparkling water?'

'I'm sure there'll be one in Claire's fridge.' Saskia's nostrils flared delicately as she drew in more of the musky fragrance of Ayesha's expensive perfume. Her eyes followed the beautiful paralegal's jaunty walk, and Saskia turned her body to keep the visual contact as Ayesha crossed to the wall unit on the other side of the office. Ayesha turned after raiding Claire's fridge and met Saskia's interested stare with a tiny frown and a hint of challenge in her eyes, as she realised that they were unlikely to have left her. She returned and set down a cold bloomed bottle of Perrier and a tumbler, in front of Saskia; at the same moment Claire arrived back with a box file. Ayesha began to study Saskia overtly after that; she sat down opposite in one of the chairs instead of next to her on the couch; she crossed her legs and rested her slim hands on the chair arms; Saskia noted consciously for the first time that her beautiful nails were painted a gleaming dark red. Her black eyes gave nothing away; Saskia searched them, but presently there did not appear to be any friendliness on offer and she looked quickly away, to the sanctuary of the documents Claire had extracted from the file and had pushed towards her. Saskia sipped some of the chilled Perrier and gave her attention to Claire Bosola.

'The Will. I'll provide you with a copy. I wrote this up when Trevor discovered that your mother had died. It's quite a straightforward document. He leaves everything to you. Here is a list of his current assets. As you can see there is his house in Thirsk. Land and a semi ruin in a place called Hoardale; that is where we will be going tomorrow. There is a sum of money in the building Society. A share portfolio. I've already had inventory valuation made of the house contents. There's an amazing art collection and lots of very risqué antiques. It adds up to quite a lot of money. The taxman will get a feed out of it, but there'll be plenty left. Are you happy with my firm conducting probate for you at very exclusive family rates?' She smiled winningly.

'I don't want any special treatment,' Saskia replied.

'Take what is on offer.'

With the oddest sense of déjà vu Saskia peered at the document.

'The Place is not mentioned here. Though I presume that I shouldn't expect it to be?'

'Correct. The law of this land does not apply to a Place. Not even one such as you have inherited.'

'Please stop. You're hinting at things.' She felt tangled; suddenly contained by events. There was riddle here too, enigma. She could feel its presence and her thoughts pressed at its mysterious surface. She shivered. She had the sense that it was waiting for her.

'This is the second time in twenty-four hours that I have looked at a will, or a copy of one, that said that everything that someone owned had been left to me. Though that person is still alive.'

'That is an odd coincidence I must admit. Who is your other benefactor?'

'My landlord. My friend Roger Lavery. In fact, he isn't my landlord, not now. He had his solicitor draw up a deed putting half of his house in my name. He only told me last night. I feel quite stunned now with all of this.'

'You mentioned that Mr Lavery? Was unwell.'

'He refused anything but basic treatment. He has some sort of morphine injection every day, a nurse comes. But they are on about a pump.'

'And you are caring for him?'

'I'm a bit pathetic at it.'

'He obviously doesn't think so.'

'There are health visitors. I stay out of the way.'

Ayesha had moved across to sit next to Saskia. She took Saskia's hand to her surprise.

'Come on, you look shattered. Claire, I think this can wait. I'm taking you home,' she said.

Ayesha brought her car to the front of the office. A new silver BMW Z4 with a lusty 3.2 litre engine. She came into reception to collect Saskia; she levelled an icy stare at Siobhan Redway before they left; the receptionist returned her look with stony indifference, before going into Claire Bosola's office to try to explain her earlier actions.

'Nice car,' Saskia commented, vehicles were not an area of expertise, but she knew a 'nice car' from an indifferent one. She leaned back into the leather; she smelled the newness, mingled with Ayesha's fragrance in the contained space; she adjusted her posture as she pulled over her seatbelt. She gasped, pain probing from her ribs and hip. She wondered if Ayesha had heard her expressed hurt; it appeared sympathy was no longer on the table.

'I like it.' Ayesha started the engine and moved out into the impatient traffic. She drove fluently but with little regard for any other driver's right of way. Saskia studied her less overtly than before, sideways glances, looking now at detail, searching for imperfections, and finding few. A tiny mole in the indent beside Ayesha's mouth, another just below her eyebrow; a slim white scar close to the joint of her wrist, exposed and hidden in turn by the movement of the half dozen rose gold bangles she wore which responded to the shift of her hand on the gearstick. Other faint white scars were occasionally visible on the inside of her right hand and a suggestion on her left, as she moved both easily around the steering wheel. She had kicked off her high heels to accommodate her driving and Saskia watched her slim bare feet on the pedals. They were of course exquisite. The nails varnished in the same dark red as her fingernails.

'I thought that you'd be done with looking at me by now.'

'No.' Might as well be honest.

'Nathan fucked you, didn't he? You can be honest with me. I won't be judgemental.' The question unsettled her, the timing of it, rather than its nature; she would have been surprised if Ayesha had not deduced the truth. But she was prepared.

'When did he fuck you? I'm not judgemental either.'

Ayesha laughed appreciatively, though a little darkly. 'We had very dirty sex on several occasions. It surprised me when it began. I genuinely have never liked him. I ended it.'

'Not on good terms. There were barbs between you, I could feel them when you clashed earlier.'

'I didn't care. He has the issue. It's called giant fucking ego. He must win.'

'He's shagging Claire Bosola, and she knows that I know because I listened to their conversation.'

'They've been at it for years. You ended it today. And I'm happy about that. Did you think it was news to me? Somehow, I don't think so.'

'It would shock me if it had been.'

'She knew what he was like, it might even have been part of the appeal. But I might not have known.'

'Maybe It was a test. You like her, don't you?'

'You won't find a better friend than Claire Bosola. And you still haven't answered my question.'

'Alright, yes, Nathan fucked me. It was the best sex I've ever had. And I didn't know that pain could be so erotic. I was vocal, I'm not often vocal. And I orgasmed a lot and they were intense.'

'Are you trying to make me jealous? Because if you are, you've got me all wrong.' Ayesha told her with cool scorn.

'I know you're angry with me. I apologise if I've offended you.'

'You haven't. Why do you think that you have? What makes you think I'm angry? What do you think you've done?'

'The way I stared at you lacked any ambiguity. And I stared at you lots.'

'I know, you still are. I get the message. I Particularly got it when you stared down the front of my jacket.'

'I'm sorry. I don't know how to behave.'

'I'm sure that you do. I'm not angry with you. Do you think I didn't enjoy it?'

'I got the impression you were turning very cold on me.'

'I wanted to get us out of the office, so that we could talk without feeling we were being supervised by mum.'

'If Claire's been shagging Nathan for the last few years, I think she's hardly that,' replied Saskia, suddenly relieved.

'Don't underestimate her, but I'm certain Nathan must have turned down the heat when he was in bed with her. He has charisma. He certainly can be charming; he was when he was around Claire anyway. It can't be that he cared for her. Nada!'

'I think he liked my mum. When they were in the order, he said that they practised sex magic together.'

'Oh my God!' Ayesha shot Saskia a sudden surprised stare, she appeared slightly shocked, and amused. 'Did you know that he'd shagged your mum? before he shagged you, I mean.' Saskia nodded gloomily. She shrugged.

'There's something dark in my psyche. It's what made me want to go with Nathan; if it hadn't been for Roger Lavery, I believe I would have you know. He scares me though, but I scare myself too sometimes.' She studied her fingernails, comparing them enviously to Ayesha's. She picked at a little bit of hard skin near the edge of an index finger. It suddenly occurred to her that she had money now; she could afford to do something with them and not berate herself for spending money she could not afford on indulgence. She decided that she was going to be indulgent. Maybe not as indulgently polished as Ayesha; or there again!

'Ayesha, when you've finished smirking.'

'Yes.'

'While Nathan was in the shower I went through his pockets. I found an antique snuff box made of horn. Inside it there were seven blackthorns each about three quarters of an inch in length. I tipped them into my palm. I got the strangest sensation from them; it felt like they were alive.'

Saskia saw surprise flicker through Ayesha's expression; her mouth set, and she frowned. Then she grinned, her eyes filling with an impish light. She removed her grin and her lip curled sardonically.

'That is old-school magic. They will have been steeped in Nathan's blood and semen and hardened in alchemical fire. His intention can only have been to hammer them into your back, at seven points of coercion. If he had succeeded, you would have become his property, and your will overridden and subject to his will. He could have done what he wanted with you. It's called a compliance of thorns. That is what he meant by you being compliant.'

Saskia regarded the empty faces of buildings beyond the car windows; streets, whole districts; hiding God knows what behind some of the facades. Her eyes were impassive, her mouth a straight line in an expressionless face as she considered what lay within herself. She knew that there were dormant things that she had not yet met, that were curled there waiting to be woken up;

familiarities too were in residence, things that most people might recoil from, but to Saskia they were fascinating.

'I find the thought of that darkly compelling.' She admitted. 'I'm sorry if that shock's you, but it's the way I am. How do you know so much about it?'

'I'm not shocked. There's nothing can shock me anymore.'

'How old are you, Ayesha?'

'I'm twenty-four.'

'That's young to claim that nothing can shock you.'

'What are you? Twenty?'

'I'm nineteen for three more weeks.'

'And how dark are you?'

'I don't know; pretty dark. Did you love Nathan? You don't necessarily have to like someone to be in love with them, according to the Tv.'

'God no! There's nothing to love. He's a bastard, though some people love bastards I know. But I liked what he did. Then it was time to move on.'

'You were willing to fight him to protect me this morning. I envy you your power, your confidence.' It had felt good too, now that she had time to reprise it.

'I wasn't that confident. I might not have won.'

'If that's the case, you are amazing. I think I may be in love with you.' Saskia half laughed trying to make a joke of her words.

Ayesha voiced a dry soft chuckle. 'You must want to get into my knickers so badly. I get it now; you were trying to make me jealous, weren't you? it had nothing to do with Nathan.'

'Okay.' Saskia shrugged attempting nonchalance. 'I admit it, I want to be your lover is there anything wrong with that? and I'll do whatever it takes.' It was direct, honest. Saskia studied Ayesha's profile with almost microscopic scrutiny, searching for subliminal response. Surprise, contempt, shock, irritation; the devil was in the detail; in the flexing of tiny facial muscles, around the perfect mouth, or across the beautiful eyelids, so darkly lashed, or the long, exquisite eyebrows. Ayesha's response was immediate, easy, relaxed, unhesitant, her face unchanged or so she believed, but Saskia saw it, the fleeting sign of pleasure that barely breathed over the lashes of her lower eyelids, a visual quantum of cruelty in the infinitesimal reduction in her pupils. And, just perhaps, regret in a compression of her perfect lips, that almost had not existed.

'Not possible. There is someone,' Ayesha replied casually.

Saskia felt a singular rush of disappointment, and then the sting of jealousy; quite a lascivious sensation she thought, not to be underestimated. She accepted the knowledge as her new instrument of self-torture and locked it away inside herself; to bring out later and enjoy at leisure. She felt the pleasure pain of desire and loss. The crush was full on. In the coming days, the ache of jealousy would expand to sensual agony knowing Ayesha was having sex with someone else. Saskia would employ subtle cunning, she would discover when, who, if she spent the night with them, or them with her.

'Do you love them?'

'Not love. Obsession. Compulsion; that word. I'll tell you about it another time when we know each other better.'

'Mind my own business, eh?'

'No, I mean I'll tell you about it when we know each other better.'

'If you say so.' Saskia spoke the words softly.

'You play the Lute.' Saskia caught a stress in Ayesha's voice, it may have been the acoustics in the car as it passed under a road bridge, but it sounded wrong for that somehow. If Ayesha wanted to change the subject, she decided to allow it.

'Lute, Mandolin, Guitar, banjo, among others. Mum taught me.
I'm told I play okay.'

'I would like you to play for me then.'

'Now you may be patronising me.'

'I would never do that. I really want to hear you play, just for me.'

'Yes, I'll play for you soon, if you really want to hear me.'

'I want to be impressed Saskia.'

'I'm not mediocre.'

'Okay, so tell me, have you no magic at all? Half of magic has no need of energised intent, though it helps.'

'I had that conversation with Nathan. I've no designing, nothing like that. I didn't have anyone to teach me, after Bernadette I had no connections.'

'You're lucky you know.'

'I don't see how.'

'Magic runs in your family. It's in the sap of the tree. Most ordinary people need to claw it out of themselves and make it work. Most never try. Most that do, fail.'

'Did you have to? Claw it out.'

'No, I'm the third variety. It just popped up out of nowhere. No family history unless it died out a long time ago and made a mysterious reappearance in me. It was awkward for a time.'

'What about Claire?'

'Family. Her family name is Bosola, she didn't take her husband's name, Marriott. She is powerful, I mean really powerful. I think Nathan envied her. No, more than envy, he was jealous. He wouldn't have made the play for you otherwise. He took a terrible risk, but he must have considered the potential rewards worth it.'

Saskia wrapped her hands around each other and rested them on her knee. She studied them or appeared to. She compressed her lips and realised that she was clenching her teeth. She tried to relax.

'I told you that I wanted to go with him,' she told Ayesha. 'I found it extremely hard not to. If Roger hadn't needed me. I would have gone. He could have done whatever he wanted with me. Yet I actively disliked him.'

'Nathan is a powerful magician, but he also has a talent for reaching inside you. He likes to own you. I like to be owned. It attracted me to him, but only for sex, otherwise I loathed him. Its why Siobhan Redway took risks for him, it probably cost her job. He won't give her a second thought and she'd do the same again. He's hard to resist.'

'Are you still attracted to him?' *Liked to be owned*, she had said.

'I've moved on. It was not a relationship. It was convenient at the time.'

Saskia wondered if that was true; Ayesha Shah believed that it was. But as Saskia knew very well, people tended to lie; even to themselves.

'I was naïve believing him, wasn't I?'

'How were you to know that he couldn't have the fetter removed?'

'Well, Bernadette said, in fact she screamed, that it was almost impossible to get rid of.'

'Did she say that? 'Almost impossible.'

'I was distraught. In tears, it was a terrible argument between her and my mum, but yes those were her words.'

'Then why shouldn't you have believed that Nathan could have it removed. He lied. Bernadette did not.'

'I think I see where you're going.'

'The word 'almost' is your solace. Take some comfort from that and keep in mind that magic has a way of reaching out to its own. Your fetter might seem insurmountable. But it isn't. I may be pre-empting Claire by saying this, but you are special and the Place you have inherited is special. If there's a possibility for you to find a way to overcome the awful thing that was done to you, it's in all of this. Don't ask me how though.'

'What time have we to be there?'

'Claire said to meet her at around midday.'

'What does it have that Nathan wanted so much? It must hold so many secrets Ayesha. And if there's a chance, I can get rid of my fetter because of it.'

'You must see for yourself; I don't know enough about it. Regarding your fetter I might be talking out of my arse, but one thing is certain it's never going to be straightforward.'

'I'm scared I admit it.'

'I know that you are. Look, you either embrace it, or you walk away which is what I gather Trevor Challoner did. Though he lacked the strength, I believe, that you have.'

'Is that what he did?'

'He rejected magic. You haven't.'

'I haven't got any. That's why I'm scared.'

'Yes, you have. It didn't just go away.'

They descended into mutual silence leaving the city behind them. Saskia decided to inflict mental self-harm on herself, by exploring her latest crush and thinking of Ayesha with her unidentified lover. Though there was light; Claire Bosola obviously thought that they would be spending several days together; in that time, she could find, or make chinks in Ayesha's armour and bring doubt to the table. She wished she had the nights too, but they were out of the question. And, if Ayesha wanted a Lutist she would have a Lutist with the devil in her fingertips. She had brought the half imbibed 500ml bottle of Perrier with her, she reached for it and unscrewed the cap. It was still pleasantly cool as she swallowed.

'Might I?' asked Ayesha.

Saskia passed the bottle to her, deliberately not wiping the mouth. Ayesha accepted it, a hint of a smile curving her lips, amusement in her dark eyes. She placed the mouth of the bottle to them and tilted her head, the tip of her tongue addressing the mouth. Saskia watched the movement of her throat and the flow of the water over her tongue, until she ceased, and she handed the bottle back, a trace of water trickling from the ripe red of her slim lower lip to her chin. Saskia raised the returned bottle to her lips and drank again.

She watched the daylight crumble in the passing scenery and definition give way to the encroaching darkness. The beams of headlights in procession worried at her vision and she looked away, searching for ache; she was suddenly aware that there was no burning inside her head and there had been none for some time. The town lights were visible ahead, another mile brought them to a large roundabout.

'Don't follow the town centre sign,' Saskia said, 'it enters a one-way system. Next right and keep going.'

'Okay. Do you drive?'

'No. I want to. I meant to take one of those intensive courses when I could afford a car. I've no excuse now, have I? There's a turning on the right about a half mile ahead. An estate and some shops. Just keep going. Carr's Lane is on the right.'

A police car was drawn up by the hedge when they arrived, and another two cars occupied the drive which usually stood empty. The lights were on everywhere on the ground floor of the house. Mrs Molyneux was peering eagerly out of her bungalow window across the road. Saskia felt melt ice trickling through her veins, and she shivered. Ayesha parked and Saskia unhappily climbed out of the car. She waited for Ayesha to brush the soles of her feet with her fingers before putting on her shoes, then together they walked up the drive. One of the cars belonged to Roger's health visitor Natalie, Saskia noted. The other had a doctor on call notice in the windscreen. Natalie met them at the door with a glum look on her chubby face.

'I'm sorry Saskia. It's Roger. I found him. He'd gone to make a cup of tea by the look of it, he dropped it on the floor. I think he suffered a heart attack.'

They went inside and Natalie escorted them through into the lounge. The fire had diminished to embers, normally the flames would have been rattling the back boiler. Roger's body was laid on the floor, partially on the rug partially on the carpet alongside his armchair. A police officer was standing in conversation with a middle-aged man who Saskia recognised as Roger's doctor from the local practise, just down the road.

'The police come out for a sudden death,' Ayesha told her reassuringly, laying slim fingers on her arm.

'I tried to revive him. I called the ambulance,' Natalie told them. 'They went a while ago. I've got to go too; I must finish my round. I've made my statement. The Doctor's here to certify death.'

'Okay Natalie. Thankyou.' Saskia was close to tears, but she was trying not to smile sadly at Roger who was standing by the Tv set, a broad grin on his face.

'I see ghosts.' Saskia told Ayesha when the undertakers had collected Roger's body.

'Is he still here?' Ayesha was dispassionate, she was an Archer of Lugh, a Sorceress. She had summoned her first entity to the circle when she was twenty. She had not doubted Saskia when she told her that the ghost of Roger Lavery was standing by the Tv set.

'No, I think he went with the body. He may still be attached.'
Ayesha nodded. 'Are you okay?'

'Not really. I feel very cold. I didn't know that they'd come for him so quickly.'

Ayesha reached out to take one of Saskia's hands in hers. It felt icy cold, and the house was not chilly. Saskia extracted her hand from Ayesha's; she went to stand near a storage heater, hugging herself. She appeared quite forlorn; at least she hoped that she did.

'You go. You don't want to be here anyway.'

'I'm not leaving you.'

'I'll be okay. Come for me in the morning. You must be sick of me by now.'

'I am not,' Ayesha protested. 'And I'm certainly not leaving you.'

Saskia's shoulders began to shake, and tears ran down her face. She looked quite stricken. Ayesha went to her and stroked her upper arms soothingly.

'Saskia what do you want to do?'

'I don't know.'

'I know what we are going to do.'

'Do you?'

'I'm taking you back to Leeds and you're going to stay in my apartment. I'll make you something to eat or we'll get something in. Okay?'

'I can't Ayesha. That estate we passed, there are lots of nice people there, but there are bastards too. There are break-ins and word will get round.'

'Surely, they won't know the house is empty. There are some antiques here but nothing amazing; I don't want to stay here, but I don't want you here on your own either.'

'In the back bedroom there are a dozen antique boxes and small leather cases. They're full of silver vinaigrettes and snuff boxes, by people like Nathaniel Mills. There are nutmeg graters and
Bilston enamels. I won't leave them.'

'Then we'll take them with us.'

'You'll do that?'

'Start believing in me,' Ayesha sighed.

'Will they go in your car?'

'We'll cram them in. Come on, you need to pack some clothes. Any documents, copies, gather them up. Show me where this stuff is, and I'll start to fetch it downstairs.'

'What an amazing apartment!'

To Saskia, Ayesha's lounge seemed vast; A stunning interior with high walls and a floor of wide, engineered-oak, lime-washed boards; they were distributed with white hand knotted Yak wool rugs. It had mostly white leather furnishings, and glass and chrome and exotic woods; There were several sculptures from antiquity on display. The walls were hung with a collection of modern erotic art, still evolving. The entire outer wall was glass, with a view over the lights of the city of Leeds. Saskia set down her bag and crossed the room to gaze out over the night vista.

'Is that the river?'

'Yes.'

'How did...?'

'How did a paralegal afford an apartment like this? I'm not being kept if that's what you think.'

'I didn't think that you were.'

'I'll dish this up, I'll tell you while we eat.' She was referring to the stiff paper bags that contained boxes of Takeaway food they had brought inside. They had stopped outside an extravagant looking Indian restaurant to pick up. Ayesha had phoned their order ahead; the owner himself brought it out for them as they drew up to the pavement, He had greeted Ayesha like an old friend and said a cordial hello to Saskia.

Ayesha lit the stretched gas fire mounted into the wall and touched the lights to a soft setting.

'Make yourself comfortable. I'll warm plates.'

It had been a journey made mostly in silence from the cottage to Ayesha's apartment. Saskia had been lost in her own thoughts and Ayesha had left her to them, sensing that she wanted to be left to her thoughts. Saskia had been surprised that she did not feel more grief than she did at Roger's passing. She did feel sad, and she had cried for a time, but Roger had always said you should save your tears for the living. She would miss him.

'Oh Roger,' she sighed softly to herself when Ayesha had gone to the kitchen. Ayesha appeared again a few moments later carrying two slender stemmed glasses of chilled white wine.

'Chardonnay. Yes?'

'Yes.'

'You must be tired,' Saskia remarked, as she went through the action of swallowing a mouthful of vegetable Tikka Masala.

'We're both tired. But I'm not too tired to enjoy this. I'm trying to become vegetarian; the ham sandwich earlier was a lapse. I blame you.'

'Blame away. Aren't you ...?'

'No, I'm not. My parents are and my younger sister and brothers. My family is from Saudi originally. Why are you smiling?'

'I'm imagining you in a Hijab.'

'Ah, I suit one. I use them occasionally as a fashion statement.'

'I think you probably look incredibly sexy in one.'

'And you'd be right! it looks fab with a mini skirt and stilettoes. They wanted me to marry a nice Saudi boy, I didn't want anything to do with any of the cow eyed little shits! My sister is married to one. And my brothers hate me. But I terrify them. When you can knock the side of a house out with energised intent when you are fourteen years old, you tend to get your own way. In the end they couldn't get rid of me fast enough and my uncle Mahmoud took responsibility for me until I was eighteen. Fortunately, my uncle Mahmoud was an enlightened man, among other things. He referred to himself as a hedonist, and he moved among other enlightened men and women. He rejected religion for instance, as do I.'

Saskia detected a sardonic note in Ayesha's words about her uncle; it had intensified when she had referred to him as an "enlightened man, among other things". She wondered how much Ayesha was not telling, not that it mattered for the present.

'Did Claire train you in magic?'

'I was mentored and partly trained by Claire Bosola, in fact it was my uncle who introduced us; also, a Magician called Khalid Taharqa, who was my uncles business partner; he introduced me to other practises.' Again, Saskia thought she detected a sardonic tone.

Ayesha swallowed a last mouthful of wine from her glass and looked at Saskia's which was standing empty on the coffee table. They had removed their footwear, and they were both curled in chairs, eating from trays.

'More wine?' She stretched for the bottle.

'I would love some more wine.' Saskia offered up her glass.

Ayesha poured for them both, finishing the bottle. She considered another but decided against. She admitted to herself a growing fascination for this young woman, but she had not yet decided to like her. She had been catapulted into the orbit of Saskia Challoner without preparation and she needed time to get her; she saw intense beauty and an ability to beguile, and she was cautious of it. She had never mentored anyone, and she wondered if this was the start of that process in Claire Bosola's mind. At present she was Saskia's guardian in the event anything unfriendly should turn up, beyond that she did not want to think.

'My uncle died five years ago. He had no offspring, no wife. He left me everything including his half of a business. Now Khalid runs the business and I'm a silent partner.'

'What sort of business is it?'

'Property development and rental. It's quite successful.'

'Why do you work, you obviously could afford not to?'

'Because I like to. And I work with Claire, and she is my friend; I don't have any others.'

'You didn't think of becoming involved in your uncle's...I mean your business?'

'Too visible, I try not to upset the family; also, my father has a high regard for people who practise law.'

'I understand, it surprises me though, you didn't strike me as the sort of person who would care. How long have you lived here?'

'Do you think it was part of my legacy?' Ayesha's voice struck a scathing note, she felt that she had been criticised; she struck back with sarcasm.

Saskia shook her head. Ayesha looked at her searchingly.

'Are you sure about that?'

Saskia felt her instinct being challenged. She held her nerve and nodded with cool confidence.

'You're written all over it. Every piece of sculpture, every piece of art.' Ayesha's eyes narrowed suspiciously. She searched Saskia's expression for needle or derision, but she met only candour. She went to the eyes, still searching, those green bewitching eyes. Mistake. Shit. Even if denied as by Saskia Challoner's fetter, magic never fully went away; part of it found a way out, a winding secret path through the corridors of the psyche and the personality, to come out behind the hot gates of the soul, and manifest in other ways; in Saskia it existed in her eyes. Saskia's eyes were distant and sultry, and there was an underlying sadness inside them. But when they found Ayesha's eyes searching them, they widened in welcome and fell on her like wolves. Ayesha fell back on the only resource left to her and flashed resentment from her own beautiful eyes.

'I never asked for your critique of my personal taste,' she snapped, a little too snappily it occurred to her.

'I'm sorry, it wasn't a critique. I'm envious of you,' Saskia frowned, she was puzzled and slightly hurt. 'You really don't like me, do you?'

Ayesha felt suddenly ashamed. 'I don't know, I'm not sure. I'm sorry. I don't like myself most of the time. It's best not to ask me. Just take it one step at a time and don't expect too much.'

Saskia smiled, relieved. 'You are beautifully odd Ayesha Shah.'

'And you aren't?' Ayesha chided gently. 'Tell me about how you see ghosts.'

'Are you humouring me?'

'I would never do that.'

'Okay, some are just memories. Some are spirits. And sometimes I see entities. Some have physicality.'

'What kind of entities?'

'Both. Entities who were once spirits, who became something else. And sometimes I see entities who have never been spirits.'

'What happens when you see the spirits, the entities?'

'Sometimes they approach me or follow me. I think that they nourish on something I own. I don't necessarily go cold, like most people do, in fact that effect is the exception not the rule.'

'Do you communicate with any of them?'

'Yes, sometimes. Occasionally more than that. My first lover was a ghost.'

'Go on. You've got my attention.'

'When I know you better,' Saskia smiled.

Three

'That is your property, and the land around it from the circle of standing stones on the right. You own the mere and the woods.'

Saskia shivered. It was an unsympathetic day and colder still at the water's edge. The mere gleamed like old, polished iron under the low hanging sky. An icy breeze skimmed across it agitating the surface. Saskia wondered how it would look in the rain. Located at its centre was a small island supporting a stand of about a dozen trees and some dense shrubbery.

'It has a very moody atmosphere,' she remarked. 'How many people live in the Dale?' She could see two distant pillars of smoke trailing into the air from dwellings further along the valley. Another on the hillside.

'That is Howlsike farm up on the brow of the hill, according to the map. There are several other properties I saw when I came up here last month. Some are unoccupied, they are on their way to becoming ruins, like your own property; Your cousin obviously wasn't inclined to spend money on its upkeep. There's a small hamlet at the end of the dale.

'Do those sheep belong to Howlsike do you think?' The grassland all around the mere was close cropped almost manicured, it was scattered with grazing sheep, a few of them had begun to pay attention to the three women. More sheep were spread over the hillside pastures below the cluster of grey buildings that was Howlsike farm.

'Yes, Howlsike has grazing rights, that's mentioned in the deed.'

Saskia gazed at the expanse of dense, old woodland that skirted half the mere, its branches mostly stark and naked, tree roots clambering down into the water. She could see crows in the trees, and she could hear their harsh calls. She had no issue with crows. Her gaze swept back across the mere and settled on the house, a seventeenth century structure in dressed local gridstone with a tiled slate apex roof, though half was missing. It was about fifty yards back from the mere on rising ground, with thin woodland behind and an orchard. It was accessed by a flight of stone steps set into the wall and rising diagonally to a heavy timber door about eight feet above ground level. Two tall chimney stacks jutted from the slates; these were arrayed with long salt glazed pots: one stack for each end of the house. Clumps of straggly grass grew from the stacks and patches of moss between the remaining roof tiles and on the surrounds of the windows, which Saskia noted were mostly narrow lancet shaped, though a few were small and square. Most were missing glass, the survivors looked to be leaded and all of them were dark and empty.

'You are entitled to call yourself Lady of the manor of Hoardale. Though it doesn't mean a great deal. It comes under Manorial title, there are hundreds of them, all totally meaningless. You are not a peer or a member of the aristocracy.'

'I understand.' Saskia smiled thinly, self-mocking. 'Lady Challoner, hardly.'

'It sounds rather cool,' Ayesha remarked. Like the other two she was dressed in a thick coat; hers was grey, with a military style and she had on a fur lined cap with drop down ear flaps; very Russian Saskia decided. Claire was in a red coat and red mohair hat, Saskia in black, but hatless. Ayesha wondered if she was warm enough, she knew that she was only wearing a thin pullover under her coat; but it was not her business. She had been good company on the journey up, feeding her squares of chocolate bought at a garage stop. She had kept her entertained and had surprised her with a knowledge of antiques. Claire was there before them, and they had arrived only a couple of minutes after midday. She had driven up in a bronze Nissan Patrol and parked on the sward between the house and the mere. She greeted them with a smile and a wave when they parked next to her, but she looked tired and wan. Saskia wondered if Nathan had kept his threat. But she thought, *we do it to ourselves.*

'I'm sorry about your mister Lavery. It was brave of you not to put this off.' To Saskia's surprise she had hugged her tightly. 'You know we'll help.'

Even in their short acquaintance, Ayesha had come to realize that Saskia could be hard to read. She studied Saskia's face as she surveyed her fiefdom for some indication of how she was thinking, but her eyes were hooded, and she was giving nothing away.

'Are you ready to look inside the house?' Claire asked. 'It's a bit of a ruin, but most of its intact.'

Saskia nodded and met her gaze. 'I know I'm being quiet. I'm taken aback, I think it's beautiful.' She treated Claire to a rare full smile that wrinkled her nose and showed her perfect teeth, it went into her eyes and warmed them momentarily; it made her look noticeably young.

'Come on then, but be careful.' Claire smiled warmly and took Saskia's arm and walked her towards the house; Ayesha raised her brows, smiled, and followed them with a little posed walk, her shoulders hugged up against the chill, her hands thrust deep into her pockets. Claire withdrew her arm as they came to the steps and climbed them in front of the others, extracting a large antique iron key from her pocket. The timber door was made of oak boards and braced with iron; it was a couple of inches thick. The key turned the ancient Banbury lock with a satisfying clunk and Claire pulled the door outwards on creaky hinges, by a large iron ring handle. They entered together, pausing on a wooden landing with a short staircase that lay straight ahead; it ascended diagonally up an interior wall to a railed gallery that circuited the room. Another staircase on the right descended from the landing into the main room which soared to more than double height into the massively beamed roof space. Only a dim light filtered into the large space from the doorway and a couple of the windows.

'There's no electricity or mains water. The house is supplied by a spring.' Claire realised that she sounded like an estate agent.

'That fireplace is vast,' remarked Saskia appreciatively, she cautiously descended the staircase to a paved stone floor and approached a massive inglenook fireplace, an iron basket grate stood cold at its centre.

'I so want to see that lit!' she exclaimed.

'Don't light it until you remove the bird's nests in the chimney,' Ayesha advised.

'Why don't you come and help me remove them?'

'I might,' Ayesha surprised both herself and Saskia with her reply. She subsided into self-conscious silence, making a show of removing her fur lined hat and stuffing it into her pocket; then flicked her hair back into place with her fingertips.

'There's a kitchen with a water pump,' Claire continued. 'Some pine shelves and cupboards. There are some gaping holes in the roof at the back as you could see from outside. It's been left to fall into ruin for decades.'

'You don't have to make excuses for the house,' Saskia reassured her. 'What right do I have to criticize anything?'

They explored the kitchen, finding this also had an old range. The other ground floor rooms were dingy and empty, with a paved passage leading to them. Upstairs was creaky and partially exposed to the sky; the roof having partly collapsed into the bedrooms where things were growing. There was no pipework or drainage and Saskia realised that there had never been a bathroom, or a toilet.

'Great house to camp out in during the Summer,' she remarked.

'If you like roughing it,' Ayesha commented.

'I don't mind it a bit rough,' Saskia replied.

Their eyes met, mutual silent laughter in them. They ended their inspection. Saskia regretted the condition of the house, but in a way, she was not disappointed; she liked the place. She had not been joking about camping in it during the summer. And the roof could be repaired. It could be made sound again. The house warmed and brought to life with fires. The orchard behind was overgrown with briars and lank grass. It had apple trees and plum trees and drifts of fallen tiles. It was simply that the house was forlorn. She had not seen any ghosts.

'I really do want to see the Place.' They were standing in front of the inglenook once again. The frigid air penetrating the room from the open door and the windows and the fireplace. Saskia shuddered.

'It must overshadow everything, I know,' Ayesha said softly. She exchanged a look with Claire, lifting her brows and taking a long breath. She directed a *let's do this* look at Saskia. 'I don't know how you imagine it to be,' Claire said.

'I have no preconception.'

'You must have a picture of sorts in your mind.'

'I suppose that I do, a crude one, a child's vision.'

'And what is that?'

'Oh, God! I don't know. A room full of secrets. A vault piled with strange artefacts. I feel stupid even saying it.'

'Would it surprise you to know that there are Places exactly like that?' Ayesha said. 'But not this one. Shall I take us there Claire?' She threaded the fingers of her left hand through Saskia's right and closed them tightly pressing their hands together, palm to palm. Claire moved to stand in front of them, facing the younger women. Saskia sensed both of her companions grow tense, alert even, they seemed to take on a readiness as though they might be called upon to act. She felt a tingle of excitement and a clutch of fear.

'It is not down in any map; true places never are.' Saskia heard Ayesha quote from 'Moby Dick' as if from a long way off, as though she might have been shouting them from the edge of the mere, though at the same time she could hear her calm clear voice reciting them next to her. Her world pivoted into whiteness and then as abruptly stilled again. She was aware of an icy wind that clamoured in her ears and raked her skin. She no longer stood in the house in front of the Inglenook because the house no longer existed. She felt a surge of panic as she realised that Claire and Ayesha were not visible, they were no longer with her. The cold and fear cut into her like a knife.

She did not recognise Hoardale; the landscape lay under a canopy of snow, drifts of it. The shape of the mere was visible, but snow lay thickly over the top of it, and for it to stand, the surface beneath had to be ice. The island in the middle might be reached on foot over the snow and ice. The woods opposite climbed right to the top of the slope, and Howlsike farm had never stood there with smoke trailing from its chimney, and above the slope towered dark hostile cliffs shot with patches of snow. The cold rushed into her body, and she clutched her coat tightly around herself, though it made little or no difference to its bite; she wished that she had dressed more appropriately, but how could she have anticipated this, she thought. She was surrounded by a ring of standing stones a hundred feet across or more, they jutted out of the snow individually like misshapen grey teeth capped in white. She recalled the much smaller ring of standing stones on the slope to the left of the house; she wondered if that ring had once been part of a much larger monument. They had caught her attention as Ayesha had driven them down into the vale. the road had passed between woodland of conifer and Scot's pine. The mystery of the place had called to her then and she had straightened in her seat and paid more attention to the landscape. She had glimpsed ancient burial mounds through the trees on either side, their shapes under grassy shrouds, and more standing stones, mysterious and tall. The ring of stones had made a powerful impression on her. She had counted them as they had driven down the steep decline into Hoardale. Twenty-four larger than man-sized tapering menhirs. Now there might be over a hundred.

    Saskia cried out against the cold which had driven all the warmth from her body; her slim fingers already felt numb. She cast about for some sight of the house; she might have missed it in the snow she thought, its stone walls and slate roof under a layer of white. It was not there.

    'Ayesha!' She yelled. She had to come. Saskia had never been so afraid. 'Ayesha! Claire!' she howled. She ranged the snow with her gaze searching desperately for footprints that might show that they were there too, and missing her gone in search of her, but nothing had disturbed the inches thick whiteness; tears came and turned to ice on her cheeks.

    'No! No! Not like this!' she yelled angrily, though there was fear, almost terror in her voice too. She had a brief dark thought that Ayesha and Claire were her enemies after all; that they had sent her to the Place to die. The sudden thought tortured her, almost as much as the cold. She knew that she would not survive for long in these conditions. Hypothermia would claim her, and she would lay huddled in the snow and fall into a sleep from which she would never wake up.

She heard a loud snuffle behind her, followed by the hoarse bark of a large dog; the sound jarred into her. Shaking uncontrollably now with the cold, Saskia turned around, though barely able. She was confronted by a massive hound at the edge of the stone ring. She saw it through eyes blearing with tears. It resembled an elongated wolfhound, only bigger, more muscularly powerful. Its coarse coat was pale, white in places, tawny at the shoulders but mostly yellowish along its back and flanks and down its long legs. It had malevolent red eyes. Its snout ridged up into a snarl, showing rows of pointed teeth as she met its stare. Twenty feet beyond it were two more, one to either side, their bodies half crouched. They were not snarling like their companion, but their red eyes were fixed, and watchful. Saskia's whole body shuddered in terror, and she could hear herself making strange little sobbing sounds at each jerky movement of it. She remembered the teeth of a Doberman Pincher within inches of savaging her as a ten-year-old; the image had never left her.

She heard a shout through the sough of the wind and the noise of her own teeth chattering. A man's harsh voice. She did not understand the words, but she heard the tone of command in it, the expectation of obedience. The lead dog ceased to snarl as soon as it heard the voice; it growled, a low murmur of threat deep in its throat, and its red eyes warned her that she should not dare to move; she could not have anyway. She saw the man emerge from the treeline then. He was stocky and powerful; he carried a spear. He was swathed in fur, over his trunk and limbs. It almost seemed part of him. He had seen her, and he was striding towards her purposefully.

'Sa...sa...sa!' It was the sound of a voice. It was not the mans. It sounded like it was coming from inside her head.

'Sa...sa...sas.' It came again. It sounded familiar somehow. Then she suddenly realised what it sounded like. Voices lost in static on the radio, just like when she tried to tune in a station one time for Roger Lavery.

The man had begun to pass between the stones. Fur extended over his neck and head like a strange hood. She could see his broad features contained within the fur as he approached her. He had a wide mouth, and it was smiling in satisfaction. He owned small hard eyes. He pulled a fur pelt from over his shoulders to wrap her in, she assumed; she felt almost detached, and there were lengths of animal hide; to bind her with, she wondered. She did not care anymore she decided, the ache of the cold was too much to endure. She could no longer stand, and she dropped to her knees.

'Sas...Saskia!' The voice was almost clear. She recognised it.

'Ayesha?' she could barely frame the word. She was aware of a shadow next to her. An unformed, unresolved shape. Shifting, moving slightly, in and out of partial focus; she had seen some ghosts behave like this. She reached out to touch it, her arm barely responded, and she was not sure if it had performed the action, she had required of it. She laughed hysterically at her own misery. Then she heard the man shout, and she looked through grainy vision at him. He was angry, baffled, hurrying forward he shouted again, a command and the dogs snarled and surged forward.

'You're frozen!' She was kneeling, shuddering on the paved floor of the house; she had Ayesha's hand gripped in hers; there was snow clinging to her boots and jeans. Ayesha dropped to her knees in front of her and wrapped her arms about her.

'Put your hands inside my coat, take my warmth. I'll give you more. We thought that we'd lost you!'

'What happened?' Saskia asked; she felt that she was able to speak coherently. She pushed Ayesha's coat away from her, feeling warmed through, the glow was too much now, she felt too hot. They had taken her to Claire's Patrol and filled the cab with heat from the started engine. Ayesha guided her into the middle seats and sat with her, palms pressed to her sides; strangely it felt like she was giving her warmth, transferring it to her. Claire occupied the front passenger seat side on. She had brought a flask of tea and Saskia had relished the hot drink, and the feel of the warm metal cup in between her shaking hands.

'The Place allowed you, but not us,' Claire told her. 'I've never experienced anything like that before. And I've been to many Places. When we tried to come after you, it denied us, and that was the most unnerving thing of all. I have considerable magical power, but I am not a craftsman of the Boundless Edge, I could not force a way. Together we could not force a way. In the end it was Ayesha who reached out and found you.' Claire looked shaken, she had appeared horrified as they took Saskia to the patrol, even guilty; though Saskia didn't see how any of it was her fault.

'I'd been close to you for the best part of twenty-four hours so in a sense we were attuned, I tried hard to reach you; at first I couldn't locate you, but I kept trying, I wasn't going to give up.'

'I could hear you.'

'Could you?'

'You were all staticky and broken up. Then I saw you, but you were just a blur, a shadow. I called out your name.'

'I heard that. I knew I had you then. And I felt your hand. You looked terrified when you came back. Did I hear dogs snarling?'

'Yes. I wasn't alone.'

'What happened to you? in your own time.' Claire said.

'Then I'm taking you home,' Ayesha told her.

'Is it a Place Claire? It felt like a world.' Saskia finished her account of her experience, now she voiced her doubts.

'It's a Place I promise. And if you ever go back after that experience, you will find that out for yourself. The man you encountered was probably simply a man, but I can't say that for certain, the dogs sound like Fen hounds, bred by the old so called 'Dark Elf' races. The Shee and the Dokk Alpha. God, I wouldn't blame you if you decided not to have anything to do with this part of your legacy, and I refuse to put pressure on you to do that.'

'Why wouldn't I want anything to do with it?'

'You have no energised intent. No other craft. After this experience it wouldn't surprise me if you simply wanted to walk away.'

'That's not my way.' Saskia insisted.

She was aware of Ayesha's eyes on her. As she replied to Claire, she saw her ease into the corner made by the back of the seat and the door. Ayesha folded her arms and gazed at her as if with fresh eyes, certainly with renewed interest; she was smiling and frowning at the same time, trying to work her out.

'By Shee, you mean Faeries?'

'The Place permeates our world at Hoardale, and the worlds of the Sidhe, where they stand in proximity; that's why they are similar. They look almost identical. It's called the Wild Saskia. That is the name of your Place. It was not made by human magicians but by the Shee. It was a gift from one of the races of the Shee, possibly the oldest of them, to your family for whatever reason. My family and yours have been linked for generations because of it, and here that link has been remade between you and me. I'm nothing more than a magician who is a lawyer, and in all honesty, I know very little about the Wild. My father knew so much more. So yes, it is a Place, there simply aren't many others like it.'

'How big is it?'

'I have a chart case in the back for you. With maps of Hoardale and some hand drawn ones of the Wild. But I believe it's about twelve miles by eight miles wide, though it is irregular in shape. It's mysterious and its old. I believe it is inhabited. Some of those inhabitants were friendly once or just less hostile, that's what my dad told me. But some simply have dark souls. It can be a dangerous place, uncompromising as you've seen first-hand. But there are supposed to be connections to a powerful kind of magic. Ancient stuff. It can be tapped and harnessed if you know how; it's what Nathan coveted.'

'Couldn't he have simply gone there? Found and taken what he wanted. He has the skill set surely!'

'No, to be frank. The key is in the blood Saskia. That's what he lacks. It belongs to you. It's your fiefdom if you want it. But you must discover how to properly own it, because I can't tell you, I don't know how. No other member of your family will have set about that task with a disadvantage like the one you have. Most have had knowledge passed on to them, mother to daughter, father to son. The female line was always the dominant one, and Challoner women always keep their name. The last hundred years has seen a male line that was quite broken, even effete. No Bacchus's or Drakes there,' she remarked enigmatically. 'You almost need to go back to square one if you ever take it on. I don't envy you. It might kill you or drive you insane. I and a few others would always be there to support and get to pick up the pieces; I suggest that you don't return to Hoardale until you are much more prepared. On a more ordinary level, I was going to suggest that we looked over your house in Thirsk this afternoon, but after your recent experience I'm convinced that it's not a wise idea; you look spent. I'm going to leave the keys with you and Ayesha, so you can drive back up when you're ready. I've some personal business I need to deal with anyway. So, I think that we should call a halt for now.'

Saskia nodded; she could not have agreed more, she both looked and felt exhausted, and the burning inside her head which had relented for a period, had returned with vengeance.

A client and friend of Claire Bosola's had once confided that she believed fairies lived at the bottom of her garden, in the vicinity of an ancient spring; that in the evenings she occasionally saw them; that they were strange and furtive; that they were visible to her for only moments at the side of her vision, and never when she looked at them directly. She said that they were normal size, not like the fairies in the books; she had seen them for years; she was not mad she promised; she had told other friends about them, and one said that she had glimpsed them too. Claire had smiled and said that there were many mysteries in the world and that she did not think she was mad or disbelieve her. How could she in all conscience, when she too had fairies at the bottom of her garden. In the wood just beyond the orchard. They did not live there, but they did visit, and Claire did not see them indirectly; she could see them in the direct line of her vision. There were ancient standing stones in her wood, most had fallen or been pulled down over time; they lay buried, just mossy bits protruding here and there. But three remained upright, a good distance apart, and in the vicinity of one particularly, she occasionally met with one or sometimes two representatives of the oldest of the Shee races, who Claire knew regarded humankind with an element of benevolence and occasional friendship, particularly humans with magic, and north of the Lloegyr: the archers of Lugh especially.

The early winter darkness had only just descended when Claire arrived at her roomy brick-built country home. She left her car on the gravel drive next to her housekeepers Land Rover; she did not immediately go inside; she went through the side gate and opened the kitchen door to say that she was home to her housekeeper Grace, and that she would be another half hour. She walked through her pretty garden, illuminated by lights fastened to the house walls; as she passed beyond their reach into her orchard, she coerced a ball of static at her fingertips, of sufficient power to light her way; she lodged it above her head. She entered her wood by way of a pivoting cast iron gate of Victorian manufacture and followed the path to the largest of the standing stones in the old wood. She could hear the light wind stirring the naked branches of the trees beyond the hum of her orb of fizzling energy; there were no stars or moon, just unseen masses of cloud. The Shee was waiting for her as she knew it would be. A pretty female, with short spiky white hair and silver-grey eyes; she looked thirty but might have easily have been six hundred, Claire had known her since childhood; she had never undergone change in that time. She was attired in black, tunic and breeches, and boots and a cloak with a silver clasp in the form of an ouroboros. She was of the Tuatha de, sometimes called the Danu, the oldest of the Shee races.

'My huntsman was not given the opportunity to acquire Saskia.' The Shee said in a soft sibilant voice; there were no formalities, no greetings.

'It certainly didn't go to plan,' Claire replied. 'I barred Ayesha's access to the Geifu-Prydain and then Saskia's return when I saw that Ayesha was reaching for her. Ayesha is strong, but nowhere near my strength. Something else was active!'

'Saskia herself perhaps.'

'She's fettered. I can't see how that would be possible.'

'Then Ayesha is stronger than you thought, or something else transpired.'

'Such as?'

'I do not know. Perhaps the Gift itself intervened in some fashion. It does not matter; it cannot be undone. I did counsel against placing her in our care. The energy did not feel proper; you must protect her now. If I can assist I will; though I do not see how.'

'I'm left with the alternative.'

'Which is not without merits. Will your brother press his seal?'

'Hal will do as I ask.'

'Does he know anything of these events Claire?'

'I'll bring him up to speed tonight, I mean, I will familiarise him. He does know about the Geifu-Prydain, and he knows that I'm still connected to the Old Path. He's trod it himself, or he wouldn't be who he is.' She intended to speak to her brother Hal on the phone that night, immediately she had eaten and on her second glass of Sauvignon. 'We'll protect Saskia with a mortal Covenant.'

'I sense anxiety. You appear tired and troubled Claire.'

'As, do you Anghyrad. Your problems far exceed mine.'

'They may yet intersect.' The Shee cautioned, she was pensive.

'How so?' Claire's curiosity became instantly aroused.

'The huntsman encountered a CaolShee in the Geifu-Prydain.'

'In the Wild! Fuck!'

'Indeed.'

'Did he act?'

'He ended it, not without difficulty. If more come, he will not seek to engage.'

'This is getting thought-provoking.' Claire remarked, choosing the words carefully.

Anghyrad compressed her pale mouth. 'That is one way of looking at it.' she replied.

After thirty minutes Saskia felt driven to say something. The burning had never been this intense, she felt like her head was going to explode with the heat. If she was going to die, she thought, she at least wanted Ayesha to know what had caused her to flatline.

'Ayesha,' she said in a soft voice.

'Mmh? What is it?' Ayesha was distracted; the events of the morning had caused her to call herself out. Saskia's silence had been unbroken, quite intense; not surprising given the morning's events, and it presented Ayesha with an opportunity to summon herself before her own personal inquisition. Saskia Challoner had figured exclusively; notably an admission that she had allowed her to burrow deep under her skin and with only token resistance on her part; more than that, she actively wanted her there; though she was determined not to let her know it just yet. She was going to prove a serious complication to her life. And presently she did not know how she viewed that.

'I'm not very well,' Saskia told her in a quiet voice.

'If you're going to be sick, puke in a bag. There's one stuffed in the door pocket.'

'I'm not going to be sick.'

'What's the matter with you?' She sounded more impatient than she had intended. She realised that she was being unsympathetic, quite callous in fact.

'I have a problem. It has affected me since I was fettered. A burning sensation deep inside my head, like a hot coal from a fire.'

'Is it with you all the time?'

'No, it comes and goes, but most days. Mostly I can tolerate it. Often, it's bad. Sometimes it's intense. But it has never been like this. It came on when Claire was telling me about the Wild.'

'Why didn't you tell me about this before now?'

'I thought I could manage it. I was trying not to bother you with it. I have a mantra. It hasn't worked. I only use it when it's really bad.'

'Can you use another word please rather than bad?'

'Okay when its fucking awful.'

'Can you wait until we get home?' Ayesha winced, realizing how mean that had sounded. Saskia remained silent. Ayesha glanced at her white face.

'No of course you can't; I was being a bitch.'

'Whilst I've been with you, I've not felt it until now. I think connection with the Wild caused it. What are you doing?'

'I'm turning into the car park of that pub.' She stopped the BMW in the furthest corner of the Matelot's carpark. She turned towards Saskia.

'Look at me.' Saskia turned in her seat to regard her. Ayesha fixed her stricken face with a cool gaze. She extended her arm.

'Lean into me.'

'I don't want a hug,' she lied.

'I'm not going to hug you. Come here. Put your head on my arm. Close your eyes, try to relax.' Saskia nuzzled into Ayesha's upper arm; Her smoky green eyes moved curiously over Ayesha's face before she hooded them; she released a shudder of breath. Ayesha rested the fingers of her extended hand on Saskia's slim shoulder. She studied the angular beauty; the narrow length of her jaw; the ear exposed by the short floppy hairstyle. She frowned and watched as the outer corners of Saskia's eyes drew in as she winced, and her breath caught at her pain.

'I think that my mum had the same condition,' Saskia murmured. 'She was always angry, and there were days...' she left the rest unsaid. 'I think it contributed to her death in the end. She went to sleep. Didn't wake up.'

'Yes, it probably did. But that's not going to happen to you.'

Tenderly Ayesha stroked Saskia's brow with the backs of the fingers of her free hand. Then she moved them to her head and stroked her dark hair and pushed her fingers through its short length, letting it collect between them; she repeated this gently, soothingly, allowing the moments to become minutes. She regarded the beautiful face, almost upturned to her; she listened to Saskia's breathing; it had been occasionally distressed, now it sounded like the softness of breath drawn and released in sleep. She studied the definition of her mouth. On impulse, unable to prevent herself, she leaned down and pressed her lips to it. Saskia's eyelids fluttered open.

'I'm not asleep you know,' she said.

'I know,' Ayesha breathed.

'You took it away piece by piece.' Saskia's eyes filled with tears, they tumbled from her eyelids and streamed down her face. 'It's left me.'

'You're not unique my darling, it happens to others now and again. Not to everyone though. Having your fetter obviously makes it chronic.' Ayesha kissed a tear as it trickled down. 'All your little energy centres are humming away. It was quite delightful listening to them as they emptied into me. I was surprised how much there was. It will come back, but you can be you for a time.'

Her voice became gently chiding. 'Next time, fucking awful, bad, or indifferent you tell me.'

'Are you hungry?'

Ayesha's BMW was eagerly eating up the miles again on the journey back to Leeds.

'You don't know what it means to me to be free of it. It's had such an impact on my life, it's made me so miserable. I know that you said it will come back, but you'll take it away again, won't you?'

'If you behave,' replied Ayesha.

Saskia laughed appreciatively. 'Yes, I'm hungry.'

'You didn't have breakfast again, that has to stop.'

'It will I promise.'

'You look shattered. I intended to take you out to eat, but I vote we get another takeaway.'

'Fine by me, my Ayesha. And it's my turn to pay. I want to play for you tonight too.'

'And I would like that very much if you're not too tired. You can call me your Ayesha, but remember what I told you, there is someone.'

'I know.' She spoke softly and turned her head away; she raised a hand to pluck lightly with her fingers at the short hair around her right ear. She looked thoughtfully at a descending dark that was leeching the colour out of the landscape. It was not supposed to be dark for another hour, but night seemed happy to step up to the table, invited by massive nimbostratus cloud forms, the colour of graphite moving out of the west. Lightening flashed, stalking between Fewston reservoir and Jack hill. Only a moment later thunder crackled malignly.

'Spectacular,' commented Saskia.

A few minutes later hail came down in a cataract and headlight beams seared and danced through it. Saskia watched Ayesha's hands tense on the steering wheel, the tension flexing across her shoulders and down her arms. 'It won't last,' she promised her.

A couple of minutes later it was over. More strokes of lightening were threading the blackness behind them, with thunder close by, but for the time being they were out of reach of the storm.

'I make a decent spaghetti bolognaise,' Saskia remarked, 'I'm sure you could add some sophistication to it.'

'I find that seriously tempting,' Ayesha responded.

They made and consumed a spicy Fusilli Bolognese, then took their chilled Chardonnay to watch in the dark from Ayesha's wall of glass, as the storm descended on Leeds. Hail came in shrouds, and rivulets of melt clawed down the glass. Violet lightnings threaded across the night exposing chunks of the city under flailing hail; they stalked the courses of the river Aire and the canal, vocal thunder ranging with them.

'It sounds pleased with itself,' Saskia remarked. She was standing; she held her glass by its stem, her other arm was laid across her breast, fingers resting in the crook of her elbow.

'At least its natural,' Ayesha replied, glancing at Saskia; she was sitting in an Eero Saarinen womb chair, one knee over the other, the toe of her slim fitted boot pointed, rising, and falling with metronomic regularity.

'Did you think it might not be?'

'The thought crossed my mind briefly.'

'You thought it had been raised?'

'First at Jack hill. But you allayed my fears, you were confident.
Then when it followed us to Leeds half an hour ago.'

'You suspected it might have been sent for us?'

'At first, not now.'

'By whom...Nathan?'

Ayesha screwed up her nose registering contempt. 'He will not just roll over. He's scared of Claire but that doesn't mean to say he doesn't have other options. There are two or three dark orders who wouldn't mind getting their hands on you once they learned about the Wild. That's why I'm babysitting.'

'Is that how you see it?' Saskia frowned, she showed resentment and the beginning of distress.

'Now you're all hurt; don't turn away, look at my face.' Ayesha allowed a slow smile to curve her mouth, she laughed silently showing her parted teeth, her laughter lit her eyes.

'Little cow.' Saskia smiled back in relief.

'No, I don't see it like that. You're not a baby, you're too much of a handful. I see my roll exactly as I described it in...' she paused while a spectacular crackle of thunder rolled overhead, her eyes widened in impish appreciation as the sound imposed itself on them... 'Claire's office; as riding shotgun,' she finished, and turned to watch a wall of hail crash into the glass and more violet lightening blast across the darkness behind it. Saskia glanced down into her empty glass; a half full bottle stood on the coffee table; she circled the couch to get it. She poured, half filling her glass. She raised the bottle offering more wine to Ayesha, who refused with a shake of her head. Saskia sat on the edge of a cushion, she untied her laces and eased off her boots; she drew up her legs and knelt into the couch resting her elbow over the back and her chin on the back of her hand.

'Do you think that Nathan or one of the dark orders will try to snatch me?' she asked.

'I wouldn't rule it out. I'm not particularly informed, but it does appear that the stakes are high. I'll try to protect you.'

'That's not reassuring.'

'It wasn't meant to be. Please, not now Saskia. We'll talk about this tomorrow, I promise. Let's watch some Tv and take our minds off things, or a DVD. You choose.'

Saskia searched the channels on the Tv for something to watch. She had few likes and occasional arcane taste. She found nothing that appealed. She resorted to Ayesha's drawer full of DVDs and to Ayesha's surprise held up the 1931 version of Frankenstein.

'Really?' She had not known what to expect. Strangely, the choice seemed right.

'Don't you want to watch it?'

'It's dated. But bits of it are cool. If you want to.'

'I've been fascinated by it forever,' Saskia confessed. 'Boris Karloff as the Frankenstein monster I mean. I had a black and white poster on my wall, and a book of stills. Occasionally I dream about it; that its watching me from out of the shadows; that it follows me. It feels quite real, but it never does me any harm. I've never seen the movie!'

'Okay, then we must watch it.' Ayesha shrugged. 'We'll drink chardonnay and eat decent crisps. We'll watch 'bride of' another night.'

Saskia was instantly awake and with a cat like instinct, fully alert. She had fallen asleep on the couch after Frankenstein, curled against the back. She recalled the storm moving away, then a little casual conversation; then obviously she had fallen asleep. Her wine glass stood empty on the table. Ayesha was no longer in the room. Something had jerked her out of sleep. Something high pitched, intrusive, and quickly cut off. The landline phone was missing from its hub. She heard the murmur of Ayesha's voice through in the kitchen. Saskia flowed from the couch; the display on the VHS player read 10.24 in red. Saskia glanced through the opening into Ayesha's Danish design kitchen. Ayesha was standing with her back to her, the upper half of her body visible at the other end of the long central island. She was speaking on her phone, while she ran the fingers of her free hand through her hair. Her voice was not hushed but it was less than its usual level. Saskia stood back from the doorway, she had the hearing of a cat; she tuned it in and listened to Ayesha's side of the conversation. She must have been standing almost next to the phone to get to it so quickly, Saskia thought.

'I do want to see you. Yes of course I do.'

'I have missed you. I've missed what you do with me.'

'Not tonight, Khalid, no you mustn't come to me.'

'Yes, I want you in my bed.'

'I know that you prefer it there.'

'Yes, I prefer you in my bed, but we can't, not for a while, not in my apartment.'

'The girl who is staying with me. She needs a safe place. Not on her own.'

'She will be here for a while. Maybe a few weeks. Khalid, it's a favour to Claire. It's a nuisance, but how can I say no.'

'Phone her, ask her.'

'I'll make it up to you, I promise.'

'I'll do whatever you want, no change there.'

'Tomorrow night. At seven then. I'll wait for the car.'

'Yes, I'll wear that scent.'

'I know which dress.'

'I know the shoes you mean.'

'No, I won't wear anything else.'

'Yes, goodnight, Khalid.'

Ayesha set the phone down on the work surface. She massaged her temples, closing her eyes. She reached for her wine glass a few inches from her phone. It was almost empty. She drained it and after a moment's thought approached the fridge. She retrieved a fresh bottle of Chardonnay and took it to where the corkscrew lay, by the twin Belfast sinks. She set to uncorking the bottle of Chardonnay, as she turned the screw into the cork she spoke.

'I'm sorry I had to say you were a nuisance Saskia. You are not. That conversation was not all that it appeared I promise you. Please will you fetch your Lute.'

'Yes Ayesha.' Saskia replied quietly from the doorway.

By the time Saskia returned with her Lute, Ayesha had made the living room ambient with softly lit lamps, they combined with the flicker of the fire in the wall. She had brought the womb chair to the fire side and poured Saskia more wine. She was standing, and Saskia wondered if she had been crying. She gave the laughter smile, to which Saskia was becoming accustomed, making her even more convinced that she had been crying. Ayesha had a remote in her hand, she pointed it towards the window. The heavy drapes drew together, closing out the night and the Leeds lights.

'Where will you sit?'

'I'll kneel,' Saskia replied. 'You sit.'

'Okay,' Ayesha took her seat in the womb chair. She gave a little puzzled frown as Saskia knelt in front of her, then laid her Lute down on the floor on her left side. Saskia lifted Ayesha's left foot and drew off her slim elasticated boot, putting it aside. She had revealed a slender foot in a close fitted black sock. She squeezed the foot between her hands, gently compressing the toes. She glanced up taking in Ayesha's pretty face; the tears had begun to tumble down Ayesha's cheeks; Ayesha smiled tenderly putting her head a little to one side. Saskia kissed the tips of her toes and placed the foot to the floor. She raised Ayesha's right foot and performed the same actions.

'Oh Saskia,' said Ayesha softly as Saskia kissed her toes.

'Now I'll play for you, my Ayesha.' Saskia picked up her Lute. *La Traditora*,' she said softly and gave a little flash of her eyes as she began to play. She followed it with *Fantasia dolcissima et amorosa* and continued, softly telling the titles to Ayesha.

'You're a bit good, aren't you?' Ayesha whispered sometime later. The playing was beautiful, amorous even. Performed so intimately it charmed her and suddenly made nothing else matter beyond the two of them. Saskia watched the intensity form in Ayesha's expression, she enjoyed the attention of those beautiful dark eyes as they moved back and forth between her face and her playing. After twenty minutes she paused, resting the Lute on her knees, she reached for her glass and drank some of her wine.

'Had enough?' she asked.

'Silly question. The last piece. It was different somehow, more visceral. Quite dark. You didn't name it,' Ayesha remarked.

'It was my own composition. It had no name until now.'

'Yours! it was beautiful. What are you calling it?'

'I'm calling it Ayesha's dark eyes.'

Saskia began to play again and surprised Ayesha by singing to accompany her lute playing, *Secreit neict*. And *Veni, Veni Bella*, in a soft lilting singing voice. After those she simply played with all the subtle skill and guile she owned, occasionally bringing it to her eyes and to her smile as she raised them to Ayesha's own. Eventually she stopped playing and put her Lute aside. She kissed Ayesha's knee and laid her cheek on her thigh.

'I'm sorry,' Ayesha told her.

'I believe you think, that you are,' Saskia replied, closing her eyes. She felt Ayesha's slim fingers run through her hair. They stayed like that for some time.

The woman had sexily sly eyes; they were narrow; blue grey. They contained a wicked gleam as she stared along Nathan's muscular body, as it jerked through orgasm and his ejaculate flooded her mouth. He articulated his pleasure with rapid explosive breaths. Her wide lips withdrew from his shaft, and she drew herself along the length of his body to study his heaving torso and grimacing face. He was sweating, his baleful eyes watched her hungrily; she was small and beautiful, with wriggling sweet hips and long brown hair, that trailed down over her white skin and pert breasts. She extended her hand and stroked the sweating skin of his muscular abdomen with slim, red nailed fingers. She returned his stare as she worked the content of her mouth, her pliant lips twisted into a half smile as she swallowed; she licked their inner surface with the tip of her tongue and drew one side of her lower lip between white even teeth. She was exhibiting a return to a mildly mocking humour she had already expressed before they had sex, when Nathan had turned up unannounced at her small Queen Anne period manor house near Cheadle Hulme. That was not unusual for him, though his visits were irregular, and sex had been habitual for several years, and preliminary to any business between them. They enjoyed sex but they were not lovers, there was no affection, not even friendliness; only the transaction and the intense activity in the woman's large circular bed, had significance.

'Unbelievable, that you lost the girl, after all the effort I went to, finding her,' she chided, satirically.

'I fucked up. I'm under no illusion.' His face hardened irritably.

'You underestimated her, admit it.'

'She was wily. I thought I had her.'

She chuckled. 'You thought she was cock struck you mean.' She taunted him. 'Your king size ego kicked you in the arse.'

'You might have fared no better. Don't let your own ego convince you of infallibility; you more than anyone should be aware of that danger.'

She frowned, a hint of rancour entering her lovely eyes. 'I think you know, I would. Hubris Nathan it was your undoing, and a pretty face with a glib tongue. If you'd left it to me, you'd have her at your feet now, tied like a Turkey, waiting to be basted, and pricked!' She issued a bark of unpleasant laughter, genuinely enjoying his discomfort. He flashed resentment at her. She glanced away; her eyes flickered towards a candle spiked on a high bronze votive stand; it was tall, in black coloured wax; eleven more surrounded the bed flickering their coy light across its occupants nakedness; they were scented amber and musk. There was no other source of light in the bedroom. She casually reached for the candle and lifted it from its spike, her hand did not quite close around its cylindrical girth. Before Nathan realised what she had in mind she had tipped the molten wax that had pooled around the wick, across his abdomen in a spatter of hot rain. Nathan flinched and hissed, his abdominal muscles flexing in response to the contact with the hot wax. His jaw clenched and he regarded her wolfishly; pure dislike filling his pale eyes. The smile she returned him was disdainful, on the edge of mocking. She turned her body away as she replaced the candle on its spike. When she turned to face him again the smile had left her face.

'What do you want me to do?' she asked; she rested her fingers over the hardened patches of wax on his abdomen; she began to lightly brush the skin between them, with the points of her fingernails. She arched her brows questioningly. 'Rectify your cock-up I suppose? Speaking of which.' She moved her gaze to his groin where his semi-tumescent penis had begun to stiffen; perhaps, she considered, in response to the stimulus of her fingers, but she decided more likely, in response to them and a combination of the reality of her pouring hot wax onto his skin. She mused vaguely what his response might have been had she streamed the hot wax over his dick. Probably best not to find out, she decided.

'Yeah, I still want the little bitch, Rachel; I want her badly,' he told her. 'I want your help to acquire her.'

'Do I need to find her?' Her fingers slid over Nathans lower abdomen, exploring; they found his erection, now pleasingly hard.

'I know where she is.'

'Then why do you need me?'

'You have connections.'

'Ah! You want my contacts. It depends on which.'

'You have links I know, with a certain dubious Order; in the past you have worked for its head, I believe.'

'The Kadman. Celia Ostermann; you must know her too.' Her fingers moved up and down in smooth strokes. She listened for the change in his breathing.

'I know her a little. You know her better.'

'I'm not getting the whole truth here. You got on the wrong side of Ostermann, didn't you? And now you want me to mediate.'

'I want a proper moot. Differences put aside. I also want you to be involved the next time I move to acquire the Challoner bitch.'

'All of this won't be cheap Nathan.'

'I'm good for it. In fact!' He twisted away from her leaving her hand empty and swung his legs out of the bed. Standing, he crossed between the candles, to the chair where he had folded his clothes and reached into his jacket, which was coat hangered across the back of the chair. He extracted something from his inside pocket. Rachel watched him with cool curiosity as he returned to the bed; he tossed her the item he had retrieved, before he climbed back into the bed. She caught it cleanly and peered down into her hand. A small vial rested in her palm, in quite heavy transparent glass, it was stoppered. It was filled with a clear liquid, Citrine in colour.

'A gift.' Nathan told her, his tone slightly sour.

'I presume not a urine sample?'

He regarded her stonily. 'You know what it is.'

'I guess I do. Wowsers! honestly! you can help me inject it later.'

'Inject it! Fuck!'

'You know me Nathan, I try to get the most out of everything. Speaking of which!' She reached for his erection again and stroked its length along the underside. She straddled him and guided it inside her, she gasped as she impaled herself.

'I'll arrange everything in the morning.' She laughed softly. Her sly eyes filled with pleasure as she established rhythm. 'You'll have your moot.'

'Good?' Ayesha was panting, the sweat coursing down her face, her dark eyes gleamed.
'Shattered!' Saskia grimaced. She grinned then and wiped the sweat from her eyes and brows.
'Had enough?'
'For now.' Saskia panted, gulping breath. She bent over resting her palms on her thighs, fingers turned inwards. She straightened and stepped off the now inactive running machine.
'Maybe you should take it a bit easier,' Ayesha remarked, her eyebrows lifted as she glanced at the reading on the machine. She passed Saskia a towel.
'You weren't exactly holding back!' Saskia remarked.
'I exercise down here three times a week. Usually at night after work when its busier. So, it is nice having the place to ourselves.' Ayesha was referring to the empty Gym, exclusive to residents of her building, for a hefty yearly fee.
'I'm out of condition. And I'm a skinny cow!' Saskia was despondent, her expression at the edge of self-pity.
'Lithe,' Ayesha smiled soothingly. 'You are not skinny; be careful not to run off the weight you want to put on though.'
'I'm a sodding mess. I feel a mess. This is not how I want to be Ayesha!'
'You had better tell me how you want to be then. Let's go and shower and have breakfast.'
'I need Gym wear too.'
'We'll walk out later. You can choose some.'

'I need athleticism,' Saskia insisted. 'Presently, I'm a stick insect; I need to be healthier and fit. I need to be polished and to feel polished. I want to be like you. I want to know which clothes to dress in, which makeup to wear, which perfume to use. I want to be stylish; Is there anything wrong in wanting that?'
'Nothing. And nothing that a good nail bar, a beautician, and in-depth clothes research under my supervision won't solve,'

Ayesha reassured her. 'It really is about maintaining a habit. And you are not lacking in style. As for being a stick insect, where did that idea come from?'

'Don't you think I'm a stick insect?'

'A praying mantis, the way you look at me sometimes.'

'Thanks.'

'It's perception. Apart from a couple of inches in height we're of similar build, you could put on a couple of kilos if you want. You've told me yourself you sometimes go a day without anything to eat. Well, not on my watch, and I hate that phrase. We'll work on you. No more skipping breakfast. A slice of toast doesn't cut it. We'll start you on Pilates for core strength, weights for building up some muscle, walking for stamina. Walk on the machine don't run. You are elegant, quite beautiful; all your equipment is in place; I promise.'

'Pilates?'

'I'll teach you.'

'Elegant and beautiful?'

'Don't let it go to your head,' Ayesha waited for Saskia to slip a couple of tablemats from a stack, then set a porcelain mug of tea down in front of her. She joined Saskia on the couch, keeping hold of her mug, preferring her tea at its hottest.

'Have you thought anymore about what happened yesterday in the Wild? I have a feeling that somehow, in the long term it won't deter you.'

'I intend to go back. But I don't know when? Not before I'm ready I suppose.' Saskia raised her mug to her mouth and sipped the strong tea. She had folded her legs onto the couch. She was in jeans, black T-shirt, and socks. That morning was the first occasion that she had seen Ayesha denuded of makeup. It distracted her, engaging her attention more than she wanted. Ayesha was beautiful. Subtlety was more at play, charm, and a built-in cuteness.

'Why wasn't Trevor Challoner under the same sort of threat as me when he inherited the Wild? He rejected magic after all,' Saskia asked her.

'No, I believe now that that is a false premise; he rejected the Wild; he simply was not inclined to practise magic. That does not mean that he never did or would not have done so if it were needed; he was not vulnerable like you.'

'That puts my situation in perspective then, doesn't it? I'm a nuisance. And I am putting you at risk.'

'Put it like this; when I went to work the other day, I didn't expect to have a lodger by the end of it; one that I needed to protect.'

'I'm sorry Ayesha, but I didn't ask for this either.'

'I resented you, I felt uptight, and I didn't particularly like you. I did it because Claire asked me to. For the first hour I was in shock; I think I covered it up well.'

'And now?' Saskia put down her mug and raised the back of her hand across her lower face, beginning to feel a sense of hurt.

'I suppose I can stand you for a few more days. Don't look at me like that. I'm only winding you up. You can stay here as long as you want to, and no I don't feel sorry for you and I'm no longer doing it as a favour to Claire.' Ayesha put down her mug and shifted closer to Saskia, she reached out and drew Saskia's hand from in front of her face, and held it between her own two hands, rested on her knee.

'I think that I needed this. This is me Saskia. I think you will find over the coming weeks that I have a pretty empty life.'

'I fulfil a need. I can live with that.'

'No, you do not. I don't need you. I want you. You've got under my skin very quickly somehow. I don't know if it just happened or if it was deliberate. And I really do not care.'

'What about your work?'

'I enjoy my work, its fulfilling. This is better. There might come a time when I want both, but that's some way off.'

Saskia smiled showing emotion; she bit her lip and widened her eyes fighting the beginnings of tears. She sniffed. Ayesha felt her fingers tighten around her hand.

'Oh, Wow! That was unexpected. I don't have to think that I should feel guilty anymore. I hope you know what you've taken on Ayesha Shah. There's a lot I need to do and so much I need to ask you, I'll drive you mad.'

'Probably. Ask anyway.'

'Alright. What do you know about the Wild?'

'You don't waste time, do you? And the answer to your question is, not much, I only found out about its existence recently myself, after Trevor Challoner died; Claire sort of recruited me when you couldn't be located, at about the same time she recruited Nathan to help find you. I had this notion that I was simply moral support.'

'How secret is it? If you didn't know about it?'

'I suspect that more people know about its existence than we think. But to most of those it may only be in a historical or legendary context, something of a magical myth. I wasn't aware of it. I would say that only a very few people know that it is a real Place.'

'Will some of them know the location? Say the dark orders.'

'It is a well-kept secret. Magic is a world of well-kept secrets. We don't all know each other either; just like the ordinaries, for example not all accountants know each other, or hairdressers!'

'Magicians are a bit different to hairdressers, Ayesha.'

'Obviously, they're bad examples.'

'Artists might be a better comparison.'

Ayesha looked down and smiled with gentle tolerance.

'Okay, Artists. Right, I personally am acquainted with a dozen or so Practisers in magic. I know of a couple of dozen more. That's mostly down to Claire. But most Practisers will not know or know of anywhere near those numbers; so, they will not be aware of most of what is taking place in their world. I know some strange stuff Saskia, but there is very much more that I don't know. And I'm probably better informed than most because of my relationship with Claire; she does try to keep her finger on the pulse, you know.'

'Are you saying that there is only me, you and Claire and Nathan who might know the whereabouts of the Wild? Plus, whoever he might have informed by now.'

'Probably. But why do you think Nathan knows where it is?'

'You think that he doesn't?'

'Why should he? Claire didn't tell him unless she is being secretive about that, and I doubt it. I only found out a couple of days ago myself.'

'I see.' Saskia frowned in thought. 'Why do you think the Wild allowed me and denied you and Claire? Would it do the same to anyone else?'

Ayesha shrugged and shook her head. 'I don't know. The Place recognised you. Places do. When it did it obviously just wanted you, no one else. That would be my reasoning. If you had known how to enter and leave, there would not have been an issue. So, I'll teach you; you don't need intent for that.'

'It is not down in any map; true places never are.'

'You remembered. That key is generic. There will be a specific key. It might be lost. I hope not, as it will have other properties. The words help. They focus. The rest is imagination and assumption. I don't have a Place. Claire has one, her father constructed it. I don't think she'll have an issue with us hopping in and out of it until you get the hang of it. Then it's up to you when you take a trip back to the Wild. You can change your mind at any point you know.'

'No, I can't Ayesha, not while I have this fetter. I don't know where to begin.'

'I'll help you in any way I can and so will Claire. Though I don't know anything about the Wild; its ancient magic, and I'm a modern magician. Its secrets are there for you to unlock but I would avoid them, for the time being. Fancy going shopping. We can have lunch out. Remember I'm out tonight.' Saskia regarded her coolly.

'You'll be safe I promise. You will have a bodyguard.'

'Another Archer of Lugh to babysit me?'

'Put away the lip Saskia. Come over here.'

Saskia followed her moodily; she was surprised when Ayesha led her to her bookshelves. Ayesha indicated the section that contained a collection of illustrated editions, glancing from Saskia to them. Saskia had browsed a few of them. She was already familiar with artists like Rackham, Crane and Dulac. Ayesha's collection had introduced her to the likes of Lear and Heath-Robinson. She wondered what this had to do with her protection. Something might be concealed inside one of them, she thought. A weapon?

'Many magicians keep guardians, and other energy forms, for other purposes,' Ayesha explained. 'Some are kept in plain sight. Others are concealed in vessels, statues; whatever. They are usually dormant, until needed. I keep mine in books. When I told you to keep the first four books in their exact location and order I wasn't being pedantic. Each volume holds an energy form of a different nature formed from my imagination and made by my intent, through Desiring. The most powerful of them is my house guardian. Claire and another good friend, who is an advanced elemental magician, constructed it for me, and I helped, and because of that it's immensely powerful. Which book do you think contains it?'

'It has to be Alice's adventures in Wonderland.'

'Of course, it is. I'm going to wake the guardian now so you can get used to the idea of it being around. It will materialize and you'll be able to see it for a time, then it will fade out of sight, but it will still be there. It is odd. But I like it.'

Ayesha extracted the first book from the shelf. A volume of Alice's adventures in wonderland illustrated by Arthur Rackham. She turned to face Saskia and held the book up in front of her balanced on her upturned palm. Saskia watched as Ayesha smiled and her dark eyes grew large. Ayesha made a fist and tapped the cover of the book with the end joints of her fingers. 'Come out! Come out!' she said. 'That's just my little eccentricity,' she explained to Saskia. 'Totally unnecessary.'

It appeared from the cover of the book like a large bubble, the size of a beachball. It shuddered and clouded darkly, and acquired an image which solidified, until the large grinning blue-black face of a cat regarded them.

'The Cheshire cat,' Saskia said, she smiled in pleasure.

'My version of the Cheshire Cat. I know, not very imaginative, but it doesn't need to be. As I said, I like it.' Ayesha watched Saskia's expression curiously. There was nothing present to show that she was even mildly astonished, or uneasy. She was fascinated and entertained.

'I forgot. You've seen it all haven't you; we need a demon from hell to phase you,' she said.

'Sounds about right. He's sweet.'

'Sweet,' Ayesha chuckled, shaking her head. 'It's staring at you now. So, you need to give me your hand.' Ayesha returned the book to the shelf and took hold of Saskia's wrist; she raised her hand and passed it through the guardian's form. Saskia felt as if a thousand tiny needles were being jabbed into the skin of her hand and along her forearm. The sensation lasted only briefly. As soon as it passed the guardian ascended. It began to glide slowly about the room above head height, wearing its broad toothy grin.

'It knows that you belong now. It will stop being visible shortly; but it will still be there. It will protect you, against almost anything. This is an extremely dangerous sustained thoughtform; See it's disappeared.'

Saskia decided not to say anything to Ayesha, but the large, disembodied, permanently grinning, blue-black cat head was still clearly visible to her.

'Now you're acquainted I'll teach you how to summon and to dismiss it. It is easy, you'll see. Tomorrow if you like?'

'I'm going shortly.' Ayesha came into the living room and regarded Saskia, with an element of defiance in her gaze, though a note of caution existed in the careful tone of her voice. Saskia had her head in a book on Paris Street-style. It had been her first purchase of the day. She dragged her attention from its glossy pages and regarded Ayesha; Saskia appeared outwardly dispassionate, inside her jealousy levels were spiking.

'Is it okay if I borrow your laptop?' she inquired.

Ayesha looked exquisite and Saskia experienced a stab of desire. She was wearing a revealing mini dress in a red leopard print; an expensive garment by an exclusive designer; she was carrying a slim red patent clutch bag of comparable credentials. A pair of expensive stiletto heels, with minimalist strapping, revealed her exquisitely maintained feet; her toenails were newly varnished, as were her fingernails, in their customary dark red.

Saskia won a hard fight not to scan her flawlessly made-up face. Ayesha searched Saskia's face, as if seeking appreciation, approval, or disapproval. There was nothing there. It was clear to Saskia that Ayesha was stressed; this was not a comfortable situation for her, but Saskia decided to be unforgiving. She could be without compassion, cruel even when the mood took her, and she had no intention of giving Ayesha any reassurance or solace. Not in this matter.

'Yes. Don't break it. Don't go out. Promise me that you won't go out.' Saskia had already promised.

'If the guardian does reappear don't worry it won't come near you.' Saskia could still see it floating about, she had not yet informed Ayesha that she was still able to see it.

Ayesha compressed her lips, then she quirked them into a small unhappy smile. She stared regretfully into Saskia's steady gaze. She searched for condemnation, disappointment, pain even. She found none of them. She felt a certain resentment, then her defiance returned.

'It's my life after all,' she said. 'I will be late. Don't wait up for me.'

She turned and made to walk out of the room. But paused in the entrance. She remained there between the unframed walls. Shoulders tight, slightly bowed, head slightly down. As though waiting.

More of her tattoo was visible on her exposed back and leg. It curled like a black vine across her shoulder blades, winding diagonally back across and down, curving beneath the dress. Exposed in the light, Saskia could see that it was not a vine, but a curling briar of thorns; wicked thorns, like rose thorns, and some of them seemed to be buried in her skin, and where they entered, slender threads of blood trickled down. Saskia found it both beautiful and cruel.

'Don't give up on me Saskia.' Ayesha said, barely loudly enough for her to hear. 'And make sure you eat something.'

Saskia almost responded. She felt tears pricking at her eyes, but she brutally put them away, and made no reply. Ayesha straightened and walked from her sight. Saskia heard the door close as she went out. She got out of her chair and crossed to the window; she watched, ensuring that she was out of sight behind the drapes. She watched Ayesha emerge and climb into a midnight blue Bentley GT. She was too proud to look up. Her shoulders were stuck in a tight line, her arms at her sides, fists clenched, as though she knew Saskia's eyes were on her.

'Fancy a look at some old maps Snuggles?' Saskia said to the guardian after Ayesha had been driven away. Snuggles bobbed, pausing in its slow weaving progress and regarded her, expression unchanged. For a moment Saskia thought there might be connection, however it lost interest almost instantly and bobbed away into the kitchen.

That morning, they had taken a taxi to the city centre and engaged in what Ayesha described as recreational shopping. Fascinating stuff, Saskia discovered. She bought several delightfully stylish items of clothing, shocked as the costs were rung up on various tills, and all going onto Ayesha's credit card. Saskia was developing a taste for Chardonnay. Initially she had accepted the wine as their drink of choice for no other reason than to not appear unsophisticated to Ayesha. She realised after a couple of thought-provoking glasses, that she enjoyed it. To Ayesha's amusement towards the end of the shopping trip, she had insisted on buying a box at Ayesha's wine merchants. *'It's only fair!'* she had remarked as they had waited for the taxi to pick them up. She extracted a chilled bottle from the fridge, together with the remains of the previous evening's pasta meal. She left her meal heating up in the microwave and went to her bedroom to retrieve the chart case that Claire had given to her.

Snuggles's fiendish cat face grinned down at her from the ceiling when she re-entered the room. She winked at it, but it remained dispassionate. It appeared to observe her as she opened the chart case; studying her as she withdrew several documents and folded maps, but she could not be certain. She heard the microwave go ping and went to fetch her food. She consumed it in silence and regarded the documents she had distributed over the floor in front of her chair, with a calculating gaze.

An ordnance survey map of the area was included with the documents in the case, and two large, folded parchment maps of the Wild, though neither were titled. Saskia spread them out on the floor. They were drawn in faded ink, turned sepia, and they were detailed with old script. Both looked to have been created by the same hand. They were peppered with symbols and legends. Saskia could see no key on the map, so she presumed it lay elsewhere, at least she hoped that it did. There were other documents, single sheets of parchment covered in script, some of it she presumed by the same hand that had created the map.

There were a couple of slim notebooks from a later age, with lined pages, again handwritten, in both pencil and some in fountain pen. They would all need to be scrutinized closely; collated. She drank wine and considered her mysterious and disturbing legacy. God Claire must be horrified, she thought, that the secret of the Wild and Hoardale lay in the least capable of hands. She poured her third glass of wine. Her thoughts kept turning to Ayesha and the conversation she had heard her have over the phone with the man Khalid; It had not sounded like they intended an ordinary hook up, not your everyday type of sexual encounter. It had sounded heavy to Saskia; Ayesha's submissiveness had surprised her, there was obviously something darkly sensual about the energy between her and this Khalid. Saskia had no objection to consensual depravity between adults, she had deviant threads of her own, but on this occasion, it affected her, and she had received a vibe from Ayesha that had disturbed her; it gave her the impression that Ayesha was torn, not emotionally committed. She pushed it from her mind, there was plenty of time to think about it later; when she could default to her fall-back position and indulge in a good gorge of sensual agony and self-torture, by imagining Ayesha with her lover, when the deviant in her would seduce her. She recalled seeing a large magnifying glass in a drawer in Ayesha's kneehole desk, ideal for scrutinising the maps. She went to get it. She extracted it and closed the drawer. She set it down on the work surface and lay her hands over the edge of one of the twin Belfast sinks. She clutched the cold porcelain with clawed fingers going white with ferocity as she fought the agony of emotion that welled up inside her. She croaked with the strain of it in her throat; her mouth stretched open, and her lips drew back, exposing her teeth. Shaking she fought the manifestation of misery with every fibre of her being, denying it voice. But then she was unable to fight it off any longer; Her cry of desolation came with all the rage and misery that she could summon. Snuggles shot into the room searching for threat, grinning. It gazed at her impassively when it perceived that there was none, then continued to hover.

'Thank you,' she told it. Immediately back in control.

She compared Hoardale on the ordinance survey map with the hand drawn map of the Wild. The two places appeared to be identical. Hoardale terminating in a natural barrier to the north. A limestone cliff a quarter of a mile across, called Hoar Scar. On the hand drawn version, no barrier existed, Hoar Scar continued along a widening eastern boundary of the Wild for a further four miles, according to distance points on the hand drawn map. Names no longer devised by historical context but given by the original map maker were present. Places with provocative names, epithets that hinted at personal experience and mysteries. A whole new terrain was mapped that did not coincide with anything on the ordinance survey map. And at the centre of the Wild lay its most prominent feature, a great mass of woodland over six miles in length and in places three wide. It was named Herla's wood; within its boundaries there were other named locations; at the very centre the word Henge; which could only mean one thing. The Wild began to fascinate her and the thought of going back to it frightened her; but it excited too. She pored over the maps for several hours, until she became tired and jaded, and she put them away.

At ten past four she sat alone in the dark, empty of thoughts; Saskia at last heard the door mechanism and the almost sub audial sound of the door being opened. She heard, almost sensed, Ayesha's presence come into the hall. She stiffened slightly, preparing for encounter. The light in the hall went on, its radiance extending partly into the living room. Saskia listened to movement, A little gasp, of pain perhaps. A sigh, then: 'Fuck!' sotto voce.

The main light came on, partly dimmed and Ayesha entered the room. She paused when she saw Saskia; if she was surprised, she concealed it; the look she gave her was cool, unformed, yet holding just a hint of challenge; no smile was involved. She looked weary, and she was slightly stooped, and her right shoulder was a little lower than her left, as though she was favouring that side of her body. Her lips formed a straight line, and her makeup was a mess. Saskia gazed appreciatively at what she saw as flawed beauty.

'I told you not to wait up,' Ayesha said. She certainly did not appear embarrassed, but Saskia sensed that she felt embarrassment; that it pricked Ayesha and goaded her towards a cold simmer of defiance.

'I didn't wait up. I simply chose not to go to bed. I've been busy.' Saskia was careful to allow no inflection to enter her voice. She was angry, jealous, and resentful, but revealed none of that to Ayesha, not in the tone of her voice or in her body language. She was relieved to have Ayesha back in her possession again, but that was a fact best not shared, she decided.

Ayesha glanced at the empty bottle of wine on the coffee table. 'So, I see.'

Saskia followed her gaze. 'I'm not drunk.'

'I didn't say that you were.'

'Just saying. I've been looking at my maps.' She glanced towards the chart case that she had propped against the wall beside the unlit fire, after she had returned the maps to it. It was Ayesha's turn to gaze follow. Her brows dented into a small frown. 'We could have looked at them together if you'd said.'

'I was compelled to get a feel for Hoardale and the Wild. Then I just sat in the dark for an hour.'

'I see. I feel dehydrated. I need a glass of water.'

'I'll get it for you.'

'I'm capable of getting it for myself.'

Ayesha propped herself against the wall with a hand; she bent and raised each knee in turn to allow herself to release the high strap on each of her stiletto heels with the fingers of the other hand; unfastened, she kicked them off and walked bare foot through into the kitchen. Saskia retrieved an envelope from behind a cushion and followed her. Ayesha got a tumbler from a slick array of wall cupboards and took it to the fridge; she drew ice water from the dispenser and drank; raising and lowering the glass in a succession of swallows; she kept the icy water in her mouth on each occasion for a few moments. Saskia studied her back and her arms, searching for the appearance of bruising that might account for Ayesha's posture, but she saw none; she could see something else, but she ignored it until she had conducted her inspection, then she focused on it. Her eyes narrowed in curiosity. Along the length of Ayesha's visible tattoo, and the surrounding area extending about an inch on either side of it, her skin appeared inflamed. Saskia drew closer and peered more intently. She saw that there were tiny blisters like those left by stinging nettles spread across the area of inflammation. She wondered, dispassionately, how much pain Ayesha might be experiencing.

Ayesha had drunk half of the water in her glass. She replenished its contents from the dispenser and turned around. She met Saskia's stare with a cool impassivity. She said nothing, made no gesture, she watched while Saskia glanced at those elements of her tattoo, on the front of her body, which were revealed by her dress. They were equally inflamed. Saskia's gaze lifted to Ayesha's face. She watched the dark eyes as they searched her expression; she was certain that they would fail to find anything; she was on emotional empty, howled and sobbed out over several interludes in the night, watched by a grinning elemental guardian.

'Here.' She produced a bundle of notes from the envelope she had brought with her and offered it to Ayesha. It held the money she had squirreled away under the loose board.

Ayesha looked puzzled. She frowned and shook her head.

'It's the money I owe you from earlier. Not all of it. I'm seventy-three pounds short.'

'Now? You want to do this now?' Ayesha said in disbelief.

'I don't want you to feel that I'm taking advantage.'

'Right now, I feel that you're taking the piss.' Ayesha was trembling; her voice tightened, and tears spilled from her eyes. 'I did that as your friend!' She snatched the bundle of notes out of Saskia's hand and threw them back into her face. 'Fuck you!' she spat, 'fuck you, Saskia!'

Saskia blinked into the flurry of notes, the smell of them forcing itself into her nostrils. A dozen different lives. She could smell tobacco, engine oil, cologne, mouse. She allowed the cluster of notes to fall to the floor, she heard them rustle on the slate tiles. She was not interested in the money; she was only interested in seeing Ayesha's reaction. Following the event to its emotional conclusion. Ayesha thrust her glass away spilling half its contents. She turned away making fists of her hands, she pressed them against the fridge door, resting her forehead between them. Saskia watched the movement of her lustrous hair as she sobbed silently. She began to crumple, and Saskia reached for her, careful of her inflamed tattoo. She turned her forcing against resistance;

she put her arms around her and held her. Briefly Ayesha relaxed into her, nuzzling. As quickly, she pulled away again.

'Let me go,' Ayesha begged, 'I stink of sex. I stink of him, I usually shower, but we argued, and yes over you.' Ayesha straightened and twisted away from Saskia's arms. She pushed her backwards, thrusting hard with the palms of both vertical hands. She stepped around her and paused momentarily. She spoke, her words sounding difficult to form.

'You know what your problem is Saskia. You're fucking feral. I'm going to shower and I'm going to bed, and I'll get up again when I'm ready. Now fuck off. Fucking praying Mantis.'

She stumbled away. But she paused again in the kitchen entrance.

'I'm sorry, I didn't mean that,' she said shakily without turning around.

'Fuck you, Ayesha!' Saskia sobbed, suddenly lost in misery. She stalked past Ayesha through the lounge and into the entrance hall and wrenched open the door. Ayesha followed into the hall.

'Where are you going?'

'I want...I need air.'

'It's not safe.'

'I really don't care.'

'Saskia! Please don't do this.'

'What have you got to cry about?' It was an accented voice, with a nasal tone. She had seen him first as she approached him along the walkway, half visible in the light from the payphone box by which he was standing, his form limned by the radiance. He looked solid. Physical, but Saskia had encountered enough spirits to recognise one, even from fifty yards away. She had walked hard and tearfully from Ayesha's apartment block. She felt angry with herself, she had thrown a tantrum, a rare event. But she had wanted to hurt Ayesha as much as she felt Ayesha's actions were hurting her, a suitable punishment. She palmed her eyes as she walked and was on the point of turning round when she saw the figure through her tears. She continued towards it. She had no coat and the cold bit, but she did not care right then.

As she approached, he moved away towards the darkened or semi-lit structures to her left, disappearing into the shadows as he sensed that she could see him. Bloody-minded and inquisitive she followed the direction he had taken, pausing only when she came to the edge of the thick darkness into which he had become absorbed. She saw him loitering in the shadows of a passage, and as she did, he appeared again and she took a pace backwards to study him, because he was very tall. He was dressed in period, in a good thick but tired black jacket, moleskin trousers, and worn boots. He was wearing a black hat with a brim, and a thick woollen Guernsey under his jacket. He had a long angular jaw that was covered in black stubble; his face wore a sinister expression; the eyes, which watched her with curiosity, were narrowed into a permanent smirk. She detected memory odours, an unwashed smell, spirits, stale sweat, and blood. He was manifested in a strong physical presence.

'Plenty,' Saskia replied to his inquiry. 'Hello. I'm Saskia, have you got a name?'

'John Pickering I'm called. Though over time hereabouts I've been called other names. Docker John. Tall John. Smirky. By them that sees me.'

'You are tall,' she agreed. She took three paces back as he took two paces towards her.

'Six feet eleven inches, they said, when they measured me for my sack and my box. They buried me but I never went away. I don't meet that many as can see me or talk to me for that matter.'

'I see ghosts. I prefer Docker John. Is that what you were?' Another two paces.

'A Longshoreman me; and I was a sign writer too and not a bad one. But I wasn't dependable at either. I had a reputation for drink and trouble. I came to Leeds for a fresh start; thirty-three years old, with four shilling in my pocket.'

'I can hear the Mersey in your voice.' Three more paces, there were cobbles under her feet. She glanced quickly behind her.

'Aye, I'm from Liverpool.'

'What year did you come to Leeds?' Her interest was genuine.

'1909 in the September. I was only here two days. They stuck me for four fucking shilling. I was up a prossie in the yard. Not that one. It's long gone now along with all the houses. I was in my last strokes too, and they stuck me in the kidneys. For four fucking shilling. They could have let me finish.'

'Bad things happen,' said Saskia. 'Life is full of disappointments. Is this where you are, or do you roam about?' Memory ghosts stayed in one place she had discovered. Sometimes powerful revenants or entities did too, but mostly they roamed, though distance limited them, unless they had other connections. More steps. She paused on the edge of the quay with nowhere else to go.

'I get about. Public houses mostly, where people gather to imbibe spirit.' He chuckled darkly and his smirk deepened. 'I look at the lasses all on display. I smell the drink and I stare around at the tap rooms, all warm. I roam both sides of the canal and the river. But sometimes I think I should go home. But I can't find the way back. If only they'd let me finish!'

'Is that the reason you stayed?' Saskia asked; sometimes it was all that was needed or sometimes nothing at all.

'I think it was,' he replied. 'Now who might this be?'

'Saskia, who are you talking to?' Ayesha was coming towards her quickly; she had thrown on her coat and pulled on a pair of trainers; she had left the laces untied in her haste. She was almost jogging. She must have agitated for several minutes, thought Saskia, before freaking out and following her.

Saskia looked back in the direction of Docker John, or where he had been standing; he was no longer there.

'You were looking up at something and talking,' Ayesha said as she drew near. She looked exhausted, Saskia thought.

'I encountered a ghost. I'll tell you about him as we walk back.' Saskia felt suddenly protective, her emotions diffused, she shivered and hooked her arm through Ayesha's. 'Come here you. I'm sorry, I was jealous, and I behaved childishly. It won't happen again.'

Four

True to her word Ayesha did not get up until late. It was after midday when she appeared from her bedroom and came into the kitchen to find Saskia. Her face was again denuded of cosmetics, she appeared wan; she had a hint of sadness at large in her dark eyes, Saskia thought. Ayesha was wearing a black silk dressing gown, knee length. She had nothing on her slim feet. She peered cautiously at Saskia. 'I'm sorry,' she told her.

'Why?' Saskia replied. 'I was a prick. And I apologise.' She gave a shy little smile. 'Good morning, Ayesha.'

'Good morning, Saskia,' Ayesha smiled in return.

Saskia had woken up on the bed fully clad. Surprised that she had slept at all. At ten past ten, almost five hours sleep wasn't bad she decided. The darker side of Chardonnay had greeted her as she awakened. After first peeing, and refreshing her mouth, she had changed and chanced a trip on her own down to the gym, with a bottle of spring water to walk off some of her head with a couple of kilometres on the machine. By the time she emerged from the shower she felt at seventy-five percent and realised that she felt very hungry. She left her hair to dry naturally. She put on black jeans and a new grey T-shirt and her new slippers; she answered the call of the kitchen. Ayesha arrived as she was in preparation.

'I'm having poached eggs on toast with baked beans,' she announced. 'Would you like some?'

'I believe that I would love some.' Ayesha replied. The tiniest inflection of relief made it into her expression, it was barely visible, but it was not lost on Saskia. Ayesha simply wanted a return to their eccentric rapport; it was in evolution, and she was growing fond of it. Saskia hid a smug little smile.

'Good, you arrived at just the right moment.' She extracted two more eggs from the carton, popped two more slices of bread into the toaster, and added the rest of the tin of beans to the jug destined for the microwave.

'How did you feel about the guardian being around you whilst you were alone?' Ayesha inquired conversationally.

'Snuggles and I got on fine. He was solicitous.'

Ayesha did not know what Saskia meant by that, but she let it go. She wrinkled her nose into a little smile.

'Snuggles,' she said to herself as she went to pour coffee, inordinately pleased to see the coffee maker already getting on with its job. She filled a mug, added a trickle of milk, and placed it on the breakfast bar, then hitched herself onto a bar stool.

Ayesha watched Saskia stack their breakfast things into the dishwasher with a softening gaze. She became aware that she felt cared for, and that it was a nice feeling. She waited for Saskia to finish and return to the bar, and as Saskia leaned across her, she laid her hand on hers to prevent her from picking up her empty mug. Saskia paused, liking the touch. Her gaze inquired.

'Saskia.'

'Yes.'

'Would you very gently cuddle me?'

Puzzled, Saskia was hesitant; a little smile flexed at the corner of her mouth. She did not say anything, but after a few moments she slid her arms around Ayesha; the lithe warmth of her body felt good, she sensed need, and enjoyed the sensation of Ayesha's arms returning her embrace, and the slim firm fingers pressed into her back.

'We really must talk,' said Ayesha at last, she disengaged and leaned back. She withdrew her arms and laid her hands on the curve of Saskia's shoulders; seated on the bar stool she was at the same height as Saskia; she gazed deeply into her calm green eyes. 'I need to explain. You need to know some things about me.'

'You don't need to explain anything to me.'

'I must. I owe it to you, before the two of us go any further along our path, because there is an us; I think. Then you can decide if you want to step back. And I would understand.' She slid from the bar stool.

'Come with me.'

She slid from the stool and walked away, confident that Saskia would follow, she walked like a gymnast, or a ballet dancer Saskia thought as she watched her momentarily. She followed her from the kitchen through the main room and to Ayesha's bedroom. Saskia felt a needle of anticipation pierce her, drawing tightly on a dark thread of possibility. She discouraged. She understood that this was no invitation to have sex, this went deeper toward a furtherance of joint understanding. Something else was at play. Like herself, Ayesha owned a dark side to her personality; she sensed that it was more evolved than her own, more completed; the demon was better sustained. She sensed that she was about to discover something about it.

Ayesha Remained with her back turned to her and came to a stop in the middle of her spacious bedroom; located next to the living room at the front of the block; though smaller, it too had a vast viewing wall of glass; this was shielded at present by its white semitranslucent inner drapes, which allowed in a softened daylight. Ayesha loosened her dressing gown; she shrugged and allowed it to slide to the floor. Fascinated Saskia watched as the dark silk denuded her. She wore nothing beneath.

'Go on then; examine it. I know that you want to. You must understand that it is not simply an ordinary tattoo.'

Inquisitively Saskia approached her. She felt her soft hairs rising and her skin tingling; the intimate caress of desire; she allowed, aware that she would not take it further. She went down on one knee and peered closely at the start of the tattoo. She was aware of the subtle tremor in Ayesha's skin, of its scent and its warmth, her lips within inches of brushing it. The tattoo took the form of a black thorny briar. It began above the bone on her left ankle and wound twice around the leg as it ascended; it emerged at the top of her inner thigh and curled across her taut rear to where her coccyx began, then across and above the flare of her right hip; it wound back and across to her spine, which it followed, threading along her vertebrae to her shoulder blades, where it divided; one branch continued to her left shoulder ending at her upper arm; the other crossed her right shoulder blade and curled from sight beneath her right arm. The skin on either side now had only a trace of inflammation, any sign of blistering had disappeared. Saskia began to straighten, to follow the route of the briar to its conclusion, but she paused, focusing her gaze as something won her attention. A small bump in the skin about the size of a textile stud was located at the base of Ayesha's back, at the place where one of the inked thorns gave the impression of piercing her skin.

'You can touch if you want to.' Ayesha said, her face turned to her left shoulder. 'I am a little tender still, I can't kill the pain with intent you see, but that's okay. There are twelve of them.'

Saskia touched the place cautiously with the tip of her index finger, she felt Ayesha's body respond, flexing imperceptibly. Saskia showed a brief smile as she saw the cheeks of her rear tauten. Saskia re-examined the vine from its start on her ankle, tracing it with the merest caress of her fingertips over Ayesha's smooth skin. As she progressed, she found more small protrusions under the skin, one at each point along the tattoo where a thorn appeared to pierce her. The first was located above Ayesha's ankle where the briar began; the second on the outer side of her knee; the third was on her inner thigh a couple of inches below the separation of her legs; another above her left buttock which had been the first that Saskia had discovered, and one by the flare of Ayesha's right hip; four more were located along the briar as it traversed Ayesha's spine, another on the separate branch of the vine in the flesh below her shoulder; one on the main branch where it crossed above her shoulder blade. Here the briar progressed under Ayesha's arm to the front of her body. Saskia circled her, transfixed. Ayesha lifted her arm to allow Saskia's fingers to trail beneath, spreading across her ribs and over her breast and curling down towards her abdomen. Ayesha widened her dark eyes as their gazes met; she seemed slightly amused, and, Saskia decided, as she noted the slightly accelerated rise and fall of her coned breasts, quite turned on. The twelfth and final protrusion was located at the side of her right breast.

'In each of those points on your body, there is something under the skin?' Saskia said, intrigued. The fingertips of her right hand rested lightly on the final thorn beside Ayesha's breast.

Ayesha remained silent but gave a little nod; she drew her lower lip between her teeth and her dark eyes flashed her continued amusement. Saskia could not decide if they held an element of derision, though at present she was not inclined to care.

'What are they?' she asked softly.

'They are spikes of the purest silver, each one modelled in the form of a rose thorn driven under my skin, though I prefer to think of them as barbs.' She studied Ayesha's beautiful eyes as they widened in comprehension and lifted to meet hers.

'Ayesha, is this a compliance of thorns?'

'That is the name it is known by.'

'Is this what Nathan would have done to me? That is why you looked at me so strangely when I told you about the blackthorns. Who did this to you?'

Ayesha gave a little suppressed laugh; Saskia thought that she detected a note of scorn. A little sardonic smile played on her mouth as she responded.

'The ink is alchemical and symbiotic to the silver of the thorns. The tattooist who fashioned it, is also a modern alchemist, the silversmith another. I supplied the most important ingredient. The process was expensive.'

She had such incredibly beautiful eyes Ayesha thought as she continued to hold Saskia's gaze; with tiny golden threads permeating the patterning in the green of the irises; they held immense power, she did not think Saskia was aware of the power they owned; occasionally they became feral, and they hunted like wolves. She watched the pupils shrink to points. She hoped that she had not overestimated this unusual young woman. She relaxed as the eyes darkened, and the green became lambent. Saskia compressed her mouth into a tight smile that wrinkled up into her nose, she shook her head and folded her arms.

'More,' she said.

Ayesha relaxed inwardly, she shrugged. 'Okay. If you had experienced the pain induced by a large rose thorn, a sharp broad tapering thorn, as it pierces your palm or fingertip, especially if pushed further in; you would know that it hurts with a certain cruel ache?' Ayesha appeared to be relating from experience. 'That pain, I find erotic.'

Saskia remained silent assimilating this revelation. She recalled a memory of her own.

'I occasionally did garden jobs for auntie...for Bernadette,' Saskia told her remembering. 'She always made me wear gardening gloves, occasionally I spiked myself on the roses; once though, I picked up an old pruning, I didn't know was there among some debris; I gripped it in my fist accidentally; so yes, I know how it hurts.' She tipped her head to one side to study Ayesha's face, concealing her thoughts.

'Can you imagine that bite of pain only ten times crueller?'

'Probably not. When did you become a pain bunny?'

'I'm certainly not a bunny!' Ayesha's eyes flashed with sudden resentment. 'I'm a fucking little pain freak!'

'Put your claws away.' Saskia said. 'I'm an ally.'

She surprised Ayesha by dropping to one knee and circling her legs with her arms, she caught up the silk dressing gown, pausing as she adjusted it to find its edges. She was aware of the presence of Ayesha's smooth pudendum a few inches from her face, the warmth of her skin and the tantalizing smell of her perfume. She straightened and drew the short gown over Ayesha's body; she checked, to find her hands with the inner openings of the sleeves, then completed the action. She did not wrap over the two edges or tie the silk belt; she left that choice to Ayesha.

'You haven't answered my question,' she prompted.

Ayesha suppressed a little shiver; she had experienced a sensual high during Saskia's actions, and she decided that if she wanted the dressing gown to remain open then so be it. Maybe she preferred the wanton look. She gave a little resolved smile. And allowed the younger woman still further in.

'My mother grew English Tea roses in our lovely suburban garden. She was ever so proud of them. When I was young and my parents were trying to force me to agree to marry, so I could pop out brats for a misogynistic entitled man with the intellect of a penis; when the angst became too much, I would go into the garden, and I would press the rose thorns into my thumbs and fingers; I know, self-harm. If I were really upset, I would clutch a full stem and hold it tightly in my fist while the blood ran out, and the pain stabbed. Then I would show it to my mum, and smile at her. To my mum the roses symbolized our Englishness and the society and culture we belonged to, yet she was enthusiastic that I should enter an arranged marriage, and I saw this as incompatible.' She lifted her hands, their palms horizontal, to reveal the white mesh of scars in their surface. Saskia was aware of their presence; she had first seen them on the journey to Roger Lavery's; they had drawn her attention regularly thereafter; thus far she had resisted making any reference to them.

'I recalled that pain as my friend, and my solace, and my revenge, and it has remained with me since. I realised that I enjoyed it. Then as I grew and became more sophisticated, I imagined what the pain would be like if it was enhanced. I learned about the compliance of thorns by accident a few years ago. I simply repurposed it, so to speak.'

'How old were you?'

'I was your age.'

'Do you never regret it?' Saskia was fascinated, absorbed.

'No, I do not.'

'Could someone exercise power over you with it?'

'I don't see how? Only I can charge the goad with intent. I belong to me Saskia.'

'I don't know what the goad is.'

Ayesha smiled crookedly. She had allowed this odd young woman so far in, and so quickly. The more analytical everyday part of her asked why, the intuitive, sensual part of her said why not?

'I took a leap of faith telling you about myself Saskia. You might have despised me for all I knew. most young women of your age would not have the maturity to reconcile what I've told you, but you aren't most young women are you?'

'The same could be said about you!' Saskia smiled satirically.

'I am a bit older than you. And I have my magic, and it does change you.' Ayesha was enigmatic. 'It leads you down strange paths and it's up to you to light them or just stay in the dark, and there are arguments for both.'

'It is not just magic which does that. You know, I think I have been an adult since I was about twelve. The fetter took away my innocence. If I ever had any. It seems that we are both dark little souls you and I; I told you I would have gone with Nathan, but for Roger Lavery. I'm glad I didn't.'

'You would have regretted it. Nathan is a brute; I know from experience. I might be a pain freak but I'm not into brutality and menace. I have no regrets about my association with Khalid. He has a wife and I know he has other mistresses, but it suits me.'

'Lucky Khalid,' Saskia murmured.

'You must understand that I do not love Khalid; I am fond of him. But there is no passion. He is the consummate sensualist. He can make you come all night, or he can tantalize you until you ache for pleasure. And he knows how to use the goad.'

'What is the goad?'

'I'll show you; don't rush me. My compliance of thorns might have inspired Nathan, he got to use it you recall. He intended the same for you, only more so.'

'You weren't with Khalid then?'

'Khalid was abroad for a few months. I needed my diversion. Nathan got lucky. He was fascinated by the compliance, so when all of this kicked off it was a solution for the treacherous bastard. He was coming for you, old school. Blackthorns.'

'Why old school?'

'He understands it better. And he had limited time to act when he found out about the Wild and who had inherited it; it must have been a surprise when he found out it was you. That did give him an advantage of sorts, he was almost certain that you would be fettered. What he had in mind for you is cruel magic, quite barbaric in fact, and very dark. Anyway, let's not think about Nathan, he's not worth our breath. I brought you in here for a couple of reasons; because it's intimate; I wanted to experience your reaction while you examined my compliance; elsewhere it would have been impersonal; here it's provocative and I must admit I wanted to wind you up; you are fascinating by the way; the way you looked at me when you examined me; your body shaping. I believe that I saw want, but I could have been mistaken.' She gave a little, darkly playful smile.

'What was the other thing?' Saskia asked ignoring the invitation.

Ayesha frowned, stung to sudden irritation by her own sense of disappointment at Saskia's response.

'My goad's in here, you want to see it don't you? You've seen about everything else,' she said sharply.

'Yes, I want to see it,'

'It's still in my bag, on the bed. Get it, it's in a lacquered black case.'

Saskia located the bag and knelt on the bed to open it. Ayesha joined her, sitting on the edge of the bed; she watched her with curiosity, her dark eyes flitting, but mostly studying her face and expression. Saskia extracted an oblong case that was coated in shiny black lacquer. It had a hinged, fitted lid. She released it by pressing a small silver stud at the front. She raised the lid and gazed at what lay inside it. Ayesha watched the green eyes widen infinitesimally as they filled with an appreciative gleam. Saskia glanced briefly to the side, finding her.

'May I?' she asked.

'Go ahead.'

The goad fitted snugly into its recess, which was perfectly cut into an internal block of black Perspex. Cautiously, Saskia inserted her fingertips at the access points provided and extracted it; she held it delicately between her fingers, treating it with studied circumspection.

'It's exquisite,' she commented softly, and it was. Carved with all the skill of a netsuke master in a dark polished wood. The goad was roughly six inches long; it had been given the form of a garden rose stem. It possessed twelve brutal looking curved thorns, all crafted in silver; each had been fixed into the wood with exquisite skill, so that they appeared to be growing from it, and they were dangerously sharp.

'Appropriate, yes?'

'I was thinking that exact thought.'

'Were you? Truly?'

'Yes, truly.'

'The thorns were created from the same piece of alchemically altered silver as the barbs lodged inside me. Mixed with some of my monthly bleed if you're really interested.'

'It's warm, it feels alive, Ayesha.' Saskia was aware of a sense of movement similar, though less insistent, to that of Nathan's seven blackthorns: the sensation of something stirring inside it. 'It's sleeping. It's beautiful!' Saskia exclaimed in a whisper; causing Ayesha to wonder if she had listened to her. 'Wow!'

Saskia was about to ask how the Goad worked but Ayesha flared irritably. 'Wow? You examine every inch of my naked body, and it's a well-maintained, excellent, fucking naked body; in fact, it's pretty fucking special, and you say nothing. I show you my goad and that gets a wow! Fuck! Are you punishing me for something? For calling you a Praying Mantis. I took that back.'

'I actually think that I like you referring to me as a Praying Mantis,' Saskia informed her.

Ayesha shook her head in mild disbelief. She half laughed.

'You also said that I was feral.'

'I meant that. I'm going to dress. Do you intend to watch?'

'Yes, I intend to watch.'

'You had better put that away then hadn't you. Be careful, I can see you've already pricked yourself.'

'How about Master and Commander at the Vue.'

'Has that got Russel Crowe in it?'

'Is he a deal breaker?' Ayesha smiled mischievously.

Saskia regarded her with contempt, which in her manifested as a face devoid of expression together with a totally blank stare.

'No, he is not.'

'You haven't been out for three days. We should go for a walk as well.'

'Two. This is day three and we've only just eaten breakfast. What is the matter? you're bored with my company, aren't you?'

'Of course not.' Ayesha frowned slightly, apparently taken by the thought. 'Actually, no I'm not.'

'You sound surprised.'

Ayesha shrugged. 'Take the compliment Saskia.'

'Okay, I will. Master and Commander's fine by me.' Saskia shrugged, she had removed their breakfast things, now she slid into place again next to Ayesha; she slipped her arm around her waist, her fingers snuggled into black lamb's wool. She rested a token glance on the newspaper which Ayesha had spread out on the worktop; as Ayesha made to turn the page, she stopped her with her hand laid on hers.

'Look.' She pointed to a kicker, a few lines near the top of one of the columns. '"Grinning ghost groped a dog walker as she scooped up doggie doo. Lecherous phantom, known locally as smirky, struck on Saturday night, when the sixty-year-old woman...yadayada...she claimed the seven-foot randy revenant merged into a solid brick wall. Police are treating the incident as sexual assault...phantom predator or prankster?" it has got to be my ghost, Ayesha! My docker John!'

'Your docker John!' Ayesha issued a little harsh laugh. 'Are you laying claim to him? Why don't you grass him up to plod. They'd love you!' She barged Saskia playfully with her shoulder.

'Interesting though, isn't it?'

'It is, I suppose. You aren't going to drag me out looking for him, are you? To persuade him to change his sleazy ways.'

'No! of course not! That's not my job. He does what he does. But he might become dangerous.'

'He already is by the sound of it.'

'I mean even more so.'

'Then, potentially, he becomes commercial.'

'Commercial?'

'If he can be jarred.'

'Jarred. What is, jarred?

'Contained in a vessel, not necessarily a jar! But often a stone jar. Any more questions?'

'Lots!' Saskia responded. Her eyes gleamed with fascination. 'You are not leaving it there. Tell me more. Who would jar him and why?'

Ayesha shrugged, compressing her mouth. 'Someone who had a purpose for him. Their own, or to sell on to someone with a purpose for him.'

'What sort of purpose?'

'I don't know. Some adepts use entities in their work. They even study them. One or two collect them, to experience them.'

'I see, I think.' A deep frown delved between her dark brows. 'I know of entities Ayesha; I have encountered several. Usually, I keep well clear. They don't exactly hide, why haven't they been scooped up and jarred?'

Ayesha became thoughtful. 'Because they slipped through the net perhaps, in some cases,' she suggested, 'or they are simply too dangerous. Maybe there's something else about them? I don't know. I'm no expert. The people to ask are Claire or her brother Hal, they'll know far more than me. I'd suggest Nathan for pure knowledge, but he's a nonstarter.'

A deviant strand of thought threaded through Saskia's mind at the mention of Nathan; part of her was still fascinated by the idea of him and the seven black thorns of compliance he had intended to hammer into her. She allowed her mind to dwell temporarily, on the particular dark rabbit hole that that would have propelled her down; into the dark matter world that composed the alternative side of her sexuality. She imagined herself Nathan's acolyte; a servant to his agenda, as well as distraction and plaything; she smiled to herself; she was not under any illusions; she would have been his creature, she knew that; his property; Saskia found that appealed to her sinister side most of all. Almost reluctantly, she pushed it from her mind.

'That's not a good smile,' Ayesha said, as she considered Saskia's expression through narrowed lids.

'Isn't it?'

'I see it when you aren't present in the room with me.' She spoke softly, holding Saskia's gaze. 'When your mind is elsewhere.'

'Does that happen often?'

'Often enough; I wonder what's going through your head.'

'Ironically, you should ask.' Saskia looked amused.

'Do I want to know?'

'I'm mostly thinking about you.'

'I see. Pardon me if I don't blush.'

'I don't expect you to!' Saskia laughed. Then her humour fragmented in a sudden wince of pain. She closed her eyes and pressed the tips of her index and middle finger between her brows.

'How bad?' Ayesha inquired.

'Just a stab, and its passed now. No burning sensation...yet.'

'Don't suffer in silence.'

'I won't. Can we go for a walk?'

Ayesha nodded. 'If you like! We can walk down to the towpath and look at the barges.'

Saskia went to brush her teeth; She fetched her padded jacket and put on lace up leather shoes; she was not really a fan of trainers. When she emerged from her room, Ayesha was in the hall, tidying the hems of her denims over suede ankle boots. Saskia cast admiring eyes over her fleece lined jacket; it was in burgundy leather with a tight little belted waist; it suited her; everything suited Ayesha, she thought. Ayesha straightened and smiled. 'Ready?'

'Let's go!'

They descended by way of the stairs and emerged into quite a breezy, overcast day; they turned left and walked chatting, until they reached culverin way, and dropped down to pass under the road bridge to link with the original towpath beside the canal. They came to the moored barges, pretty and well maintained. The design and the detail appealed to Saskia. There were only a couple of people about; the sound of laughter and conversation came from one of the boats. There would be community here Saskia decided.

'I thought of living on one not so long ago, If I could afford to,' she remarked. 'I enjoy the alternative lifestyle they offer; or the idea of it, I suppose.'

'That one is called Lethargic Spirit,' Ayesha chuckled. 'What would you call yours?'

'I don't know, the Little Cow.'

Ayesha laughed appreciatively. 'Have you ever stayed on one?'

'Straight answer, I've never even been on one.'

'I've travelled on one for a couple of weeks, not in the UK. In France. I liked it, and before you ask, yes, I was.'

'Was what?' Saskia asked, playfully feigning innocence.

'With someone I was fucking at the time.'

'Were they special?'

'Special? He was a damn good fuck if that's what you mean!' Ayesha's eyes flashed as she indulged in the memory; she searched for a jealous reaction in Saskia. 'He was French actually, looks and muscles; I met him in York when I was doing some work for the firm. He was there on some private security assignment, for a company called Santalla, I believe. He picked me up. We saw each other during the evenings and spent the nights together; he asked me to come and stay on his boat, Peniche, they call them there. I was overdue some holiday time, so I said yes.'

'Is he out of the equation now?'

'For fucks sake Saskia! He was never in the equation. By day eight he was boring me to death, and he knew it. The trip wasn't. Just him.'

'He might have been special for all I knew,' Saskia reasoned. She managed not to wince as she felt another stab of pain behind her eyes; she had experienced several now, and the familiar burning sensation had started not long after they had left the apartment; it had been growing more intense since they had dropped onto the towpath.

'Well, he wasn't then, and he isn't now.'

'Good. I'm pleased,' Saskia said softly. The canal barges had been a distraction from the burning to begin with, but it was no longer possible to ignore.

'Are you okay? You look as white as a sheet of A4.' Ayesha was looking intensely at her, suddenly concerned.

'It's my burning. I've only once known it get so awful so quickly, and that's when we drove back from Hoardale; usually it begins like an itch and gets worse through the day. I don't often get the stabbing pain either, but I've had it a few more times and its beyond what I've experienced before.'

'You should have said.'

'I know.'

'What are you like Saskia?'

'I'm sorry.'

'Don't be.'

'It's changed. It's scary? I keep thinking about what happened to my mum.'

'I drained your energy centres! It had never been done before! the energy has been creeping back in, impeded by your fetter, but also prevented from dissipating for the same reason. Its acting like a valve. It appears to have reached the: I'm going to burst your skull open stage.'

'How reassuring.' Saskia released a shaky breath; she frowned in discomfort. 'But what you're describing is the reason for it, and I don't disagree. It does not account for the fast onset, or the speed of build-up. I think I know the answer, what caused it to change. We had best go back.'

'It's too far,' Ayesha insisted. 'There's a bench a bit further along; come on. So, tell me what you think brought about this change?'

'The Wild of course. It happened when I visited the Wild; soon after that the pain became unbearable; you saw that.'

'You know this for certain. Instinctively.'

'I know, Ayesha. Going to the Wild changed me in some way.'

'Okay, for what it's worth, I think you might be right. I think the Wild is more than simply Place; it's high magic. You should ask Claire. Sit down.' They had arrived at a solid looking bench made of varnished teak, with an attached memorial plaque dedicated to somebody called Emily. As she sat, despite her pain, Saskia wondered if Emily ever visited, if this was presumably a favourite location; she was not aware of anything vestigial. Ayesha sat down next to her; her knees turned in towards her. Saskia adjusted her position so that they were facing; she watched Ayesha's eyes search her face, she saw an unfamiliar tenderness in them; they fixed on her own and remained. Lightly, Ayesha rested her left hand on Saskia's right forearm, fingers spaced. Once again, she resisted the urge to tell her that she found her gold threaded eyes quite beautiful, though it was a close-run thing. She stroked her paper white cheek with the tips of the fingers of her right hand; deftly, she slid them beneath her dark brown hair. Saskia caught a sharp little breath in reaction, as though ice had touched her naked spine. Unexpectedly she nuzzled her cheek into Ayesha's palm. Ayesha felt tiny spikes of energy penetrate her body as she began to draw off Saskia's centres; she was aware of resonance, a subtle ache; some light headedness, but that would pass. Suddenly something was trilling, muffled, surprising her; she felt the vibration of it close to her body; her mouth curved in a half smile as she recognised the source.

'It's your phone, inside your pocket,' Saskia told her. 'Are you going to answer it.'

'No, I'm not. I'll finish what I'm doing,' she replied. Mentally she dismissed the muffled ring tone, and the soft vibration against her hip.

'It might be important,' Saskia suggested.

'Not more important than you,' she said and watched darts of colour form in Saskia's cheeks.

Ayesha's phone ceased to ring at the very moment she completed her task. She withdrew her fingers from Saskia's hair; as she did so Saskia turned her head so that her mouth brushed their undersides; Ayesha smiled and gave a tiny shake of her head. Her phone was in her left side pocket, she raised the loose flap and retrieved it; she opened the screen and glanced down. When she looked up again her lips quirked into a wry smile, that had sorry written everywhere in it.

'That was him, wasn't it. Khalid.' Saskia's words were phrased as a statement, not a question. Ayesha searched Saskia's face for condemnation, at least a sign of disapproval or judgement, but she encountered only a blank stare.

'Little point denying it. He chooses his moments,' Ayesha replied, she felt uncomfortable, but she decided that she was hiding it well. She wondered what Saskia was concealing behind her impassivity. 'I'll phone him when we get in.'

'Aren't mobile phones for that? Why don't you call him back now?'

'Is that what you'd like me to do?'

'I think I'd prefer it.'

'Okay.' Ayesha gave a little poignant shrug; she compressed her mouth, which Saskia recognised as indicative of irritation; her nostrils flared delicately as she exhaled hard from them. She opened her phone and returned Khalids call. At first, she thought he was not going to pick up, the phone at the other end rang and rang. She had four numbers logged in her contacts for him, this one belonged to his private office phone. She could almost feel Saskia willing her not to end the call; she let it ring well beyond what she would ordinarily have permitted. She almost flinched in surprise when Khalid eventually picked up and she heard his voice answer.

'Hi, Khalid, it's me. Look I'm sorry but I need to be brief, I'm in the middle of something.'

Ayesha kept the conversation as short and to the point as she could. Khalid Taharqa enjoyed being in control; it was in his nature to impose himself and to order Ayesha up like an expensive food delivery, but Ayesha felt embarrassed and exposed, and suddenly so not in the mood. She fielded and pared their conversation to the bone. She watched Saskia's face as she spoke; she looked so tired, but her colour was returning; as for her expression, it gave nothing away; simply returning look for look.

'Okay Khalid. Goodbye.' She ended the call and slid her phone back into her pocket. 'I'm sorry Saskia.' She said quietly. She looked quite forlorn, Saskia thought.

'I know, no movie. You have your own master and commander tonight.'

'Very droll! Khalid might be many things Saskia, but my master, he is not. Please, let's not talk about it.'

'Let's go home.' Saskia surprised her by taking her hand in hers and standing up; Ayesha allowed herself to be drawn to her feet. She felt the strength of the breeze now they were facing it. Saskia's hand felt comfortable in hers, somehow reassuring. She blinked at tears induced by the cold breeze, at least that was what she decided had prompted them.

Ayesha spent the rest of the day in a silent misery of her own construction; she was aware that her relationship with Khalid was symbiotic, it held no warmth, no tenderness; certainly, no love. But there was sensuality and inventive sex; most of all there was a gut-wrenching need for her chosen pain, and the fulfilment of it led to the perception of being dependant on Khalid for her fix.

'There's something else, in ways, even darker.' She told Saskia, speaking suddenly, as if halfway through a conversation. Saskia had her head buried in a book on cave art; she looked up attentively when Ayesha placed two glasses of Chardonnay on the table and slipped into the opposite corner of the couch she occupied. She was dressed for her rendezvous with Khalid, in a short, flared, blue velvet strapless dress and naked stilettos. Saskia felt a bitter hit as jealousy tried to claw its way out like a needy bitch; she denied it, her face continuing to be a mask of self-possession. Ayesha continued to speak conversationally, but with conviction.

'That, being the need, you get me? the craving, for someone to inflict it.'

'Inflict what?' Saskia asked, playing mildly dumb.

Ayesha frowned almost peevishly. 'Pain of course. I tried inflicting it on myself to begin with, and it hurt! But I knew immediately it was imperfect, even derisory, and I knew why. It lacked the orchestration of another will, and the abstention of mine.'

Saskia set aside her book; her knees were drawn up in front of her and she rested her back against the arm of the couch. She was wearing black ankle socks, and she studied her toes as she scrunched them. 'What made you choose Khalid?' she inquired.

'That was easy. It was the obvious choice given our history and I knew he was a cunt.'

'And if you'd chosen badly?'

'I would have found someone else. But I absolutely knew he was the right choice. Saskia the car will be here soon, it's always on time. I need to know that we are okay. You've not mentioned Khalid once since our walk, until just now.'

'Don't look so worried. I'm proud of you; you really do look remarkably beautiful.'

'Don't.'

'Utterly stunning, in fact.'

'Saskia, please.'

'I'm cool Ayesha; I got over myself; trust me. Go to your man.'

'He is not my man. Never that.'

'He is for a few hours, during which I will feel incredibly jealous, but I promise you I can handle it. It will just be for a few hours, then you will come home to me.'

Ayesha searched Saskia's face for signs of muted anxiety or bitterness, but she found nothing; Saskia was cool; in control; she appeared totally at ease, as she had been throughout the day. 'I must go now,' Ayesha told her.

'I know. Go on.' Saskia's voice was soft in tone, almost soothing. 'But I will wait up for you.'

Ayesha nodded determinedly; she stood; she smoothed her dress; perfect red nails against the blue. She drew a deep breath and turned away, missing the tiny twitch in Saskia's eye by a mere microsecond. She walked from the room, and a minute or so later, the apartment. She had left without touching her wine Saskia noticed. She reached for her own glass, tears trickling.

'Not 'appy is she?'
'Compelled I would say.'
She had observed the young woman as she climbed into the chauffeured car. Her sly eyes studied the intense moodiness of her beauty, the determined compressed mouth; she puzzled at the hint of despondency. She had not long ago parked on Culverin way herself, maybe twenty minutes previously. She was there to look, to see, evaluate; what, she did not know until she knew. She was about to get out of her Audi Spyder, slip on her coat and shoes, and walk for a while; then the Bently had been driven past her, and on a whim, she followed it, stopping on the forecourt, a few metres away. Rachel Zimpara had habit of being in the right place at the right time.
'You can hear me. Can you see me?' the voice was chiding, mocking, Liverpudlian accented.
'I can smell you.' She twisted in the low seat and tilted her head to the side, peering at him with birdlike intensity. He filled her passenger side where she had sensed him materialise a few moments ago, his long body jack-knifed into the seat. He exuded stale dampness, the smell of the docks, urine. His squinty sinister eyes roved over her, lecherously she decided; they dwelled too long on her short-skirted thighs. She readied intent, preparing to defend herself if necessary; this was much more than a conventional spirit; she could sense physicality crawling out of it; he was approaching entity.
'She doesn't see me.'
'Who?'
'One you was watching.'
'Was I watching her?'
'Seemed to me you was, hard, when you saw her.'
'She's a beautiful woman.' Nathan had sent a photograph of Ayesha Shah to her mobile, a somewhat compromising one, another of Saskia Challoner, not so clear, playing a Lute, busking in the street.

'T'other lass can see me and talk to me you know, like we are doing.'

'Can she?'

'Ay, she's still inside.'

'Oh. Is she? Out of interest, have you ever seen her come out on her own? The other lass.'

'Once. Late in the night after the other one came back. I approached her, and we talked. Then the other one came looking for her.'

'She could see you as well as I can. Communicate.'

'Just as well. I get about. I felt the urge to see them after that, strong like. But there's something else up there where they live, and it scared the blue fuck out of me.'

She had already discarded any thought of entering the building and personally acquiring the Challoner girl. The disembodied merely confirmed what she already suspected; that there would be a powerful guardian in situ.

'I'm sure your motives were honourable,' she commented, not disguising her cynicism.

His smug smile broadened appreciatively. 'Nah, I wanted to watch them fucking.' He chuckled to himself, evidently taken with the thought. He grinned showing a mouth filled with the stumps of rotting teeth. 'I'll be seeing you,' he said, surprising her.

'Wait, I've...'

He had already distorted and smudged into a smear of brown smoke, beginning to exit the car before her words were formed, leaving only a residual stench.

'Fuck!' Her reactions were fast, her actions efficient, she had the car door open in an instant; her petite body issued from the Audi in one fluid movement. The cool air reached for her; it had started to rain, the sort of really wet rain that filled the air like aggressive mist. It quickly soaked into her red suit and wetted her face as she ran to the passenger side of the car. Her slim feet were bare for driving. She made it as her declining ended; and time within her vicinity quickened again.

'That's a new one,' he said as he emerged smirk first from her car.

'In that case you are moving in the wrong circles,' she replied sarcastically. She watched him as he assumed full form. The smirk never seemed to leave his face, but there was puzzlement in his eyes now, and above all, caution. His almost seven feet of height towered over her five feet nothing, five foot three had she been wearing the high heels which were tucked under the driving seat.

Docker John peered suspiciously, down into her sly eyes.

'You have no idea what you are dealing with.' His voice had taken on an element of menace.

'I, so do,' she replied coolly. 'But you do not.' She glanced briefly up towards Ayesha's penthouse. There was no sign of Saskia Challoner, but she did not want to take the risk of being seen; not when the girl was able to see ghosts. 'Not here. Over there. I only want a few moments of your time. So don't risk it for a biscuit will you if you get my meaning.' She winked, then indicated the entrance to the subterranean car park, not visible from the penthouse. She led the way and paused at the edge of full streetlight; her eyes never leaving docker John, as he reluctantly followed.

'Hereabouts is basically your haunt?' she said. The rain was soaking into her suit and trickling down her face; she regretted not having the brolly she kept in the car within more easy reach; lesson learned; she hated getting wet.

'Not as much as it was. Recently I've got about a lot more.'

'I'm sure you have.'

'My death was down there, in a yard.' He pointed along the walk with a big hand, its fingernails edged in black. 'They broke its old bricks to build with new, and they broke my chains too.'

'I see. Fortunate for you. By what method did you die?'

'By the knife, as I got my hole!' His face broke into a salacious grin. 'They could have let me finish.'

'Spare me the details.'

'What have you got to say? I've places to be.'

'I'm sure you have. Things to see!' she flashed her wet eyebrows at him and allowed her wide mouth to curve into a winning smile. 'It's your eyes I want, or the use of them.'

'To watch them lasses?'

'Perhaps perform other tasks too, but mostly that. I know people who will pay well.'

He chuckled, mocking her. 'What the fuck do you pay the likes of me with?'

'When are you most active? I presume the night.'

'Hours of darkness. Though not all of them.'

'I presume that you would prefer to be. Active I mean.'

'What the fuck do you think?'

'I am willing to bet that when you show yourself to anyone, those that can't ordinarily see or hear you, like I can and the girl, for whatever reason, it uses up a tremendous amount of your strength. What happens then?'

'I get bone weary. I cannot move around. Then I sleep. I hate sleeping, it is like death!'

'You don't dream, do you?'

He answered her with silence. He shifted in and out of focus, she watched him carefully in case he bolted. He responded to her question with a slow shake of his head.

'What is your offer? What's your coin?'

'More time. More opportunity. Less sleep.'

'I'm listening.'

She relaxed, sensing genuine acquiescence from the ghost. 'There is someone I want you to meet. I am going to phone him now. I think you will get along, even though he won't be able to see you. We'll drive to meet him. Unfortunately, that means you getting back in my car.'

She ignored docker John's snicker of laughter from the passenger seat, as she climbed with as much waterlogged elegance as she could muster, back into the driver's side. She pressed rainwater from her eyebrows so that it trickled down the sides of her cheeks, then retrieved her phone from her bag on the floor; she opened her contacts and rang Nathan Xavier.

'Twenty minutes,' she said as she returned her phone to her bag. She glanced at him, dubiously, but also resolutely. 'Now, there's one more thing.'

'And that might be?' The ghost inquired suspiciously.

She drew a long breath and released it as she spoke. 'I need to ensure we can communicate; that means I must create a bond between us, so that you can find me when you need to.' She had already considered the consequences of this; the reality that this would give the ghost access to her home; but boundaries could be discussed later; he was after all an opportunity not to be missed.

'How does that work, then?' His eyed bored into her; the interior light had dimmed and in the semi darkness the smirking features had taken on a malevolent cast.

She gave a little shrug; her wide mouth curved into a smile, with a hint of the satirical; her lips parted over white teeth; her retracted incisors slid into position; as sharp as needles.

'That's different,' he remarked.

She pierced her lower lip with her incisors and immediately withdrew them; the blood welled, filling the front of her gums and reddening her teeth; it trickled down her chin and dribbled onto her clothing. She breathed a burst of wheezy laughter, bubbling blood, and saliva through her teeth.

'This is the part where you kiss me, lucky ghost! Do not overthink it!' He was fascinated and he did not hesitate; he moved towards her; his mouth pressing down on hers. The touch of his lips burned cold, and he tasted like wet fish on the turn; the sort of fish that has a glazed eye as it lies on the fishmongers counter, festering and getting smellier with each passing hour. As she felt herself bind with him, she withdrew from him. She smiled in satisfaction as she wiped her bloody chin and mouth on the sleeve of her jacket; she started up her Spyders engine.

Saskia allowed herself a masochistic hour of emotional torment; during which she established the certainty that she truly hated Khalid Taharqa, and she would do him harm if she could. She resented Ayesha too, seeing her as aloof and detached; a selfish little bitch who could not care less how much hurt and anguish she caused her; she knew there was no foundation of truth in that, it felt good to think it though. She ran it through her thoughts in little fragments of self-torment; Ayesha's remembered words and looks, and an imagined cruel kind of impassivity; but that was a house built on sand; Ayesha was neither cruel or impassive; the whole lot came tumbling down and she was left with the aching desire for a beautiful young woman, for whom she cared a very great deal, and the darkest thoughts she could hold for a man that she had never met, whom she loathed utterly. She tried to detach, indulging in some self-loathing, and a guilt trip in the making about roger Lavery. She drank wine, including Ayesha's untouched glass, with a bitter determination; she emptied the bottle, but it only made her sullen. She sulked, and read some Yeats, a variorum edition apparently. She set aside Yeats, feeling dissatisfied and delved into the more esoteric section of Ayesha's library; she had had her eye on some volumes relating to Austin Osman Spare, the artist occultist, he looked interesting, she thought, and she was not disappointed. She played some ELO, keeping it background, and then some Sting. Ayesha called Spare an ordinary, with talent. Eventually Saskia returned the Spares to the bookshelves; by which time it was just after two; she made tea and selected a movie to watch, choosing Night of the Demon made in 1957. She curled on the couch to watch it in the dark; she enjoyed noir, and it proved to be an excellent choice. Afterwards she remained where she was, in the light of the blank television screen; she allowed it to endure for a time and then gave it the mercy of the power off switch on the remote. She closed her eyes, experiencing a build-up of tension, and a sense of anticipation. It was almost four, and Ayesha would not be long now; Saskia refused to twitch the drapes and watch for Khalids car as it moved along Culverin way, and then the walk, bringing Ayesha home.

  The click of the door catch took her by surprise, her eyes shot open, and she wondered if she had fallen asleep for just a few seconds. The clock display read fourteen minutes past four. She exited the couch in a lithe flow of movement and went to stand in the open doorway of the living room. The light in the hall was subdued; Ayesha leaned with her back against the closed door; her coat was black, with wide lapels and collar; she had pushed it back over her shoulders; it looked as if she had intended to take it off and stopped half way through the action; her Chanel bag was trailing on the floor, held by its strap in her left hand; her feet were bare; she had kicked her stilettos away from her across the floor;

she was pale and looked almost haggard. She regarded Saskia wearily, with caution.

'Saskia, I don't want a fight.' She said quietly; her eyes almost pleaded with her.

'That's the last thing on my mind.' Saskia moved from the doorway and scooped up Ayesha's bag, placing it on the hall table. She caught her reflection in the wall mirror that hung above it; black baggy jumper and black jeans, dark hair framing her moody face; always so serious Saskia. She dismissed the appraisal of her reflection and returned to Ayesha. She took the weight of the expensive coat at its collar and lapel; Ayesha regarded her gratefully and eased her body out of it.

'Oh, I ache!' she told her.

'You look utterly done in,' Saskia commented. She regarded the inflammation along the course of Ayesha's vine tattoo attentively; the rash, like nettle stings, was still pronounced.

'He was angry Saskia. He concealed it until we went to bed. He could not help talking about you though, I could feel his jealousy; he tried to conceal that too, but it just poured out of him.'

Saskia felt herself stiffen; she forced herself to relax. 'What happened?'

'He's always full on, he owns the bed; tonight, he was rough with me though; when he used the goad, he was quite ruthless, spiteful almost; he prolonged the pain well beyond the usual, and it felt harder somehow, and it went deeper; I didn't know he could do that; that it was possible even.'

'I'll make you some tea,' Saskia said lamely; it was all she had to offer right then.

'I don't want any tea. I just want to go to bed. I'm so stiff.'

'It's my fault!' She felt desperately sorry for Ayesha. She didn't know whether to register shame or concern. Part of her, a mean piece of herself that repelled her, even felt a tiny prick of satisfaction.

'It's not your fault. This is on me.' Ayesha padded along the hall towards her bedroom; she was holding herself, arms wrapped, her movements pained. Saskia followed, carrying her coat to hang away. She went into the dressing room and hung it on the rail on a coat hanger; when she emerged, Ayesha had stepped out of her unzipped dress and was climbing into bed in just pretty, black lace briefs. Saskia went to her own room and undressed. She brushed her teeth; she did not get into her own bed but returned to Ayesha's bedroom buttoning up a short blue linen nightshirt. She climbed carefully into bed beside Ayesha. Ayesha turned, she smiled drowsily.

'Thank you for coming back.' She snuggled cautiously into her. 'I'm sorry Saskia.'

'What for?'

'For being me.'

Saskia gently slid her arms around her; she held her. 'Go to sleep.'

'Are you awake?' Saskia inquired softly.

'I am now.'

'Sorry.'

Ayesha chuckled a little croakily. 'No need. I've been awake a few minutes. You can see the clock; what time is it?' The room was dim, only a small amount of light penetrating past the blackout drapes. They were snuggled down, facing one another on their sides.

'Seven minutes to one.'

'Gosh, that's a good sleep. I could get used to this.'

'Us sleeping together?'

'We should get up I suppose. Are you hungry?'

'Not really, are you?'

'No, maybe just some toast.'

'Yes, some toast.'

'With honey.'

'Ayesha.'

'Yes.'

'Last night you said Khalid was jealous of me.'

'Yes, he is. You have dented his massive ego and got right under his skin, without even trying.'

'He punished you because of me.'

'Yes, I think he did. He was cruel, much more than usual. It does not matter. I told you; it is not on you.'

'If you say so.'

'I do. Don't think about it. Last night I felt like I'd been beaten, and I couldn't quell the pain because its alchemically driven. Now I feel okay. It doesn't last. Come on, get your arse out of my bed.'

'What are you working on now?'

They were in the kitchen, seated apart at the island. The day had gone nowhere after their late start. The darkness of another night had collected outside without them being aware. It was almost six and Saskia had been waging war with the spider scrawl script on the documents, written, she assumed, by an ancestor of hers, about the Wild. They gave no timeline and seemed to lack any continuity. She was extracting what she thought might be useful to her and transcribing it in her own neat hand, with a slim black fibre tip into a notebook. It was proving heavy going. She had started a file on Ayesha's laptop too, transferring the information to it. The office had contacted Ayesha over the phone in the afternoon and she had got them to send over some paperwork for her to work on. She had been processing documents, scribbling busily with an expensive ball-point, occasionally referring to her calculator and sometimes typing on her laptop computer, a Toshiba, which she had claimed back from Saskia, in a rapid clicking flow, which Saskia found relaxing. Eventually, tired of squinting, with a bit of an ache between her eyes and in need of tea and possibly food, Saskia decided to break off from her task. She stared at Ayesha, working opposite, cute in a cashmere V-neck jumper in sangria red; it was slim fit, the sleeves of above elbow length. She was wearing rimless glasses by Gucci or some other designer name, Saskia was not sure which; Ayesha had applied makeup that day with a light touch and the glasses added a frisson to her beauty, Saskia decided.

'Did you ask me something?' Ayesha raised her gaze from the paperwork and peered inquiringly. There was no smile, she had been intent on her work.

'I asked you what you were doing?'

'I'm working.'

'I can see that. Those spectacles really suit you.'

'I know.' The mouth relented, she smiled. 'I am only being mean to you. Fancy making tea?'

'Yes, I was going to ask if you wanted one. What about food are you hungry?'

'I would like to finish this, so about another half hour. Can you hold out?'

'Yes fine. What shall we have?'

'I could take you out, I know a nice Gastro pub, not far away actually.'

'I'm not keen on pubs.'

'You'll be with me. It's more of a restaurant anyway.'

'Okay.' Saskia looked doubtful. 'Should I wear my new dress?'

'No. That's much too nice, I'll take you somewhere classy in that. Smart casual. I won't be long; part of this is work for you.'

'Is it?' Saskia raised her nose, peering.

'Yes, two lots of probate. I don't usually do the whole thing, I've got an assistant, but as its for you. I'm working on the inheritance tax documents presently, filling in what I can. And you will be paying tax. Lots relatively speaking. But we do need a contents valuation at your cottage, there are antiques. I'm not declaring the haul we brought away, unless you want me to?'

'No, definitely not.' Saskia chuckled. 'What am I worth?'

Ayesha laughed at that, paused, refrained, then continued. 'Enough. There's money in banks and building societies. Shares. The cottage, the house at Thirsk. The Hoardale land and Lake; I know the building is a ruin, even so. And the contents valuation at Thirsk, you lucky lass.' She scribbled a figure and held it up for Saskia to see. 'Ball Park, that is after death duties. At present.'

'Oh, my god.'

'Why are you crying? I need to finalise the figures with an expert valuation of the Lavery contents. And I know we brought documents away, but there could be more. The cremations on Friday, we can go to the cottage beforehand. There will only be you and me at the service. I thought you were making some tea.'

Five

'Is it far?'

'Ten minutes. Arm.'

Saskia slid her arm through Ayesha's. The toughened glass entrance door to the building swung to and locked behind them. It had rained and the expanse of modern cobbles across the Canal Court landing were still slick. They took the footpath along the side of the canal; its surface glinted a few feet below and reflected the lights.

'It's the Bowman, it's on the other side of the river. It used to be a real dive. Blood and sawdust on the floor. It was a coaching Inn in the past; they used to host cockfighting in the stable yard. That's apartments now.'

'You sound regretful?'

'Maybe I am, but not for the cockfighting.' They walked for a few minutes without conversing. They could hear the background noise of the traffic across the river beyond the canal to their right, and beyond the buildings to their left; these were the rear access to retail outlets, with shuttered delivery doors, windowless walls. The intermittent sound of ambulances and police cars bullied through the hum, blue lights flashing. A motorbike roared to life between the buildings as they neared the road and the sight of the bridge; it revved unnecessarily and pitched its headlights into the street; nosed into the traffic on the road and took off over the bridge. Saskia glanced towards it as it passed them, distracted. Her brows indented as she glimpsed docker John by the building wall, the ghost's form drained by the light of an overhead lamp. He faded even as she saw him, his smirk dark and knowing. Saskia gave a little shudder.

'It may seem like a very great deal of money Saskia.' Ayesha said unexpectedly, snatching her back into their reality. 'But it can dwindle, and you are only just coming up to twenty. I'm just saying invest it carefully. Any plans? I know it's a bit soon.'

'I have thought about it; though it feels a bit wicked, particularly where Roger is concerned,' Saskia responded.

'Good for you. It is not wicked; just remember Roger Lavery had your interests at heart; he would want the best for you.'

'But what about him, his ghost, what if he thought he would be coming to visit me in the future to catch up and I wasn't there? He knew I saw ghosts.'

'How often does that happen to people? Any idea? And I do not think that Roger Lavery thought like that at all.'

'I don't know. Roger saw his wife Jenny, she visited for a few weeks before he died. I don't know any other people that see them.
There is a clairvoyant in the high street back home, he claims to. But I don't think he does. I see them all the time.'

'I think you have more magic than you realise. It's probably you that enables them. If you lose the fetter and regain intent, you might lose that ability.'

'I hope so,' Saskia muttered.

The Bowman was not too busy for Saskia's taste; it was welcoming, what was the word? Convivial. Even so she would have preferred to eat in, she decided; Ayesha had seemed determined however. Saskia decided to make the effort to enjoy the experience, she was with Ayesha after all.

There was no difficulty getting a table and Saskia spied one by the window in the corner and headed for it. Ayesha shrugged apologetically at a tall waiter, name-tagged Joe, who tried to direct them to a vacant table closer to the bar. She followed Saskia. Unfazed, Joe brought menus and left to fetch two glasses of Stella Artois.

They sat opposite and hung their coats over the backs of the chairs next to them. Ayesha had kept on the clothes she was already wearing to go out; Saskia had changed into a long sleeved slim fit jumper in a graphite-coloured cashmere that Ayesha had selected for her when they had shopped. Both had chosen to wear lace up shoes. Saskia opted to sit with her back to the wall; she sat with her hands clasped between her knees and with her shoulders hunched slightly forwards as she scrutinised the menu laid on the table in front of her, with a worried intensity. Ayesha was about to nudge Saskia back to their embryonic conversation about her inheritance, but Saskia pre-empted her.

'I think that I'm going to rent out the cottage.'

'It would provide you with steady income. Interest rates are crap. You will need to spend some money on it.'

'I know. I would not know where to start with that.'

'I would.'

'You'll help me?'

'You know that I will.'

Joe the waiter returned with their drinks, two stella's in tapering glasses.

'I've decided what I'm having,' Ayesha announced. 'The big steak pie,' she prolonged the word pie and added a dark inflection which made the word sound quite sinister. 'And chips.'

'I'm convinced,' said Saskia. 'Make that two.'

They spent the next fifteen minutes in girl chat, music mostly, with a brief excursion into tattoo art prompted by an elegant well inked girl at one of the tables; Ayesha altered tack and rested her chin on interlocked fingers, elbows on the table. She peered interestedly at Saskia. 'So, come on then, what else would you like to do, now you have money? Will you do something with your music?'

'I never thought of that.' Saskia frowned briefly in thought. 'I don't think so, other than buy more instruments. I'd like a business in antiques, but I'm not ready yet.'

'You've got a head start. Is that because of Roger though, and all that stock we brought away? Wait until you see Mocking-beck.' Mocking-beck was the house she had inherited in Thirsk, from Trevor Challoner.

'No. I got to know Roger years ago because I was interested. He said I should go to Newark Antiques Fair, that it was massive. I said that he should take me there. It never happened. You could go with me; but you'll get sick of me before then.' It was a strange thing to say, Ayesha thought. Probably said to test her, or out of low self-esteem, though she doubted that.

'If you continue talking that way. Just recall the things I've said to you...'

She broke off abruptly, as a lean athletic young man in a grey suit dropped into the seat beside her in a waft of Aramis. He was dark haired and designer stubbled, and somewhere in his early thirties. He was good looking, but with a slightly oily complexion.

He had dark entitled eyes. He glanced from Saskia to Ayesha and smiled confidently.

'A girl called Elaine tried to direct us to another table, but we saw you two sitting here, and we thought wow! Why would we want any other table? Isn't that right Jed.'

'That's right Rod,' his companion agreed. Jed was red haired; he was about the same age and height, but he did not have Rod's lean build; he was powerfully built, more solid; he looked as if he belonged in the back row of a rugby team, Ayesha decided. He had cold blue eyes and he lacked charm. He had an indifferent mouth; it was too small and surrounded by messy reddish facial hair. He too was in a suit, his was more of a silver grey. Saskia watched him from the corners of her eyes, she caught the hint of a sneer as he sat down next to her.

'I'm sorry,' said Elaine apologetically, she had followed them and approached the table as Jed sat down. She looked confused and worried. 'I couldn't stop them. They saw you when they came in.'

'It's okay Elaine,' Ayesha told her smiling. 'But please don't offer to fetch them drinks.'

'That's not friendly,' commented Rod.

'I don't want to be friendly.'

Saskia peered at both men with disdain. By her criteria, it would be another ten years at least before these two no longer needed nappies, and probably beyond that; if ever. They were office types at play, a couple of predatory males chancing their luck; not all men were the same, she knew that, but too many thought they were special. There was a fine line she thought, between thinking you were exceptional and knowing you were exceptional, and those who knew had no need to frequent pubs and clubs, and the usual hunting grounds. These two would be better in the town centre, where many of the girls who knew no better, fed near the bottom.

'I do not want to listen to your crap either. I want you to leave our table. I can see several others that are unoccupied.'

'They don't have the attractions that this one has.' Rod seemed oblivious to Ayesha's annoyance as irritation flashed in her eyes; simultaneously she spared Saskia a concerned look. She was not sure how she was reacting to this situation. She had not wanted to go out. She looked cool enough, but she might just be hiding her nerves well.

'C'mon, we'll eat together. Have some drinks and a few laughs; get to know each other. Don't miss out,' Rod stroked Ayesha's arm with a forefinger, he grinned revealing surprisingly small white teeth. Ayesha pulled away.

'We are way above your paygrade, now please go away.'

'Have you mislaid your alpha male?' Saskia inquired suddenly, surprising Ayesha with her intervention.

Jed gave a little snort of derision. 'It speaks Rod,' he declared.

'It does Jed. Classy too, a bit raspy. I thought mine was slumming it.'

'Before you crudely interrupted our conversation, my girlfriend was about to remind me how much I had enjoyed the intimacy we shared just a couple of hours ago.' It was a lie, but it suited her purpose. 'I don't think you have anything we want.'

Rod had leaned forward to stare at her, his face lifted, and his head tilted to one side as he listened. He nodded slightly as he heard her out.

'We could share.' There was no ambiguity in his voice or expression; there was no doubting that he meant the offer. He watched Saskia with intensity. 'Don't tell me the thought doesn't turn you on, I can see that it does.'

Ayesha's gaze darted to Saskia's face, she searched her eyes, and her expression. She found nothing there to identify with Rod's claim. But she still felt suddenly uneasy. She watched Saskia's eyes as they levelled into Rod's and relaxed; this was a feral cat, she thought, defending what belonged to it. The realization shocked her. Saskia spoke softly.

'I am so not interested; I've too many plans for her tonight.' Saskia leaned towards him, almost conspiratorially. 'A little boy like you would only get in the way.'

Rod licked his lips, he looked as though he wanted to respond but some thought held him back; briefly a cold anger had crept into his eyes, with an effort he closed it down. He shrugged and glanced towards Jed.

'Time to move on mate. No joy here.' He got to his feet and Jed mirrored him, he purposely shoved his chair into Saskia's as he got up. Rod stared sardonically down at Ayesha, and very deliberately winked.

'Maybe another time,' he said.

Ayesha shook her head and looked away irritably. Without another word Rod and Jed moved away and occupied a table to themselves, close to the centre of the serving area.

'What was that about?' said Ayesha in bewilderment.

'They hadn't been drinking either,' Saskia pointed out.

'Do you want to go home?'

'No, I want to eat.' Saskia's eyes searched the bar area, in the hope that their food would magically appear. Her eyes focused on something familiar at the bar.

'What's he doing in here?'

'Who?'

'Docker John.'

'Docker...? Oh, the ghost.'

'Yes, he's standing at the bar, he's smiling, he's given me a little wave.' Saskia wondered if he had followed them; she allowed a small half smile to lift the corners of her mouth in response. She watched as John detached from his position at the bar, where he had been standing next to a young couple; they were engrossed in their own conversation and each other. He passed fluidly between the people near the bar, towering over all of them; then he came between the tables.

'He's moving, I hope he's not coming over,' said Saskia between her teeth.

She saw John make for Rod and Jed's table where the chairs were set on all four sides; he sat down in a vacant chair between them and rested one elbow on the tabletop; he placed his long, bristly chin in the gap between his left thumb and first two fingers. He appeared to be paying close attention to their conversation, his eyes going first right then left, his sinister smile never leaving his face.

'Where is he?'

'He's at the wankers table. He's listening to them. I believe he must have been watching them at our table. I think our foods on its way!'

Saskia had pushed down her jeans and panties and had just perched on the toilet to pee, when Docker John's smirk appeared through the cubicle door, followed by the rest of him a moment after.

'There's not a lot of room in here,' Saskia remarked, moving her upper body back from her usual position of elbows on knees. She was suddenly self-conscious of her urine stream hitting the water in the toilet bowl. She regarded Docker John dubiously.

'Is this what you do? Hang around the ladies in the pubs to get an eyeful?'

'Needs must. I wanted you on your own.'

'Oh,' Saskia was suspicious, she felt the hairs on the nape of her neck begin to rise. 'Why is that?'

'The lass you're with, she's sold you out.'

That was the very last thing that Saskia expected to hear, and disbelief flooded her expression. She shook her head, but she felt the cold dagger of fear slide between her ribs anyway.

'That's nonsense.'

'It's gospel.'

'She wouldn't. Why would she?'

'No good asking me. I only knows what I heard.'

'Tell me.' Saskia was now oblivious of the fact that she was sitting on a toilet in a tiny cubicle, only inches away from a smelly six feet eleven-inch manifestation. Her hand shook as she retrieved her fresh wipes from her bag and wiped between her legs.

'I listened to them little shitbags spout. A man is coming for you, he's not alone either. There's some sort of arrangement been reached with that lass. She's devious; she's no friend of yours.' Docker John's sinister smile widened even further showing discoloured teeth. 'They have plans for you. The man who's coming is called Nathan. They're afraid of him.' John chuckled maliciously.

Saskia was on her feet. She drew up her panties and her jeans and fastened them with shaking fingers, cursing them when the zip snagged, and she had to start again; she willed herself to calm.

Her world was suddenly imploding, she felt sick. Nathan was coming, to drag her away and to hammer thorns into her; to make her compliant. And Ayesha knew, and she was going to let him take her.

'Let me past,' she ordered Docker John. She walked into him, but he felt viscous, resistant. She had suspected that he would; he owned physicality, he was more than revenant, he was on his way to becoming entity; imminently.

'I need to pass.' Unconsciously she wiped her fingers and palms with another sanitary wipe from her bag.

He nodded encouragingly. 'You need to run lass. There's a door to the back. Or walk out the bar. But I'd get going while you've time. Before they come.' He receded, merged with the door to the cubicle, and transited beyond it. Saskia slid the catch and pushed open the door, forgetting to flush. As she emerged from the cubicle, she heard the hand dryer start up; an older rotund woman in skirt and pullover eyed her dubiously; she walked straight past the nodding grinning figure of Docker John, dropped her wipe in the bin and exited the toilets. Any thought of running lasted only moments. All hope had gone. The thought that Ayesha had betrayed her was almost breaking her in two. She felt tears pricking her eyes. She did not want to get away. she only wanted to confront Ayesha before they came for her. Then they could do what they wanted with her.

'Why are you doing this to me?'
Ayesha looked up and smiled at the sound of Saskia's voice; her expression changed to a frown of concern when she saw the look on Saskia's face.

'You bitch! You've hung me out to dry!' Saskia hissed.
'What are you talking about?' Ayesha frowned, shaken.
'Don't give me that big eyed innocent look.'
'What could make you think that I would hang you out to dry. What am I supposed to have done? What's happened?' Alarm had spread into Ayesha's eyes.

'You're in league with Nathan!'

'That is such bollocks! Why are you even thinking it?'
'Docker John told me.'
'Docker John, the ghost?'
'In the ladies.'
'In the toilet? What was he doing in there?'

'He followed me. He's been listening to Rod and Jed, they're in it with Nathan, and so are you, you brought me here to hand me over to them. Now Nathan's coming with others. I know I'm fucked; I didn't think that you would be the architect.' Saskia's voice began to break up. 'Docker John tried to persuade me to get out, just to leave, but I wanted to confront you! Look you in the eyes. Why Ayesha? What's in it …?' Saskia fell silent as though something inside her had flicked a switch; she left her sentence unfinished and dropped into the chair beside Ayesha, her eyes were filled with dismay.

'What incentive could they offer a ghost to cause it to lie?' she asked. 'And I know that you haven't betrayed me.'

'You thought that I had until the truth hit you. How do you know I haven't?' said Ayesha, relieved.

'You're too into me.'

'Am I?' Ayesha retrieved her Sony Ericson mobile from her shoulder bag which was hooked onto the back of her chair. Her eyes did not leave Saskia's.

'Utterly. You could have given me up anytime in the apartment too; we're in trouble, aren't we? I was supposed to do a runner out of the door wasn't I? Before I thought it through.'

Ayesha directed an indecipherable tense little smile at Saskia, she shook her head and drew a deep breath before she peered down at her phone. She texted rapidly and sent.

'Is that to Claire?'
'Yes. I texted: At the Bowman, help! Heading home!'
'How long will it take her to get here?'
'Too long. It will not be Claire that comes.'
'Who will come then?'

Ayesha shook her head. 'I honestly do not know. But I know that we must buy them time somehow, because I do not believe we can make it home.'

'Why are Rod and Jed still here? They should have gone, surely, when I went to the loo?'

'I think they were here for me, to delay me coming after you.'

'They harassed us. They could have stayed in the background.'

'I think it was a bit of theatre, so that when John sat at their table, it would add impact and believability to his story later.'

'Do you think they can see him?'

'Doubt it. They don't need to do they?'

'And if I hadn't gone to the loo?'

'Most of us go to the loo in a pub, you, have had two Stella Artois. If you hadn't gone, I would have, logically. I want to go now in fact. He'd have found a way though; he might have come to the table; I'd have not known. I think he's been stalking us, who would make a better watchman than a ghost. They must have someone who can communicate. Not far off either.'

Saskia glanced over her shoulder at Rod and Jed; they returned her gaze, with smug stares; Rod leaned back in his chair showing his teeth in a mocking grin; he raised his glass to her and drank; Jed had turned his upper body around in his chair, his arm rested over the back, elbow bent; his small mouth showed an ugly and mean contempt. Saskia cast them both an evil look. She turned back to Ayesha.

'I wish that I'd ordered steak now,' she said bitterly, 'I could have stuck a steak knife in one of them and hoped for an artery.'

Ayesha tilted her head slightly as she regarded Saskia, she was about to say something, but her phone announced the arrival of a text, it distracted her. Ayesha glanced at the screen and showed it to Saskia. 'Twenty minutes. We just need to occupy time. But I doubt if Nathan will allow that.'

On cue another text arrived. Ayesha peered at her screen and frowned.

'It's from Nathan, he's here. It reads: 'Outside. You have two minutes.'

A moment later another text followed. Again, from Nathan.

Ayesha read it out. 'I will come. Fuck the witnesses.'

'I suppose that it's no good calling the police?' Saskia said.

'You nailed that one. Come on let's get out of here.' Ayesha tossed some notes onto the table for their meal. Saskia took her cue and stood. They both grabbed their jackets and Ayesha led the way. They donned their jackets as they went and shouldered their bags. Saskia glanced back in the direction of Rod and Jed; they too had risen from their table. They appeared leisurely, she thought; they were confident.

'If we are going to stand any sort of a chance don't challenge what I ask you to do,' Ayesha said urgently, speaking as they walked. 'I promise you I know what I'm doing. Nathan has made the mistake of not coming for us at once. He obviously would prefer to avoid going public, but in the end that won't prevent him from entering the building.' Saskia heard the buzz and crackle of coerced static, she blinked at the fierce sphere of energy forming in Ayesha's hands; she could feel the tingling as her own electrical field added to the energy. Coerced static was the very beginning of the skill of energised intent; she had possessed it once; before she had been fettered; it was the first rule breaker of a theory of physics, that was lacking an entire dimension of laws. They were in a wide carpeted passage, it led to the toilets on the left, and the kitchen and a stairway on the right.

'Go up the stairs.'

They mounted the stairs. Saskia could hear Rod and Jed's voices behind them, exchanging mocking banter, pitched loudly enough for them to hear. She glanced over her shoulder, but they were not in sight. At the top of the stairs Ayesha pushed through a fire door into a corridor.

'They do bed and breakfast here.' Ayesha explained keeping her voice low. 'There's a fire escape at the end of the corridor into the yard between the Bowman and the apartments. Yes, they will be watching. I hope they believe that we are cowering in the toilets.'

'Memorise the number of doors, just in case.' She flicked the angry ball of energy at the nearest light. Energy discharged into the socket and wiring with an angry bang and plunged the whole of the Bowman into pitch darkness.

Saskia felt Ayesha's hand reach out for hers; she opened the fingers of her left hand to allow Ayesha's fingers to slide between them. She could hear muffled voices below as staff reassured the Bowman's clientele. Ayesha led her through the darkness to the end of the corridor, she released her hand; Saskia heard the door mechanism disengage and the swoosh of the door as it opened over the carpet, to reveal the lesser dark of the night beyond. The side wall of a building stood opposite; it had three levels. The space between was less than ten feet, it was well lit; it black iron railings sealing the river end and a tall black iron gate allowing access from the street. Saskia could see the sides of balconies attached to the front of the building. This could only be the apartment block Ayesha had told her about, where the stable buildings had once stood, and they had held cockfights.

'They are down there,' Saskia heard Ayesha's voice close to her ear, barely the sound of a breath. Saskia followed the pointing finger of her silhouette, to where three figures standing by the gate: a powerfully built man in a thick shirt, a woman with red hair, and a slight well-dressed woman with long brown hair.

'The gate is for residential access. It's always locked, but that was no problem to them,' Ayesha whispered. She pointed to the balcony opposite; there was one other above. 'The gap between the fire escape platform and the balcony railing is about five feet. The balcony is a couple of feet lower than the platform, making it easier. Can you make the jump? I can. The owner of the apartment spends his winters in the south of France. It will be vacant.'

'Yes. I can make the jump,' Saskia assured her softly.

'We cannot afford to hang about, but don't rush the jump. I'll go first. Shoes off; throw them and our bags to me when I'm over. Watch what I do, I'll be waiting to grab you if necessary.' Ayesha bent to unlace her shoes.

'Don't worry about me.' A narrow stream ran past the end of Roger Lavery's garden, at the other side of it there was woodland where she used to like to go walking; it was crossed by a couple of steppingstones, but when it was swollen after rain it had to be jumped, and she had made that jump several times. That distance was greater than the present one demanded of her, and she was agile; admittedly it did not involve a fifteen-foot drop onto dressed stone paving slabs either. She watched Ayesha zip up her leather jacket and clamber noiselessly over the railing. She perched for a few seconds in her socks on the edge of the checker plate steel platform, her heels between the vertical railings. She pushed herself forward and jumped, clearing the railings on the other side, and landed elegantly on one foot and with a couple of forward steps, before she steadied. She had performed the jump in absolute silence. She turned and approached the railing, her hands extended. Saskia had enclosed the shoulder straps inside the bags, and in under a minute Ayesha had safely caught shoes and bags. Saskia zipped up her jacket and climbed over; she rested her rear on the rain dampened handrail and slid smoothly into position. She was breathing fast, and her heart hammered. This was harder to do mentally than she had thought it would be, but she was determined to make it look as easy as Ayesha had made it. She pushed forward at the same time as she heard Docker John's Merseyside accent call out from below.

'There's the lasses, up there! open your fucking eyes!'

Totally thrown, Saskia botched the jump as she half glanced in the direction of the voice. She made the distance but hit one of her ankles on the inside of the balcony handrail, she landed on the ball of one foot but had no stability and she threw her hands out to protect herself as she pitched forward, smothering her cry of pain. Ayesha grabbed her as she fell, she stalled her descent and prevented her from going down headfirst to the ground.

'What happened? You were distracted.'

'It was docker John!' Saskia hissed; she was furious.

There were shouts from below. 'Nathan! they're in the other building. The ghost saw them.' It was a woman's voice.

Nathan's voice cracked out, impatient and angry.

'John, get your arse up there after them.'

'Tell him to fuck off!' John replied. 'The little cunt'd turn me to smoke.'

'God, Nathan's here!' Saskia growled, she winced at the pain in her ankle. 'Docker John shouted to them when I jumped, there's someone down there who can hear and see him!'

'If they came to an arrangement with him, one or more of them would have to.' Ayesha spoke as she breached the balcony doors by desiring.

'Bring our shoes. Come on we can still get out of here!' She shot into the unlit apartment. Saskia loped behind, wincing at the pain biting her ankle. Saskia could barely see a thing, she was aware of space, the smell of leather and polish; she felt thick carpets under her sock clad feet; she was aware of Ayesha ahead, and of her threading between furniture; she decided to follow blind. They came to a door into a hall; Ayesha did not try to find a light switch; she seemed to know where she was going.

'Why don't we hold up here?' Saskia asked.

'We'd be cornered!' Ayesha snapped. 'We need to be in the open, for when help arrives or back in the apartment, though there's no chance of achieving that.'

Saskia heard a hissed obscenity as Ayesha desired a security lock, the mechanism grated and snapped. Light filtered in from the communal space as Ayesha wrenched open the door into a broad corridor with marble tiled walls and plush grey carpets. Ayesha led her to the right along the corridor, they passed the end of a central corridor on their left. They could hear voices approaching and the noise of hurrying feet on the stairs. They passed another apartment door on their right. Saskia wondered where they were headed; there was no obvious exit ahead of them. Ayesha increased her pace, she seemed about to run into the wall when she turned into a recess at the very end on the left. The door of a service cupboard was framed at the back of this and on their right there stood a narrow fire door, fitted with an arm spring.

'It's a service door to the ground level, it also gives us a way out. Listen they're almost in the corridor, it will take them a couple of minutes to find this. Run like hell.' Ayesha already had the door open; Saskia followed onto a short landing as she re-locked; they descended a narrow stair and for a few moments only the sound of their breathing and their feet pattering softly on the stairs, echoed in the space. Two doors were visible at ground level; one exited the building to the right, the other was the internal access, as they neared ground level this to their horror opened, and Rod appeared. He looked disconcerted when he saw Ayesha heading down the stairs towards him, but he reacted swiftly by unleashing intent; he focused it with an angry diagonal strike of his right fist across his body. As Ayesha had progressed in magic and perfected the use of intent she had employed a snap of the fingers to focus its deployment; she occasionally still used it for effect, on this occasion she was forced to react too quickly to adopt that indulgence; she snarled and discarded his intent with an ease bordering on contempt, lobbing it back at him like a grenade with the addition of her own. Rod had opened his mouth to shout out; he tried to deploy Aspis instead, but he was too late; energy unravelled, lifting him off his feet and throwing him backwards with brutal force; he reminded Saskia of a fish being brained against a rock, in an angling programme that she had watched with Roger. His lower body crashed up into the door frame, his upper body and head impacted the ceiling, smashing plaster and board, spraying blood. He smacked onto the floor with an ugly sound. He lay twisted, his body twitching; blood welled in his hair and ran out of his ears and mouth. Ayesha crouched in readiness anticipating the appearance of Jed, but there was no sign of him.

'Come on, that might have been heard or felt,' Ayesha snapped; she desired inside the lock mechanism to the exit door and opened it to the outside.

'Do you think he's dead?' Saskia asked, staring inquisitively at Rod's twisted body as she passed him. Her ears felt tight inside, and they were still ringing; the effects of intent unleashed in an enclosed space.

'Maybe. I didn't intend to kill him,' replied Ayesha. 'Are you bothered if he is?'

'Not really,' Saskia admitted.

'I'm toast if they catch me anyway,' Ayesha told her.

On the other side of the door a narrow pathway ran alongside the building from a screened bay for the wheelie bins down to the river. It was surfaced in concrete and felt cold under their bare feet. Ayesha paused as they neared the corner.

'Shoes on, less likely to get an injury that way,' she said. 'Let's kill a couple of minutes here and buy some more time. This path continues along the front of the building and stretches to the bridge. Keep listening.' she was bent low tying her laces; Saskia pushed her feet into her own shoes, she was shaky and felt clumsy. They were both stressed, adrenalin pumping, their breathing elevated and pushing oxygen rich blood into their muscles for fight or flee. Saskia tucked her laces into her shoes and straightened. They waited; watched and listened. She was aware of Ayesha's hand tight on her wrist. Saskia counted in her head, evenly. She made it three minutes.

'Ready?' said Ayesha, she grinned at Saskia, conveying a look somewhere between fear and excitement. 'Docker John is a threat, he's unpredictable. If you see him, make sure I know where he is, and I'll take care of him.' She glanced at her watch. 'Help in ten, if they're on time. We still need to be visible, and we could be cornered here just easily as in the apartment. Nathan's mob handed; if our help is delayed or inadequate, were stuffed anyway! All we can do is try to get back to the apartment. Now move!'

Saskia ran hard, to her ears their shoes thudded like hammers on the concrete; they must be heard she thought. Her ankle throbbed, the pain worsened by the impacts, but it was only that. She was able to run and sustain the pace, she could hear Ayesha's shoes thudding on the ground behind her keeping pace with her. Saskia accelerated, feeding on the adrenalin rush; she recalled how the running machine had exposed her limitations the previous day and she eased back. Ayesha would not thank her if she hit a wall halfway across the bridge. They passed the side of the Bowman. Some of the lighting had been restored; it was likely that Ayesha's surge had only blown some of the fuses, probably simply tripping the remainder. Another thirty metres and the wing wall of the bridge jutted in front of them, and their footfalls began to echo; they saw narrow stone steps ascending in two half flights up to the roadway. Saskia eyed them with dismay; but Ayesha pressed on; they did not break stride as they continued up the steps; Saskia was aware of Ayesha moving ahead of her where the stairs broke midway. They climbed to where an antique iron gate gave access to the bridge; It complained as Ayesha opened it and passed through to the pavement on the other side of the parapet. The steps had drained Saskia's legs, and her ankle was throbbing quite badly. She kept her pace, grimly determined, but knowing that if Ayesha required her to sprint, it was not going to happen.

They were exposed now; the traffic was not heavy, but the headlight beams were almost spotlighting them, and the bridge lighting gave them no shadows to hide amongst. Docker John materialised in front of Saskia; his sinister smile was if anything shiftier than at any time before. She wondered generously if it was his way of expressing a little bit of contrition. But discarded the idea instantly.

'You fuck bastard!' she yelled. 'You absolute lying, fuck bastard.'

'I've heard them say in the pubs it's a dog-eat-dog world. They're not wrong are they lass. Needs must,' he replied. He shrugged and became a smudge of darkness that raced along the parapet towards the Bowman, at considerable speed.

'Where is the bastard?' Ayesha demanded, she halted and wheeled about when she heard Saskia's invective. Her shoulders had risen, and she looked like a hunched bird of prey.

'He's gone. He turned to smoke; he's at the Bowman by now. Keep running.'

'You're limping.' Ayesha ran beside her, a look of concern on her face.

'I hit my ankle on the balcony railing when I jumped. I'm alright, but this is as fast as I'm going.'

'They're coming.' Saskia and Ayesha had almost reached the end of the bridge. Ayesha had cast her gaze back, intuitively certain that she would see them coming. They were there; they had strung out across the bridge, six of them, three to each pavement, loping like hounds. She recognised Nathan on the right.

'We're a long way ahead, we can outrun them,' Saskia reassured her. 'And you said we'll be safe in your apartment. Oh, I don't believe it.'

Her eyes had fallen on Jed, and a pretty, pink haired, skinny girl in a pink Puffa jacket and blue jeans with torn knees; they were waiting together at the end of the quayside walk; Jed's expression was smug; his small mouth curled. The pink haired girl stared insolently; her hands were thrust deep into her jacket pockets; elbows stuck out. Neither of them moved to bar the way.

'They are letting us past' Saskia remarked; Ayesha had slowed to a walk, and she fell into step beside her. 'You don't have to explain Ayesha, they know we won't run; it would be like turning our backs on a gun.'

'I would take my chances with a gun,' said Ayesha grimly. She walked quickly in front of Jed and the pink girl and kept eye contact. They were about thirty feet away. She kept Saskia on her left as she turned into the walk. The pink girl and Jed at once began to move towards them; Ayesha at once slowed and turned and began to walk backwards. Saskia mirrored her. She glanced at the figures on the bridge, they were approaching rapidly.

'Saskia, run to the apartment, you can make it,' Ayesha encouraged her. 'The guardian can protect you there. I can hold them back.'

'Forget it, I am not leaving you. I would rather surrender myself to them. And it's not up for negotiation.'

Ayesha voiced a funny little bark of laughter in response. 'Yeah, and I sort of knew it. Stand away from me then and well back, they will not hurt you unless you run.' She handed Saskia her bag, smiled and added wryly: 'They want you alive.' She shook her head and grinned as she unleashed vis ultima.

The pink haired girl deflected giving a little gasp of effort, turning the intent onto the cobbles directly in front of a heavyweight galvanized municipal bin. Twenty of the cobbles were driven several inches into the ground, the rest of the unravelling energy sent the fifty-kilo bin sailing up into the air, narrowly missing a seagull as it wheeled its lonely way through the dark; it flew away calling out as the bin splashed into the river.

'Whoa!' laughed Jed. 'I'm impressed.' He glanced towards the figures on the bridge and licked his small lips. 'I hope Rod saw that.'

'Rod didn't, I can guarantee that,' said Ayesha unpleasantly.

Jed frowned, the sneer disappeared from his face; it was replaced by sudden dismay and anger.

'Fucking bitch!' he yelled and unleashed his own vis ultima. Uncannily coordinated, pink girl unleashed her own. Ayesha deployed Aspis. She yelled out with the effort of baffling two combined vis ultima and staggered backwards into Saskia.

'I told you to stand back. Do it! Keep moving.'

'Okay! Okay!' Saskia backed off, her ears felt tight, they were ringing with the effects of unleashed intent; her eyes strayed from Jed and pink girl to the bridge. The others were only moments away now.

Jed and Pink girl struck again, alternating their attacks in quick succession. Ayesha snarled in frustration and effort; Jed was strong, the pink girl powerful, this was taking a lot out of her. Her energy centres felt on fire and her heart was hammering. She felt a perverse kind of relief, temporary though she knew it to be, when Nathan arrived, panting, with the others, and the sustained attack was temporarily suspended. She felt her shoulders fall and her breath came in gulps; her legs shook, and the ache that was inside her, she compared to a bad period pain.

Saskia wanted to go to her, but she held back, knowing that would be the last thing Ayesha wanted right then. This was not over. The five who arrived with Nathan were a mixed group, a couple more non-descript office types like Jed and Rod; a slim red-haired girl in her thirties, wearing a duffel coat and jeans; she had stood in the yard between the buildings; also, a long, gaunt faced man in his fifties, dressed in a padded coat and brown corduroys. Lastly a muscular powerfully built man, who had been the other occupant of the yard. His face was darkened by thick stubble, and he kept himself a little apart from the others; he was dressed in a thick padded shirt, jeans, and site boots; He had a brutal sort of look Saskia decided. He saw her looking at him and he challenged her with an unwavering stare. He would not be kind in bed, she thought, because that was her way; *and in another life*: she pushed the dark thought away; she flushed and looked down, looked quickly back again as though drawn and she saw that she amused him.

They stood in a pack a few feet away, breathing hard from their run across the bridge; all eyes searching from Ayesha to Saskia, but mostly looking at Saskia; she was the prize after all.

'Hello Saskia, good to see you again,' Nathan said, his face was loaded with smug satisfaction, he seemed barely able to contain himself. 'I'm looking forward to renewing our acquaintance.'

'Don't feel bad if I don't share the sentiment,' Saskia responded. 'In fact, fuck you.' Nathan moistened his lower lip and raised his brows to her, his pale blue eyes widened with amused promise. He turned them on Ayesha. They played over her mockingly. He was almost laughing.

'The last time I saw you looking this exhausted Ayesha, you were on top of me,' he remarked cruelly, causing laughter among some of the others.

'Nathan.' The powerful man had brown gleeful eyes and a deep throaty voice; he smiled maliciously. 'How about some entertainment.'

Nathan inclined his head; his eyes did not stray from Ayesha.

'Two minutes Steven,' he replied.

Steven nodded appreciatively; he struck at once with vis ultima. Ayesha discarded it with a hiss of effort and tried to hit Nathan with it. But he chuckled, amused, and ducking back he deflected it into the river.

'Count me out,' said the red-haired woman, disapprovingly.

'Oh, for fuck's sake Gabby lighten up,' sneered pink girl, she snapped her fist closed impatiently and released intent at Ayesha who flailed it away.

'Sod you Marcie,' said Gabby. She turned her stare on Saskia and continued to stare at her curiously while the others, apart from Nathan, indulged in their malicious form of fun.

It was a cruel entertainment. Six of them formed a crescent facing Ayesha and one by one they unleashed vis ultima on her; they took turns in a circuit and then began again, only a moment separated each strike. She retreated and they followed. Saskia fell back too, keeping her distance. Ayesha had begun to cry out with effort, she could only deflect, she was too overwhelmed by numbers and the intensity of strikes to respond. Saskia watched miserably, in tears, feeling utterly hopeless. She wanted to close her eyes, but they were kept open against her will as they watched the torment with a horrified sort of fascination. Most of the deflected intent struck into the ground, tearing a sequence of huge gouges out of the cobbles that in turn sprayed and rattled the buildings to the left or rained into the river on the right, as they moved along the walk. The payphone where Saskia had first encountered Docker John was a casualty; blown to pieces.

Sixty metres from the door to the apartment block Ayesha's legs could no longer carry her and she fell to her knees, utterly done in. She had deflected fourteen strikes. Saskia had agonisingly counted each one of them. Ayesha's entire body shook and although Saskia could not see her face, she knew that she was sobbing and distraught. Vaguely, Saskia was aware of a sweep of beamed light, then of music, incongruous in the circumstances; the kind produced by a radio or a player; she ignored it, dismissed it, right then it was the least of her concerns; it stopped suddenly.

Jed stepped forward, claiming the coup de grace. His malevolent little eyes levelled at her; they showed no pity.

'I think that's enough, don't you?' inquired a male voice, raised loudly enough for Jed to hear. 'It will end badly for you if you strike. And she will still be alive.'

'Fuck you!' Jed spat his words venomously, angrily turning around. 'Who the hell are you?'

'Careful Jed,' warned Marcie, 'I believe my mum would prefer her order to continue to exist.' She had turned around and her attention was no longer focused on Ayesha.

Everyone had turned around by then. Steven looked about to comment, but then thought better of it.

A lean man in a black evening suit regarded them coolly from about five metres away. His white shirt was unbuttoned at the collar; he wore a black leather belt around his narrow waist; it had a plain silver buckle. He was about five feet ten, but he looked taller, and he had dark un-receding hair, expensively cut. he was tanned and fit. There were deep lines either side of a mouth that did not slide easily into humour. He was prepossessing without being good looking. He appeared to be about forty, and he had large thin protruding ears. But nobody ever mentioned them. He had one green eye and one grey, and nobody ever spoke about those either; their stare held a frisson of conceit, and not a quantum of ambiguity. He had emerged from a silver-grey Porsche 911 GT3, pulled up on the quayside walk a few metres away. A beautiful woman sat in the driver's seat, she had straight platinum coloured hair to her elegant jawline and regarded what was happening with a cool gaze, through silver-grey eyes.

'Fucking hell,' said the gaunt man, he obviously recognised the newcomer to the party.

'There is so much intent being chucked about, I swear I could feel it on Armley road.' The newcomer commented. 'My ears are ringing!'

'Hal this is my business,' said Nathan, but without conviction.

'It's my business now. Seven hours ago, I pressed my seal into a tablet. A few minutes ago, as we drove here, Amelia promised the same resolve. We have five names: Geburah. There is a mortal Covenant. Now, I have a roulette wheel turning inside my head like a spinning mantra. And I want to return to it. You have ten seconds to make up your mind Nathan. Or none of you will walk away from this.'

As he spoke the woman emerged from the Porsche; amazingly long legs preceded a lithe spray tanned body, that would have been the toast of any catwalk. She was wearing a short beaded red halter neck dress, and red Prada stiletto heels that she did not need to raise her height to above six feet. Music emerged with her from the car system. It was the Kinks, performing *sunny afternoon.* She did not close the car door or approach, but watched, placing herself in front of the car, one Prada shoe turned slightly outwards, and her arms folded low. Saskia noted that she had long beautifully maintained nails; these were painted white. She had a single understated diamond in platinum in the hollow of her throat, another on her wrist, and a third on her left ankle. A simple platinum wedding band encircled her finger.

'You're running me off Hal?' Nathan was breathing hard with stress; he compressed his mouth and worked it vigorously.

'I am running you off Nathan; do you want to do something about that?'

'I'm not that fucking stupid!' Nathan hissed, he stalked away his shoulders stiff and hunched; he did not so much as glance at the others.

Saskia went immediately to Ayesha, she knelt facing her, she put her arms round her and pulled her close to her. Ayesha still sobbed, she was white, her face stricken; she returned Saskia's embrace, resting her head on her shoulder.

'It's alright sweetheart,' Saskia told her. 'It really is alright.'

'Let's get out of here!' Marcie called out. She followed Nathan, the rest trailed after her, a couple wore sullen looks, the others were openly scared. Jed was the last to leave, he threw a bitter look at Saskia and Ayesha before he turned and followed the others. As he passed Amelia, she spoke to him.

'Six to one.' She said in a smoothly toned voice; there was a hint of steel in it. 'Are you proud of yourself, you cowardly little fuck. You do not understand how brave that was, that young woman is worth any number of you. Fetch six more of your best; I will wait.' Jed did not respond, he cast his eyes down, He was no fool, he knew this beautiful woman's words were no empty threat. He walked away; his stride quickened, and he drew level with Nathan who was now hanging back behind the rest; separating himself from them. He glanced sideways at Nathan's face; saw mouth and jaw working; his stare was fixed straight ahead and lambent rage flooded his eyes. But Jed could sense the fear in him, it was almost palpable; He knew Nathan by reputation only before tonight; until that moment he had thought that Nathan Xavier was a man who would not know the meaning of fear. Nathan became aware of him, but he did not glance round at him. Instead, he spoke. 'Fuck off!' Nathan hissed. Jed hurried on, suddenly fearful, catching up with Mel.

Hal approached Saskia and Ayesha; he crouched down in front of them. Saskia found herself gazing at his shiny, black, handmade leather shoes. She raised her head and looked into his strange eyes.

'Hello Saskia Challoner,' he said.

'Hello Hal, thank you,' she replied uncertainly. She felt relief, but she was still quite confused by the turn of events.

Hal nodded; Saskia thought that he was almost tempted to smile. He reached out with one hand and lifted Ayesha's chin with the tips of his fingers. He scrutinized her strained, tear-stained face, a little concerned, but she returned his gaze with a trace of defiance.

'Are you alright Ayesha?'

'I'm fine Hal,' she gave a weary half smile.

'That was bravely done.'

Ayesha shrugged. 'They'd have killed me anyway.'

'It bought time. We came as fast as we could. Now, I was creative with the truth when I spoke to Nathan, I was assuming at the time that you would choose to put your seal to our mortal Covenant.'

'I don't know; she's a real pain in the arse,' Ayesha growled.

'I can see that in her. I knew that you would. We need your seal, sometime in the next twenty-four hours. And on that premise, it was voted unanimously that you will continue to sleep at her door.
Can you make it back to your apartment, okay?'

'We can try.'

'As quick as you can then. The police will come soon. You caused a lot of noise and damage, and some people will have seen. I know they cannot touch us but best not draw attention if we can avoid it.'

'You had better go too then.'

He nodded; stood and walked away without another word. Saskia watched him as he went back to the Porsche. Amelia smiled at her and gave a little wave as she clambered back into the car beside him. A moment later and they had driven off. Saskia saw Amelia offer a straight upright finger through the window to Nathan, as they drove past him near the end of the walk.

Ayesha began to climb to her feet, Saskia helped her, but when she was upright, she shook Saskia off impatiently.

'I'm okay. I can walk.' She began to walk unsteadily towards the apartment block. Saskia remained attentively close to her, a little stung that her further help had been rejected.

'Don't feel hurt,' Ayesha told her as though sensing her injured thought. 'It's pride. Otherwise, I'd appreciate your arm around me.'

'Who is Hal?' Saskia said to Ayesha, she felt a bit of delayed shock begin to manifest; she had begun to tremble. It would pass.

'Hal Bosola. He's Claire's brother. That was high calibre help. Come on let's get inside; I can hear a siren.'

As they neared the apartment block, Saskia glimpsed Docker John watching them from the shadows stacked at the corner of the building.

'We're not done you lying creepy fuck,' she called out to him. He returned nothing but his characteristic smirk before he drew back and melded with the night.

Six

They rode in the lift to their floor. Ayesha supported herself against the interior side and said nothing. Saskia respected her silence and tried not to stare at her. By the time the door slid open Saskia had stopped trembling. Inside the apartment they removed their jackets. Saskia hung them on the rack in the entrance hall. Ayesha made for the living room. She phoned Claire, speaking briefly, tersely. They were safe. There had probably been a death; it had been unavoidable. She would speak with her again in the morning. Ayesha replaced the phone and opened her drinks cabinet in the unit against the wall. She selected a chunky looking whisky glass and a bottle of triple malt from the array of drinks. She unscrewed the top and pointed the bottle in the direction of Saskia, who stood watching her.

'Want one?' she said.

Saskia shook her head. Ayesha shrugged and poured herself out a half glass. She drank it neat, straight down and poured another. She replaced the bottle and closed the cabinet. She gave Saskia an indecipherable look and brushed past her, carrying her glass. She took it to her bedroom, followed by Saskia. In her room she turned and confronted Saskia.

'Is that what you intend to do, follow me?' she demanded.

Saskia stared at her, she felt lost, she did not want to be alone at present. Her face set and she turned to walk out.

'Stop. Where are you going?'

Saskia came to a halt, she turned around, her shoulders were slightly raised, her arms straight at her sides. 'You told me not to follow you,' she said shakily.

'No. I asked if you intended to follow me. I did not tell you not to.' Ayesha's stare was unyielding.

'Then it wasn't a fair question.'

'I suppose it wasn't. You can pull a long face when you want.'

'You can be very unkind when you want,' Saskia replied with a hint of defiance.

'I'm not feeling good. Do not expect me to be kind to you. I didn't ask for all of this, so don't expect me to change for you.'

'I'm sorry; I'm under your feet; I'll leave tomorrow, and you'll be rid of me.'

'There you go jumping in again. I did not ask you to leave. I said don't expect me to change for you. In any way. For fuck's sake Saskia I want you under my fucking feet! I want you here. Don't you get it? I really like you. I fancy you like crazy and each day I've fallen a little, and by that, I mean a tiny bit more in love with you. In a small way I resent it, but that doesn't matter, it doesn't to me, so it shouldn't to you. Remember that first day when I was horrid to you, and I said: you must really want to get into my knickers? Well, do you know what? You can, tonight if you want to. And I want you to.'

It was unexpected. It was said in part conversationally, and in part with passion; and it was said with a burning eyed sincerity that was unmistakable, and the impact on Saskia was intense. She felt lightheaded; strange flares of unexpressed thought were going off in her mind. She felt as if she had been punched without pain in her solar plexus and she wanted to smile, but she could not get her face to work. She tried to think how to reply.

'How did you know about the jump across to that apartment? You were remarkably familiar with the area and the set up.' She heard herself say the words. It had been a question she had intended to ask, but she had not meant to speak about it then, she had intended to save it for the right moment, with an option for never. She heard herself ask as though someone else had spoken for her. She had not even felt it that important to her. Obviously, some obscure part of her did.

'You really want this now?' Ayesha spoke incredulously. Her eyes were wide with disbelief.

'I'm curious, how did you know so much about the man who lived there?' Saskia listened to her own voice; it was insistent, it held a note of peevishness, and she had no right to be annoyed. She expected Ayesha to look angry. But instead, she looked devastated.

'I don't know why you want to go through this now.' When Saskia saw Ayesha's reaction, she felt clarity return and she regained her sense of self, ousting something, an unfamiliar part of herself, that seemed to belong to another person; it did not go easily, and it went away baffled. It was something that had panicked and forced its way in; it gave off fear and had thrown warnings and confusion at her; it had felt almost purposeful. Something perverse and insecure; out of these thoughts emerged threads of a familiar identity, and she was not comfortable with the sense of the personality that it hinted at. She had sounded like her mother, and it felt as if some tangible part of her mother existed within and was trying to interfere as she always had. This was everything she hated in her mother, because she took everything to such extremes. And she was disturbed to think that these aspects might be present in her too. Underlying this was the requirement that her instincts served her interests, not those of some rogue sub personality. She took a moment to regain her composure before she spoke.

'I don't want to. That was not the real me speaking. You don't have to tell me anything, you don't owe me any sort of explanation. It's not my business. If you never tell me anything else, I will never ask.'

Ayesha looked puzzled, and there was even gratitude in her expression, but then she drew a shuddering breath, and her shoulders slumped; she looked suddenly forlorn.

'You're trying to let me off the hook; I can't think why. Maybe I do owe you an explanation. You do deserve to know what you are getting into; so maybe it is the right time.' She retrieved her glass and gulped down half the contents.

'Okay here goes and this is hard for me. I used to fuck the guy who owns that apartment, I spent a lot of time there. I was fifteen then, I think he was in his fifties. He was one of my uncle's many friends; the guy had a dominant personality, and he took possession for a time. And I told you I like to be owned.' Ayesha sighed and closed her eyes, drawing herself together. 'I was fucked by several of my uncle's friends; you see I was passed around until I was seventeen; my uncle knew, and he didn't care; I was an asset I suppose. God I was a proper little whore!' Tears spilled from Ayesha's eyes and ran down her face adding to the devastation already caused to her light makeup. She finished her whisky in one at that point.

'I was saved. Though I didn't think at the time that I wanted to be saved.'

'Who saved you?' Saskia's voice was quite hushed.

Ayesha drew a very deep breath before responding. 'It was Hal, he recognised what was happening. At one of my uncle's famous soirees, and he rarely went to them you know; he saw a couple of guys take me into a bedroom; then later a woman and a man led me away. I haven't the excuse that I was out of it at any time; I was complicit Saskia because I thought that it was what I wanted too. Hal found out the rest there and then; he seriously kicked off; I was really scared that night. He told my uncle he would pull him inside out with intent if it didn't stop, and he could do that you know, and he meant it. He confronted Claire. She had missed it completely; I wasn't exactly the highest thing on her agenda, why should I have been? She hardly knew me though she always spoke to me, and I liked her even then; she knew my uncle well, and lots of his friends, she was mostly there but she was not part of that, in fact most of them were not. It was only a certain group of them; it had simply gone under Claire's radar.'

'And your uncle! Did he abuse you too?'

'What do you think?' Ayesha said stonily. 'Anyway, it doesn't matter now. That's when Claire began to mentor me and then later, she took me into her firm. I was a high achiever despite all the other stuff going on. Six A levels at sixteen. I got my degree at Leeds while I worked with Claire. I think she's still on a bit of a guilt trip. Lovely person, poor taste in lovers. I'm one to speak.'

'Good for Hal is all I can say.'

'He is an arrogant son of a bitch. But he is a good man, he really is. I hated him at the time, and I told him so. I owe him so much.'

'Do you have any feelings for him Ayesha?' Saskia inquired soft voiced.

Ayesha smiled reassuringly. 'No, I have not. I'm grateful to him and to Claire. But what really hurts is that they both know what I was.'

'That wasn't your fault.'

'Abused people blame themselves. I didn't know that I was being abused at the time. But I feel that it's my fault. So, there you have it. After that do you really want to be a part of my life, my lover? Or do you just want to use me for sex? Maybe there is no difference.

Maybe that's all it is, you just want sex with me. You can use me Saskia, I don't care.'

'Hey! Stop!' Saskia's voice became sharp. 'Ayesha I absolutely care; don't worry, it's an equally major surprise to me. We are both broken. I have an enormous crush on you. But that's relenting because I am falling in love with you, and the two things are not the same.'

'I'm not sure about broken.' Ayesha narrowed her eyes in thought. 'Altered maybe. Re-shaped. Warped is good.'

'That is what we are then. We don't owe it to anyone to conform. Do we?'

'I suppose not. You're surprising me. God, I want a bath, I ache.'

'This pain in the arse intends to run it for you.'

'I was joking about that.'

'I'm not sure you're being entirely honest, but we'll let it pass. What did Hal mean about you sleeping at my door?'

Ayesha chuckled which made Saskia smile in relief.

'In days of yore when knights were bold,' Ayesha chuckled. 'A knight who championed a lady would sleep across the doorway to her bed chamber; with his sword drawn. Why are you laughing?'

'Why did he say it to you?' Saskia smiled.

'He was being slightly mean to me. He was not to know that I like championing you.'

'I thought I was a pain in the arse.'

'Well, you aren't. You don't have to do that for me I'm perfectly capable.' Ayesha raised her voice a level as Saskia disappeared into the on suite and turned on the taps to prepare her bath. She appeared a few moments later and dropped to her knees in front of her. Ayesha had perched on the edge of her bed; she had rested her elbows on her knees and her fingers were thrust deep into the sides of her luxurious hair. She watched while Saskia unlaced and removed her shoes, then drew off her socks; she squeezed the toes together; Ayesha gasped enjoying the sensation.

'I wonder whose championing who,' she remarked.

'What does Mortal Covenant mean Ayesha? How does it affect me?'

'It's a game changer for you, it's meant to give you freedom of action without fear; it means: Touch Saskia Challoner at your peril. But it's more than that; its traditional respect for the choice of those who are signatories to a mortal Covenant. The Orders will back off, and Nathan, and any other individuals who might have had designs. As much from tradition as fear. Claire must have really turned on the big sister act to Hal; setting your seal to a mortal Covenant is not an action taken lightly. As its Hal, more will follow.'

'How will everyone know that I'm protected by mortal Covenant?'

'We hang a big sign in your aura.'

'No kidding.'

'Yes, kidding dafty. Word of mouth. Chinese whispers. Everyone who is informed is expected to tell five others, more if they want to. Even Nathan, now that is hilarious. He probably won't do it, even though tradition is a big part of him.'

'Those people with Nathan, they were obviously part of an Order.'

'The Kadman, I think. God, have you got a thing about my feet?'

'They were afraid of Hal.'

'They should be. He's a real power. As is Amelia. But Hal is something else. There's only Theo Bacchus beyond his level; but he's from south of the Lhoegyr.'

'It doesn't mean you'll be going back to work, does it?' Saskia felt a sense of alarm at the thought, wondering what the Lhoegyr was. Note to ask, later.

'Relax, I'm mentoring you. I am your champion remember. It will be weeks and I can always work from home if I need to. Stop massaging, I want you to stop.'

'Really?'

'Yes really. Show me your ankle.'

'It's okay, the throbbing's gone. I'm just aware of it now.'

'Show me anyway.'

'Okay.' Saskia gave in with moderately bad grace and put Ayesha's foot to the floor; she tugged up the leg of her jeans and rolled down her sock to show Ayesha the injury she had sustained. An angry red bruise covered her protruding ankle bone; in the middle a flap of skin had been lifted in the downward collision with the front railing. Blood had run down the side of her foot and underneath it. It was unpleasant but there was no severe damage. Ayesha nodded and Saskia cautiously covered her injury again.

'It does need a plaster,' Ayesha remarked, disappointing Saskia that she was not more sympathetic. 'I can manage the bath. I am feeling okay. What I would really appreciate is another glass of triple malt.'

'I would recommend tea.'

'Don't worry I'm not a wannabe alcoholic about to binge drink.
One more and that's it.'

Saskia shrugged. 'Okay, if that's what you want.'

'It's what I want.'

Saskia rose to her feet. A small, crooked smile played on her mouth as she went to fetch the whisky; this was the weirdest twist of fate she thought; that two such damaged personalities should be thrown so closely together. A few minutes later, having removed her shoes and jumper, she returned to Ayesha in jeans socks and a camisole top; she carried a chilled glass of Chardonnay in one hand and Ayesha's fresh glass of whisky in the other. She found her not in the bedroom, but in the on suite, naked, in the huge stone bath, leant against the back, partly immersed in hot water into which she had poured scented oils. She had washed off her makeup, a discoloured towel lay on the floor. The taps were still filling, and the level was climbing but it had only reached the undercurve of her small, separated breasts; the sheen of luxury oils lay on the surface, but the water was clear. She had dimmed the lighting to an ambient level; it felt more intimate, softened in the mist of rising vapour.

'I have never liked bubbles, they conceal,' Ayesha told her.

Saskia set the glasses down on the broad stone platform of the bath's rim. Ayesha accepted her glass, she drank a single mouthful, then placed it on the side of the bath on her left. Saskia was about to kneel beside the bath on the woollen rug, but Ayesha's next words stopped her.'

'Join me.' It was a softly spoken invitation; Ayesha tilted her head to one side, her hair falling over one eye, hinting at coquettishness.

'I'm not into water sports usually,' Saskia remarked aiming for lazy indifference. This was exciting she thought.

Ayesha raised her eyebrows in surprise. 'Have I got the wrong idea?'

'No, you haven't. I'm just not into sex in water. It's a waste of good sex, in my opinion.'

'I see.' Ayesha gave her an enigmatic stare. 'Join me anyway.'

'It looks hot.' Saskia commented.

'Not too hot.'

'I'll get blood in the water.'

'I don't care.'

Saskia crossed her arms and drew her camisole over her head; she denuded her upper body and exposed her small, neat breasts and the bruises to her ribs. She unfastened and unzipped her jeans; she pushed them down and leaned against the bath side as she tugged the narrow fit from each leg. She bent each knee in turn and lifted her feet, to remove her socks. She wore simple black briefs; she slid the waist below the level of her hips and allowed them to fall, so that she could step out of them.

'Now you can see me naked.' She laughed, but she felt insecure. exposed to the stare of this beautiful young woman.

Ayesha had studied Saskia's body as she revealed it. Saskia seemed to have developed a flawed perception of its obvious charms. She saw herself as skinny even unattractive; Ayesha saw a beautiful symmetrical body, its lithe lines showing a potential to athleticism. It could be made more toned; it could be tanned and smoothed. It could be perfected. Saskia was always going to be feral, but that could be hidden under a sophisticated veneer of cosmetics and style, in a structured evolution of the self. Something Ayesha never thought to oversee in another. She realised though, that it had already begun; it had sneaked up on her. *Suck it up Ayesha,* she thought. If you are going to have a plaything it may as well be made as beautiful as it can be.

'Climb in next to me, it was designed to take four, but there's only ever been me in it. Yes, there you go tilting your pretty head my little praying mantis, taking it in. This apartment is my sanctum. I've never even let anyone stay here before you. Now it's our sanctum. Never bring anyone back here. Only Khalid has visited. He has never stayed. And I promise he will never visit again. I'll tell him, he won't like it, but tough. And no one else Saskia, you have my word.'

Ayesha reached out for Saskia's hand. Saskia smiled into her pretty face, took the hand, and allowed it to support her as she climbed into the bath. she tentatively lowered her toes into the water. She gasped.

Cautiously she immersed the rest of her foot and her damaged ankle. 'Ow,' she breathed softly, wincing as the hot water touched her torn skin.

'Does it sting?'

'Yes, it stings, it'll go off.' Saskia realised that Ayesha was looking closely at her legs, she had shaved recently, but the hairs were growing back.

'Don't look at my legs, they're all spiky.' Saskia was embarrassed, self-conscious. 'Look at you, you're smooth, you're like silk everywhere.'

'Saskia, you are so full of self-doubt, it's like someone else inside you is challenging the self-belief that I know you have.' Ayesha smiled, reassuring her. 'Take it from me, you are hot, believe me. You merely need finishing, polishing. I'll help you, of course I will, and I'll introduce you to the joys of waxing!' she smiled a little thoughtfully. 'You'll probably enjoy it.' She stretched, reaching to turn off the flow of water, stilling the room.

Saskia lowered her opposite foot into the water and slowly immersed her lower body. She gasped again as the hot water surrounded her; Ayesha released her hand as Saskia eased back into the space next to her; she rested the back of her head against the stone and breathed deeply as she adjusted to the heat. She closed her eyes, as she allowed relaxation in. She was aware of Ayesha's fingertips trailing in her hair, stroking from the front of her scalp to the back of her head, then drawing out and beginning again. It felt good; so very good.

'I like what you're doing.'

'I hope so. This hair needs conditioning. Is this how you want to keep it?'

'Don't you like it?'

'Do you, more to the point?'

'It's convenient I suppose. But I want to change it. I want to change me, I told you. Unless you prefer me as I am.'

'I like what you are, but I'll like whatever you become too, because I'll have had a hand in it.'

'Amelia was amazing. I think I want to be more like her.'

'You'll have to grow ten inches. I think we could get you a more edgy hairstyle. Is that what you want?'

'I want a French bob.'

'Then it needs to grow a little more; we're in for a busy time ahead by the look of it. I'm almost excited. I can't think why.'

Saskia's mouth curved into a pleased smile. It faded and she became reflective as the gravity of a thought struck her.

'Ayesha.'

'Yes, little mantis.'

'You were prepared to sacrifice yourself for me tonight, had I chosen to run when you told me to.'

'I'm not usually altruistic. I don't know what came over me. I felt good when you refused to leave me though, even if I was terrified for us both and angry with you too.'

'There was no way I was going to leave you.'

Ayesha could feel the effects of two and a half large glasses of whisky beginning to wash through her system. She lined up her thoughts before they became diluted and before they focused on desire. She smiled with a wry affection at the beautiful creature next to her. She resembled a sexualized marionette with her eyeliner splodged, the effects of sweat and steam causing it to run down her face; and she would be aware of it; Ayesha had watched her glance at her own makeup soiled towel cast onto the floor; Saskia had chosen not to wash off or cleanse her own. *Focus Ayesha. Do not look at the sweat trickling down her skin.*

'You realize that I will not change who I am for you. I will not stop seeing Khalid,' she announced; she had not wanted to sound defiant.

'I know.'

'There may be others. In fact, there will be.'

'When are you seeing Khalid again? Do you know?'

'Not until next week. Let's have a quiet day tomorrow little Mantis.'

'I would like that.'

'The day after we should drive up to Thirsk and look over your house there. And I'll talk to Claire; then I can introduce you to her Place.'

Saskia nodded, partly distracted. She went silent, gazing through partly hooded eyes. Ayesha watched the movement of thoughts over the younger woman's face for some time, in the subtle shifts in her expression; whilst her abstracted gaze played over Ayesha's nakedness beneath the water. Ayesha saw hidden thoughts, and cruel thoughts, and jealousy and self-mockery. And the indication of a darker persona that fascinated her. This was no pushover.

'I've always had a promiscuous side; though I'm not profligate. And it will only be about sex,' Saskia responded eventually.

'Are you threatening a quid pro quo?' Ayesha said, surprised.

'Not a threat; far from it. I can't help being what I am. No more than you. I'm winging this Ayesha, and it scares me in a way I've never been scared before; about wanting someone in my life.'

'I do get it, I suppose. I indulge in games, erotic games, sometimes of an extreme nature. But they are only an extension of my sexual self. When I finish with them, I go back to being who I am; and that is the person in this bath with you. I really do not know why you are different. Why are you different Saskia? I do know that I am not going to drive myself crazy thinking about it. I would rather just enjoy you.' *Time to enjoy the ride. Time to kiss her.*

Saskia surprised her by pre-empting her, she leaned across and set her mouth to hers. It was a prolonged kiss. At first pliant and warm; after a few moments she opened her mouth to moist intimacy and Saskia's gently probing tongue. After several minutes they drew apart. Ayesha stroked the sweat from Saskia's dark brows as she searched her eyes just a few inches away. She saw laughter in them and desire and a little wonder. Saskia leaned forward and kissed her again needily. Ayesha was aware of her elevated breathing; her own too. Saskia frowned, puzzled as Ayesha gently pushed her back, her fingertips pressed against her breast. Ayesha smiled; she spoke, head to one side.

'Isn't it time you fucked your hot little Arab bitch?'

Addendum

'You blew that!' She was disparaging.

'Hardly my fault! A fucking Mortal Covenant and fucking Hal!' The muscles of Nathan's face worked viciously; she could see he was almost salivating.

'Rage won't help.' She had pulled the Spyder up beside him, its passenger window wound down, as he returned to the carpark where he had left his Daimler.

'You stayed clear.'

'I did my part. Do you blame me?'

'Not really.' He made to get in the passenger side door, but she had locked it. 'Really?'

'I'm going looking for the ghost, he's disappeared, and you need the walk.'

'Fuck you then!'

'Yeah, fuck you too. Goodnight Nathan.' She drove away with a gesture; the second woman to give him the straight finger that night. He glared as he watched the Audi disappear. He continued, his anger and frustration twisting inside him. As he entered the car park, he aimed intent at a tortoiseshell cat as it emerged from beneath a Peugeot; it sprang out of the way, surprised by his habitual gesture, flicking his thumb hard from within his jerking hand like he was striking a match. Some redeeming part of him felt relieved he had missed; though he felt no remorse for the owner of the car whose wheel his intent had ripped off, shredding away its tyre too.

'If that had been my car Nathan Xavier, I'd have been very peeved.' The woman's voice came from behind him and off to his right. He whirled about preparing intent. She was darkly dressed, hair neatly tied back; her five feet three inches elevated three more inches by her heels. He was more than familiar with the lovely, rather cold features, that were revealed in the inadequate lighting of the car park.

'Get real!' She spoke scornfully. 'I would hardly speak if I wanted to attack you. I am prepared to forget our differences if you are. Pax.'

Nathan relaxed. He straightened from his unconsciously assumed fighting stance. Perhaps something could be salvaged after all, he thought, clutching at possibility.

'Pax. Bernadette O'Hare.'

'Good boy. Now tell me everything you know about the Wild, and Saskia Challoner's connection to it.'

Thank you for reading The Lutist. If you liked it and you want to read more about Saskia. Book Two. **A Compliance of Thorns,** is coming out soon.

Authors note. I make no apologies for creating locations in the fine city of Leeds that do not actually exist.

Glossary

Place: A room or zone that exists between realities.

Static coercion: The deployment of static as a weapon or light source.

Energised intent: Often shortened to intent, drawing force from energy centres (chakras) and using it to defend yourself or to harm.

Desiring: Energised intent imagined into an invisible form.

Aspis: Desired intent purposed as a barrier. A shield.

Grim intent: Desiring in the form of a weapon like a club or a hammer.

Deflection: Parrying or turning aside thrown intent.

Discard: basically, the same as Deflection, but the intent is caught and deposited where required.

Declining: The apparent, temporary interruption of the illusion of time in the immediate vicinity by desire. It can be sustained no longer than 4 or 5 seconds. Not every practitioner of magic can acquire this skill.

Vis ultima: The most powerful use of intent available to an individual, usually mortal in effect.

Order: A lodge or group, larger than a witchcraft coven, let by an adept.

Fetter: An alchemical/elemental restraint; it denies a practitioner the use of their magic.

Guardian: An elemental/alchemical creation of formidable power designed to protect an individual in their home.

Elemental magic: The employment of intent, elemental substance and etheric matter, combined to create a visualised form, for a desired purpose. It can be deployed almost as quickly as intent dependent on the skill of the practitioner.

A compliance of thorns: Old magic, which employs alchemically altered thorns or spikes, driven under the skin to control another individual, by inducing pain or the imposition of the will.

*Ayesha's is a modern variant, her own adaptation to enable her to enjoy her need for a specific form of pain.

The Wild (Geifu Prydain): A Sidhe place of mysterious unresolved power.

Shee: Ancient Faye races. Sidhe. Fairy. Long lived.

Mortal covenant: An oath or guarantee, it must not be broken or defied. by universally agreed consent.

Geburah: Its meaning is strength in the cabbalistic tree of life.

The Lloegyr: Early Welsh. Considered to be a region of Britain south and east of an imaginary line between the Humber and the Severn estuaries. Not including Cornwall and Devon. Used now to define the north south division between magical practitioners, but inclusive of Devon and Cornwall in this instance, and including Wales as part of the northern zone.

The Archers of Lugh: A loose association of female magical practitioners, inclined to help ordinaries against dark magic or high-level supernatural intrusion. Not an Order.

Ordinaries: People who have no magic. Everyday people.

The Boundless Edge: Everything. All universes. All planes. All dimensions.

Printed in Dunstable, United Kingdom